"C'mon, Gypsy, c'mon and dance."

Elizabeth hesitated, then bent down and took off her sandals. She didn't look at Dan.

She tossed the shawl aside. *Listen to the music*, she told herself. Forget you're Elizabeth. Pretend to be Isabela the Gypsy.

She raised her head to the sun and closed her eyes. She began to dance to the haunting strum of the guitars, to the music that stirred the soul, that spoke of loneliness and despair—and of passion and a love so hot and wild it could not last.

She danced, her slender arms above her head, undulating, sensual. Her lids were slightly lowered over her pale green eyes, her full lips moist and parted.

The people on the grass in front of her grew silent.

Dan's heart pounded against his ribs, and an intense heat spread through his loins, as driving and throbbing and hard as the music. His mouth went dry with desire.

He'd never seen anyone as blatantly, vibrantly female as Elizabeth was at this moment.

She was a Gypsy.

She was Isabela.

Dear Reader:

No doubt you have already realized that there's a big—and exciting—change going on in Intimate Moments this month. We now have a new cover design, one that allows more room for art and has a truly contemporary look, making it more reflective of the line's personality.

And we could hardly have chosen a better month to introduce our new look. Jennifer Greene makes her second appearance in the line with *Devil's Night*, an exciting and suspenseful tale that still has plenty of room for romance. Old favorites are here, too. Barbara Faith's *Capricorn Moon* and Jeanne Stephens's *At Risk* show off these two authors at the top of their talent. Finally, we bring you a newcomer we expect to be around for a long time. Once you read Kaitlyn Gorton's *Cloud Castles*, you'll know why we feel so confident.

In coming months, look for favorites like Marilyn Pappano, Nora Roberts, Kathleen Korbel and Paula Detmer Riggs, as well as all the other authors who have made Silhouette Intimate Moments such an exciting—and romantic—line.

Leslie J. Wainger
Senior Editor

Capricorn Moon

BARBARA FAITH

Published by Silhouette Books New York
America's Publisher of Contemporary Romance

SILHOUETTE BOOKS
300 East 42nd St., New York, N.Y. 10017

ISBN: 0-373-07306-2

First Silhouette Books printing October 1989

Printed in the U.S.A.

Books by Barbara Faith

Silhouette Intimate Moments

The Promise of Summer #16
Wind Whispers #47
Bedouin Bride #63
Awake to Splendor #101
Islands in Turquoise #124
Tomorrow Is Forever #140
Sing Me a Lovesong #146
Desert Song #173
Kiss of the Dragon #193
Asking for Trouble #208
Beyond Forever #244
Flower of the Desert #262
In a Rebel's Arms #277
Capricorn Moon #306

Silhouette Special Edition

Return to Summer #335
Say Hello Again #436
Heather on the Hill #533

Silhouette Summer Sizzler

"Fiesta!"

BARBARA FAITH

is very happily married to an ex-matador whom she met when she lived in Mexico. After a honeymoon spent climbing pyramids in the Yucatán, they settled down in California—but they're vagabonds at heart. They travel at every opportunity, but Barbara always finds the time to write.

Prologue

There is a story that has been passed down through the ages, that in the years when the Moors ruled Spain, a Gypsy queen ruled beside her king. And it is said that this is how it came to pass.

One day a caliph was approached by his trusted manservant, who said, "A jewel of great beauty has come into the possession of the trader Don Bernardo."

"I do not deal in slaves," the caliph said. "Besides, I already have more than enough women in my harem."

"But she is a rare creature, sire, a Spanish Gypsy whose form and face have surely been created by the gods themselves."

The caliph, though intrigued by what his servant had told him, refused to go to the slave trader.

One evening in the following week, he went at twilight to walk in the magnificent gardens of his home above the city of Granada.

This was the caliph's favorite time of the day, and he never tired of watching the sun set upon the most beautiful of Spanish cities. As he stood there and looked out upon the distant mountains and the city below, he heard a rustle of leaves. When he turned, he saw a young woman moving silently toward him. The sun was at her back, and she emerged through a bower of roses. And though she was barefoot and her Gypsy clothes were poor, there was something about her that made the caliph's breath catch and his throat go dry.

Behind her he heard his servant say, "Go forward, girl, and bow before your king."

She hesitated, then instead of bowing her head, she raised it and looked directly into the caliph's dark eyes.

A shock ran through his body, for it was as his servant had said, her form and face must surely have been created by the gods.

He knew in that moment that he must have her, and he said, "Pay whatever Don Bernardo asks. Do not haggle, for surely she is worth all of the jewels of Babylon. Tell the women that she is to be dressed in the finest silks and that her skin is to be scented with the most expensive perfumes from the Orient.

"Go with my servant," he said to her. "When you are properly attired, I will send for you, for now you belong to me."

The caliph expected, as was his due, that she would thank him for the honor he had bestowed on her. Instead, she said, "You may send for me and I will come because I have been ordered to. And because you are stronger than I am, you may force me to do your bidding. But know that I do not come willingly, nor will I ever give myself willingly."

"Be quiet, Gypsy!" the servant said, and raised his hand to strike her.

But the caliph stayed the servant's hand. "Be warned," he said in a deadly voice, "that not you nor anyone will lay a hand on this Gypsy. She is mine. If ever punishment is to be meted out, I will be the one to administer it."

But the caliph had pleasure, not punishment, in mind when he bade her go.

They brought her to him the next night dressed in a pale green gown to match her Gypsy-green eyes. Her skin had been perfumed, and her dark hair had been brushed until it glistened and fell in soft waves around her slender shoulders.

The caliph looked in wonder. Then he went to her. He cupped her face in his big hand and tilted it so that he could kiss her. Unlike all of his other women, she did not respond. Instead, she remained as still as a statue, distant and aloof.

The caliph, this man who others said was handsome of both face and figure, who was such a skillful lover that his concubines fought among themselves for his favors, was more intrigued than angry. He determined then that he would never force her; rather he would seduce her.

Night after night he had the Gypsy brought to him. Night after night he wooed her with tender caresses. But she would not yield. Though at times she trembled and her heart beat like a captured dove's within her breast, she would not yield.

The caliph became angry, then frustrated, then sad. But although he thought his body would burst with need, he did not send for any of his other women. It was the Gypsy he wanted, only the Gypsy.

But at last he knew that he could not have her, and so he decided to set her free.

On the night when he would tell her, he had her brought to his chambers for the last time. She did not speak as he opened an ivory-encrusted jewel box and took from it a diamond and ruby necklace. He fastened the necklace around her throat and clipped the matching earrings to her ears.

Her green eyes widened as she touched the ruby that hung between her breasts, but still she did not speak.

He took her hand and led her to the velvet sofa where he had tried so often to seduce her, and when she was seated, he took a diamond bracelet from the ivory-encrusted box and fastened it around her ankle. Then he looked at her and said, "Go now, little Gypsy, for you are free. I will not bind you to me."

For a moment she did not speak; she only looked at him with her Gypsy-green eyes. Then she reached out and touched his face, and the caliph shuddered as though it had been his heart that she had touched.

A smile trembled on her lips. She lay back upon the velvet sofa and lifted her arms to him. "Come, sire," she said in a voice of liquid honey, "come make love with me."

It was a night that had been made in heaven. He had never known such ecstasy, had never felt a woman respond as she responded. Her perfumed skin was as smooth as satin. She was fire and ice; she was all the things he had dreamed a woman could be. She did not merely submit as his other women did; she was wild and wanton, as giving as she was demanding. She offered her pomegranate breasts for him to suckle and held him there while she whispered her pleasure.

When at last the moment that is unlike any other moment came, they climbed the peaks of ecstasy together.

"Never leave me," the caliph said.

"But you have given me my freedom, sire."

He sighed against her lips. "Only tell me what I must do to keep you."

"I must always be free."

"Yes, I agree."

"And you must send your concubines away, for if I am to stay, then I must be the only one."

The caliph stilled. His hands tightened threateningly on her slim body. For a long time he did not speak, then he said, "It will be done."

Thus it was that a Gypsy queen came to rule beside the caliph. They had children and grandchildren, and legend has it that they were lovers until the day they died in each other's arms.

Chapter 1

This is the Pool of Myrtles, where the lovely odalisques of the harem bathed each day to prepare themselves for the evening to come."

The guide, Alberto Rodriguez, a pencil-thin man with a sallow face and straight black hair, winked at the assembled schoolteachers. "After the caliph had feasted, he would summon his concubines. While his musicians serenaded and his poets sang their songs of love, the caliph would gaze upon the loveliness of riches before him until finally he made his choice."

Rodriguez looked at Elizabeth. "And the fortunate girl—" there was heavy emphasis on the word "fortunate," and a glimmer of a smile that showed two gold front teeth "—would know that she had been selected to share a night of unbridled passion with her lord and master."

Elizabeth frowned and looked away. She'd had enough of Señor Rodriguez these past ten days to last her a lifetime. She was sick to death of his sidelong glances and his two gold teeth. She'd come to loathe the sight of the pea-green umbrella that he held aloft as a signal for the hapless teachers to follow him, and she had vowed that the next time he uttered the hated words, "Hurry along, *señoras*," she would snatch the green umbrella out of his hands and bean him with it.

She wished now that she hadn't agreed to take this two-week tour. Before she'd left the States for her six-month sabbatical in Spain, she had made arrangements to join some of her fellow teachers, because she'd thought that after having been alone for a month she might enjoy being with a group. But she hadn't enjoyed it.

The breaking point had come four days ago in Salamanca. Elizabeth had looked forward to visiting the university there, but Rodriguez had stopped the bus in the Plaza Mayor and said, "We only have time for a quick look, because we have to be in Avila by five."

And today, here in the beautiful city of Granada, he'd led them through the magnificence of the Alhambra, the place that had been described as a paradise on earth by the Moors, without giving them a chance to pause and admire the beauty around them.

This visit to the Alhambra was one reason Elizabeth had taken the trip, but she'd barely had time to look at the intricate, lacy wall carvings or the brilliantly tiled walls before Rodriguez had said, "Come, come, *señoras*. Let's move on."

Never again, Elizabeth told herself as she slipped away from the group and headed for the Alhambra gardens. Tomorrow, when the other teachers flew out of Málaga back to their homes, she would stay here in Granada so that she could see the Alhambra on her own.

The flowers of summer had been replaced by the blossoms of fall. The trees and hedges that lined the paths were still full, and palm trees swayed in the afternoon breeze. Because it was late in the season, there were no other tourists around, and after so many days of traveling with thirty-five other women and Señor Rodriguez, it was sheer heaven to be alone.

More relaxed than she'd been in two weeks, Elizabeth tucked the guidebook in her shoulder bag. It was enough to stroll in the quiet here, to take pleasure in the orange and bronze chrysanthemums and the sparkle of water from old stone fountains.

It was all so peaceful. So— A sudden, harsh clap of sound cracked through the silence.

Elizabeth stopped. Momentarily frozen, she whirled around when a man crashed through the maze of shrubs and trees in front of her. Head turned to look behind him, he slammed hard into her. She spun around, grasped at a tree branch, missed and flailing at the air, stumbled back and would have fallen if he hadn't made a grab for her.

"What the hell . . . ?" he started to say, just as a bullet whistled over Elizabeth's head. He tightened his grasp on her arm, and before she knew what he was going to do, he yanked her down into a crouch and shoved her ahead of him toward the shrubs.

"Wait a minute," she tried to say. "You can't—"

But he already had.

He pushed her to the ground, then one arm went around her shoulders, holding her still. She struggled against him, her heart beating hard against her ribs, her mouth gone dry with fear. From somewhere nearby she heard men shouting, then rapid-fire shooting.

Flat on her stomach now she raised her head and glared at her captor. "What do you think you're doing?" she managed to say before he shoved her face against the hard, cold ground.

She'd caught only a glimpse of him, a fleeting impression of a two-day growth of beard, dark hair and eyes and a mouth drawn straight in anger when he snarled, "Shut up!"

There was a crashing in the bushes near where Elizabeth and her captor lay. A man's voice said in Spanish, "There was a woman. Did you see her? Why wasn't I told there was a woman involved?"

"How was I to know he worked with a woman?" another man said gruffly. "He never has before."

"We've got to get them." A third voice, out of breath, gasped, "He's probably got the jewels on him."

"I've never killed a woman before," one of them said nervously.

"First time for everything," the gruff voice answered.

"I didn't know there'd be killing. You didn't say anything about killing."

Elizabeth twisted her head enough to see three men through the thick foliage. One of them wore the uniform of the Guardia Civil. She opened her mouth to call out, but before she could scream, the man beside her shoved her face back down into the dirt.

Wait a minute, Elizabeth wanted to tell somebody. Wait just a damn minute. You're making a terrible mistake here. I'm a schoolteacher from Ohio, minding my own business, just out smelling the chrysanthemums. But she couldn't say anything or do anything. She couldn't even move, because now this brute of a man who'd grabbed her had thrown his body over hers.

She heard the three men murmur among themselves. Then one of them said, "Come on. Let's spread out."

Elizabeth couldn't breathe. She tried to shift her body under the weight that held her pinned.

"Wait," her captor whispered.

The seconds ticked by. He moved slightly, then, his face close to hers, his lips against her ear, he said, "Okay. We're going to make a run for the car."

Before Elizabeth could respond, he got up and pulled her to her feet.

"Listen—" she said, but with a hand fastened tightly around her wrist, he began a headlong dash out of the trees toward the distant parking lot.

There was nothing Elizabeth could do. This had all happened too fast. The grasp on her wrist was too tight for her to pull free. If she didn't want an arm pulled from it's socket, she had to keep up with him. He was tall, well over six feet. He had on jeans, a white sweater, a suede jacket and scuffed boots. His lean face was tense. And he had a gun.

She stumbled and almost fell. He swore at her. From somewhere behind them, a cry rang out. Elizabeth tried to wrench free. A spray of bullets hit the dirt near her feet. She gasped, then sprinted forward, needing no urging to keep up with him now.

The parking lot loomed in front of them. She saw the tour bus, a Volkswagen bug and a black sedan. They reached the bug. A bullet ricocheted off the back fender. The man with her opened the door, thrust her inside and scrambled in after her. He grabbed a key ring out of the pocket of his jacket and stuck it into the ignition. The car started. He jerked it into Reverse, backed out and with a wide swing shot forward.

Elizabeth saw the three men behind them. One of them stopped and took aim.

"Get down!" The man beside her hit the gas pedal and the car careered away from the men.

A shot pinged a fender. Elizabeth screamed and tried to scrunch herself as far down as she could in the tiny car.

"Hang on," her captor said.

To what? she wanted to shout. She reached for a seat belt. There wasn't one. She grabbed a handle above the door, straightening in time to see her tour party emerging from the Alhambra grounds. She had a fleeting glimpse of her companions, mouths agape, and of Señor Rodriguez waving his pea-green umbrella as the three men, guns at the ready, ran toward the black sedan.

The next few minutes were so terrifying that all Elizabeth could do was hang on and pray. The narrow road that led down to the main city of Granada was filled with sudden twists and sharp curves. Her companion sped around the twists and took the curves on two wheels. Once Elizabeth darted a look behind her. The black car loomed close. One of the men half hung out of the window, gun in hand, waiting for a chance to get a shot off.

The Volkswagen rounded a sudden curve, slid sideways on two wheels, righted, then shot to the other side of the road into an overhang of trees and shrubs.

Her companion cut the engine. "Down," he ordered, then with a hand on her head, he shoved her down so that her face was against his thigh.

Elizabeth scarcely breathed. She heard the roar of the approaching sedan and dug her fingernails into her captor's leg.

The sound receded.

"It's okay." The man whose leg her hand was clutching said, "I think we've lost them. Let go of my leg, will you?"

She took a deep, shaking breath and cautiously raised her head.

"Are you all right?"

All right? Elizabeth glared at him. She was bruised, scratched and scared out of her wits. Her gray skirt was torn, and she'd ripped the sleeve of the matching jacket on a bramble bush. Her long black hair had come loose from it's clasp, and two fingernails were broken.

Taking another deep breath to steady herself, Elizabeth said, "I demand that you release me at once."

A straight black eyebrow raised. He ran a hand across the dark stubble of beard and shook his head. "I'm afraid I can't do that. They've seen you. They think you're in this with me. For your own good, I'll have to keep you with me for a few days."

"For my own good?" Fury overcame fright as Elizabeth turned on the seat to face him. "I don't know what this is all about, but I'm not having any part of it." She looked down at the gun that lay between them and shifted toward the door. "I don't know why those men were after you, Mr. . . . ?"

"Thornton," he said. "Dan Thornton." He looked at her. The black hair that had been pulled so tightly back when he'd first seen her had loosened around her dirt smeared face. He didn't know who she was, but he wished he'd never laid eyes on her. Castro and Sanchez were after him—not only that, but they had a guy from the Guardia Civil with them. To do what? Make it look legal when they killed him?

He slammed his fist against the steering wheel in frustration and wished he'd never heard of the Anzaran jewels. Three days ago he had taken them out of Castro's hotel room in Córdoba. He'd managed to get here to Granada to the Alhambra, where he was supposed to meet Thomason. Thomason hadn't shown up, but Castro and Sanchez had, along with their pal from the Guardia Civil. And this woman.

He frowned at her. "What's your name?" he asked.

Her lips pursed as though to say it wasn't any of his business what her name was, but then she said, "Elizabeth Kensington."

He nodded. "I'm sorry as hell about this."

Her eyes sent slivers of green ice his way. "Not nearly as sorry as I am."

"I've got friends who'll hide us out. When it's safe, I'll put you on a plane and—"

Elizabeth reached for the door and opened it. "This is where I get off," she said.

She was halfway out of the car when Dan pulled her back in. Elizabeth swung at him. He ducked, grabbed her hands and held her while she struggled against him.

"Dammit, woman, quiet down."

She freed one hand and smacked the side of his head with the back of her fist. Dan muttered under his breath, dodged, then recaptured her wrists. Quickly then, while she sputtered and twisted and tried to break free, he grabbed the silk scarf that was looped around the strap of her shoulder bag, and shoving her arms behind her back, he tied her wrists together.

She screamed in protest and tried to kick him.

"Cut it out," he said. "I don't want to hurt you." He pushed her back against the seat and closed her door. "Behave yourself," he snapped, then started the car.

Elizabeth shrank back against the seat, twisting in discomfort while Thornton wheeled the car out of its hiding place and began to speed down the mountain road to the city.

She darted a glance at him and knew that she was more afraid now than she'd ever been in her life.

His face grim, his knuckles white, Dan headed down the mountain, praying that Castro and the other two men were already in Granada. If he was alone, he'd dump the car and go on by foot. But he couldn't very well do that now, not dragging a woman along with him.

He was sorry she'd gotten in the way, sorry for her and for himself, because he didn't need the extra baggage. But he had no choice now; if Castro and Sanchez got their hands on her, they'd try to make her talk. They wouldn't believe her when she told them she'd never seen him until this afternoon. By the time Sanchez got through with her, she'd thank him for putting a bullet through her head.

Ernesto Castro, one of Europe's well-known jewel thieves, and Paco Sanchez, international hit man. What a team. In spite of the situation he was in, Dan smiled, thinking how furious they must have been when they'd discovered he'd stolen back the jewels.

This had all started a month ago in the Washington Hotel suite of Señor Enrique Calderon, a Spanish diplomat who had been commissioned by his government to bring the famous Anzaran jewels to the Smithsonian on a cultural loan.

Someone from the State Department had contacted the insurance company Dan worked for, and the jewels had been insured for $6.5 million.

The day after the robbery, Dan's boss tracked him down in Puerto Vallarta. Dan had been as relaxed as a man could possibly be. A beautiful, scantily clad blonde had been trailing a margarita-dipped finger across his lips when he'd made the mistake of taking the call from his office.

He'd been about to tell his boss, big Joe Jewlensky, that he wasn't interested, until Joe mentioned the $6.5 million. Ten percent—his cut—would come to a tidy $650,000. For that amount of money, he could almost buy Puerto Vallarta.

It had been almost too easy. Because it was the kind of job Castro specialized in, it hadn't been all that difficult picking up the Spaniard's trail. He should have known there was something different about the heist, though, when he realized the Columbian was involved.

Paco Sanchez wasn't an ordinary hit man; he was international big time—the kind of expert, if he'd been around then, that somebody would have hired to knock off Hitler.

Sanchez made Castro look like a choirboy, and Dan knew he'd earn the $650,000 if he managed to come out of this alive.

He looked at the woman beside him. She was scared and he didn't blame her.

"What are you doing in Spain this time of year?" he asked.

"I was on a two-week tour." Elizabeth shifted in the seat so she could face him. "I don't know what this is all about, but I promise you I won't go to the police. If you'll just let me out of the—"

"I can't do that." They had reached the heart of the city, and Dan eased the small car into the traffic. "When's the tour over? When are you supposed to go back to the States?"

"I'm not. I'm here on a sabbatical leave. I'm a high school teacher. I just joined the tour for a couple of weeks. The others are going to fly out of Málaga tomorrow." Elizabeth took a deep breath and tried to speak reasonably. "Look, it's none of my business what kind of crook you are."

"I'm not a crook."

"Of course not," she said sarcastically. "That's why the Guardia Civil is after you."

"I don't know how long you've been in Spain, lady, but hasn't it occurred to you that the Guardia doesn't go around shooting civilians?"

"But he was wearing a uniform," Elizabeth protested.

"And shooting at us."

"Because you're a jewel thief."

Dan shook his head. "I'm an insurance investigator."

"Sure you are," Elizabeth scoffed. "And I'm the crown princess of Romania."

She wasn't the crown princess of anything, Dan thought sourly. She was a schoolteacher from Podunk High, a plain-Jane who hadn't heard that even high school teachers no longer wore dark gray flannel suits and sensible shoes. Some of them had even been known to style their hair and wear makeup.

Damn! If he'd had to kidnap somebody, why couldn't it have been a gorgeous dark-eyed Spanish *señorita* with a little warm blood in her veins? The woman next to him looked as though ice water flowed through hers.

But whoever she was, she was his responsibility, and he'd do his damnedest to protect her.

"I really am sorry that you got involved in this," he said. "I'm going to do my best to get you away from here just as soon as I can. In the meantime I've got to keep you with me. We're going to stay with some friends of mine for a few days, but I promise you that as soon as I can, I'll put you on a plane for wherever you want to go."

Elizabeth leaned back against the seat and shifted, trying to get comfortable. It was late afternoon now, and darkness had begun to settle upon the city. "Where are you taking me?" she asked.

"To the caves," Dan Thornton said. "The Gypsy caves of the Albacín."

Chapter 2

The narrow, winding streets of the Albacín were just barely wide enough for the Volkswagen. At this hour of the evening, the shopkeepers had already taken in their wares. Little had changed since the days of the Moorish caliphs, and it seemed to Elizabeth as though she'd stepped back in time four hundred years. The flavor of an ancient Moorish village was all around her.

In spite of her fear, she looked with interest at the whitewashed, red-roofed houses, with their flower-filled balconies and surrounding gardens. She could see the Alhambra outlined in the last rays of the setting sun, and in the distance the snow-covered Sierra Nevada rising majestically against the darkening sky.

The sky turned from mauve to deep blue, and ahead of her, through the glimmer of the street lamps, Elizabeth saw Sacromonte, the place of the Gypsy caves.

The fear she'd known earlier gripped her then—fear of the man beside her, of what he planned to do with her. Fear of the caves of the Sacromonte.

For as long as Elizabeth could remember, she'd hated closed-in places. The idea of tall windowless buildings and of modern windowless schools appalled her. She remembered the pleasure she'd felt as a child, sitting at her desk in school, looking out the window at the first snows of winter and sniffing the fresh scent of the air at the beginning of spring. She felt sorry for children in their closed-in schoolrooms and for the office workers in their steel buildings.

Ahead of her she saw the caves, like the grottoes of Arab legends, against the chalky cliffs. This was where the Gypsies had lived for four hundred years.

Dan stopped the car. Through the open window Elizabeth could hear the distant sound of church bells. When the bells stilled there was only the silence of the night.

"I'm going to untie you," Dan said. "It would be foolish of you to try to run away. We're in the Gypsy quarter now. You'd be lost in a second, and when I passed the word that you were my woman, you'd be brought back to me. Now turn around."

Elizabeth shifted and he untied her hands. She flexed her shoulders. "Please," she said, "please take me back to the city. I swear to you that I won't cause you any trouble. You said before that I was in danger because those men saw me with you. I don't know whether or not that's true, but if you think it is, I'll leave town. I'll take the bus into Málaga with the tour group then go on to Almeria. I—"

"No." Dan shook his head. "I'm sorry. I've got to keep you with me for a few days."

She opened her mouth again, but before she could speak, he started the car.

In the dim light from the dashboard, Dan saw that her dark brows were drawn together and that her lips were tight. He knew she was still afraid, but there wasn't any way he could ease that fear. He wished he'd never seen her, but he had and so had Castro and Paco Sanchez. Her life was as much in jeopardy as his now; he had to take care of her.

He stopped again, this time in front of one of the cave-houses, and switched off the engine. "We're going to stay with friends of mine," he told Elizabeth. "Pilar and Jonas Belmonte. They—" Dan stopped, for a group of children had suddenly appeared and surrounded the car. Hands out, chattering like a group of magpies in both English and Spanish, trying to jostle each other out of the way, they cried, "Hey mister, you want to see flamenco? I take you. Okay? Good show, mister and misses. Best flamenco in Spain."

Dan got out of the car. Ignoring the children for a moment, he took Elizabeth's hand. "Come on," he said.

Reluctantly she followed him out to face the bevy of boys and girls.

"Who knows Jonas Belmonte?" he asked.

"I do," a boy said. "I take you there. Okay, *señor*?"

"Okay." Dan tightened his hand around Elizabeth's, and with a murmured, "Come on," he followed the boy to one of the whitewashed doors.

The boy pounded on the door. It opened. "*¿Quién es?* Who is it?" a voice called out.

"Dan Thornton," Dan said. "Is that you, Jonas?"

"Dan? *¡Dios mío!* I can't believe it, *hombre*. Come in. Come in."

Dan gave the boy some money, then he positioned Elizabeth in front of him so that she was in the house before he greeted his old friend with a Spanish *abrazo*.

The man returned the embrace, smacking Dan hard on his shoulder before he called out, "*Vieja*, old lady! Come see who has dropped from the sky."

Jonas Belmonte was half a head shorter and twenty years older than Thornton. There were deep creases around his eyes, and he had a prominent nose. His mouth was wide, his teeth were big, and his smile seemed to warm the whole room.

"Why do you shout, old goat?" A woman came through the beaded curtains that separated living room and kitchen. She was taller than her husband, big of bosom and wide of hip. Though not beautiful, her face was striking. Her eyes were large and of a deeper green than Elizabeth's. A nose that was almost as large as her husband's was softened by her generous mouth. Her black hair, only slightly touched with gray, was pulled into a thick bun at the back of her head.

She looked at Elizabeth, then her gaze went to Dan.

"Thornton!" Her voice was as strong as her face. "You *cabrón*! I can't believe it is you." She pulled him away from her husband in an embrace that almost lifted Dan off his feet. She laughed, then looked at Elizabeth.

"This is Elizabeth..." Dan hesitated.

"Kensington," she said dryly.

"A friend of mine," Dan finished.

"Welcome to our home, *señorita*." Jonas kissed the back of her hand. "*Mi casa es su casa*. My house is your house."

"Gracias," Elizabeth said, not quite sure now whether she was a prisoner or a guest.

The walls of the cave-home had been freshly whitewashed. A thick, richly colored rug covered part of the linoleumed floor. There were framed photographs hanging on all of the walls, along with bullfight banderillas and posters, a big picture of the Virgin Mary and dozens of gleaming copper utensils.

"Jonas and Pilar," Dan said.

"Mucho gusto." Elizabeth nodded.

"You speak Spanish?" Pilar asked.

"Yes, I'm a Spanish teacher in the States."

Pilar's dark eyes studied her, but before she could speak, a naked little boy and girl of six or seven ran into the room. Pilar bent down and smacked the boy sharply across his bottom. "Paquito!" she said. "Where are your clothes?"

He howled and tried to squirm out of her grasp.

"Mama was giving him a bath," the girl said. "But he heard someone come in, and he wanted to see." She looked curiously at Dan and Elizabeth.

"They are our daughter Adelita's children," Jonas said. "She lives here with us, now that her husband is gone." He picked the small boy up in his arms. "This bad boy is Paquito. Rosalia is his sister." He laughed at Paquito and said, "Don't cry, *mi niño*."

"She hit me," the little boy wailed.

"Don't make such a fuss." Pilar took him from Jonas, kissed both his tear-streaked cheeks and said, "Now go get your bath and get ready for bed before I really give you something to cry about." To Dan she said, "We will drink some Manzanilla, yes? Then we will eat."

"Yes, yes, let us have some wine." Jonas motioned to one of the rush-bottomed chairs while Pilar went to get the bottle of Manzanilla. "Sit down, *señorita*," he said to Elizabeth, and when Pilar returned he poured the dry sherry into four glasses and handed one to his guest. "To your good health," he said politely.

Elizabeth took a sip of the wine. From somewhere back in the cave-house, she could hear the high-pitched voices of the children, then a woman's voice raised in a shout.

Jonas, acting as though he didn't hear them, turned to Dan. "It has been over three years since I have seen you, *amigo*. How does it go with you?"

"Most of the time it goes well, Jonas. At other times not so well." Dan hesitated. "I have trouble," he said. "The woman and I need a place to stay for a few days."

Jonas reached into his pocket for a half-crumpled pack of cigarettes. He took a kitchen match from a pile on the table beside him and struck it. After he had lit the cigarette and inhaled, he said, "Of course, Dan. There is no problem. You will stay here."

Elizabeth looked around the small living room. She hadn't seen the other rooms, but she couldn't imagine that there were more than two or three. Enough for Jonas and his wife, their daughter and the two children. How could there be a room for her and one for Dan, as well?

Dan and Jonas talked while Pilar prepared the evening meal. Elizabeth sipped the Manzanilla and wondered how she was going to get out of here. Pilar put the dinner on the table, then called out, "Adelita! *¡Ven!*"

A young woman of perhaps twenty or twenty-one pushed aside the curtains that separated the living room from the rest of the house. She paused there, one arm raised against the wall, hip out, hand on her waist. Dark-skinned and sloe-eyed, her face showed the blood of the ancient Arabs as well as that of her Gypsy ancestors.

"Come, Adelita," Pilar said. "You remember Señor Thornton, don't you? He and his woman have come to stay with us for a while."

Adelita looked at Dan. She put a hand under her long black hair and lazily flipped it back off her neck before she focused her full attention on him.

"Of course I remember Señor Thornton," she said in a low, throaty voice. She lowered her thick black lashes, then opened them to give him the full benefit of her dark eyes. She took a deep breath, and her bosom swelled.

Elizabeth stared at the young woman, who had not even bothered to acknowledge her. She'd never seen such a blatant exhibition of outright sensuality before, so obvious it was almost laughable. She glanced quickly at Dan Thornton. He wasn't laughing.

"Well, well," he said. "Little Adelita." He cleared his throat and offered his hand.

Elizabeth saw Adelita's hand close over his, then slowly, lingeringly, slip away.

The four of them talked and laughed all through dinner, while Elizabeth sat silently, barely touching the food in front of her.

She studied Dan Thornton. More relaxed now that he was here with his friends, his face did not seem as hard as it had this afternoon. He had a good tan, which seemed to accentuate his masculine features. His black eyebrows were heavy, and his eyes were a deep brown. His nose was long and straight, and his lips had just the right amount of fullness.

There was no doubt about it, Elizabeth thought; some people would find Dan Thornton a handsome devil.

Neither Jonas nor Pilar asked Dan what trouble had brought him here or why he had a woman with him. When the meal was finished, Pilar pushed back her chair and said to Elizabeth, "Come, *señorita*, I will show you where you can sleep."

Elizabeth looked at Dan.

"Go along," he said. "Jonas and I have a lot to talk about."

She stood wanting to ask him where he planned to sleep and how long he planned to keep her here. She said, hoping it would work, "I really think it would be better if I went to a hotel."

"I don't." The deep brown eyes flashed a warning. "Go with Pilar," he said. "We'll discuss this in the morning."

Jonas shot an inquiring glance at Dan, and Adelita lifted one curious eyebrow. Pilar moved closer to block any movement Elizabeth might make.

The fear came again. Elizabeth clutched the back of one of the cane chairs for support. Then Pilar took her arm, and with a barely increased pressure of her fingers, said, "Come along."

The room Pilar took her to was dark and small. Pilar lighted a fringe-shaded lamp that stood on a wooden crate beside the bed. "You will be comfortable enough here," she said. "I'll bring a nightgown and a basin of water so you can wash."

Elizabeth moistened her lips. "Thank you," she managed to whisper.

"I do not know what the problem is," Pilar said. "But Thornton is a good man. It would be better to do what he says."

Without waiting for a reply, she went out and closed the door behind her.

Elizabeth sat on the edge of the bed, hands clasped tightly together in her lap. She thought about the tour group and about Señor Rodriguez. Surely he had gone to the police; surely the police were looking for her. But how could they find her here in this Gypsy quarter? And what about the men who had shot at them? Elizabeth shivered. There had been no doubt in her mind that they had shot to kill. And if they were criminals, why was there a member of the Guardia Civil with them?

Elizabeth was still puzzling over the questions that ran around and around in her mind when Pilar came back with a basin of water and a bright red, slashed-to-the-waist nightgown.

"It is Adelita's," she told Elizabeth. "You would get lost in one of mine." She hesitated a moment. "Whatever the problem is," she said, "Thornton will work it out. Things will be better tomorrow."

Then she went out and locked the door behind her.

Elizabeth picked up the bright red nightgown, not quite believing that anyone, even Adelita, would wear it. With a frown she hung it on a hook on the wall and began to undress.

The gray skirt had been torn, but that could be mended. She wasn't so sure about the jacket, because one sleeve had been ripped half-off. The stockings were ruined and one of her knees was scraped.

Elizabeth folded the skirt over the chair that stood in one corner of the room, then took off her plain white blouse and hung it over the red nightgown. She scrubbed her face and bathed as best she could in the basin of water, then brushed her long, dark brown hair.

"Thank God for your eyes and your hair," her mother had often told her. "They're your only good features."

Elizabeth had never liked her hair. She wanted it to be blond, like her younger sister's.

"Paula's the beauty; Elizabeth's the brain," her mother was fond of telling everyone.

Elizabeth was two years older than Paula, and for as long as she could remember, people had stopped to admire the younger girl. "What a beauty," they always said. Then they'd pat Elizabeth on her head and say, "You're a nice little girl, too, dear."

It's a wonder she hadn't grown up hating Paula. She had when they were both in high school. Then one day Paula said, "Don't you think it's just as awful for me as it is for you? Every term a new teacher tells me she hopes I'm as bright as you are, and then she's upset because I'm not. I want to be like you, Elizabeth. I want people to like me for what I am, not for what I look like. I hate it when Mother tells everyone how smart you are."

"And I hate it when she tells everybody how pretty you are." Elizabeth had smiled and added, "You really are pretty, you know."

Paula had hugged her. "You're more than pretty, Elizabeth. You've got something that nobody else has, a kind of beauty that shines all the way through. Maybe Mama doesn't see it, but I do."

Elizabeth had never been jealous of Paula again.

She'd been her sister's maid of honor when Paula married Harold Skinner, an accountant who was eight years older than she was. Harold, whose face was almost as round as his belly, adored Paula and their three boys, and Paula was mad about him. They were a happy family, and they shared their joy with Elizabeth whenever she was with them.

Elizabeth put the hairbrush down, and for a moment her eyes clouded with tears. She wanted to be back in the States and safely married, too. She wanted to be anywhere except here.

At last, Elizabeth, still dressed in her white slip, lay down and pulled the patchwork quilt that covered the bed over her. She tried to relax, and finally, in spite of her anxiety, her eyes drifted closed. But they flew open when she heard the lock click and the door swing open.

"I thought you'd be asleep by now," Dan Thornton said.

"What...?" Elizabeth sat up and clutched the quilt over her breasts. "What do you want?" she managed to say.

"To get some sleep." He locked the door with a key and put the key in his pants pocket.

Her pale green eyes widened in alarm. "Where? You can't sleep here."

Dan gave a long, drawn-out sigh. He tossed his suede jacket on the chair and started to pull off his sweater. "There are two bedrooms," he said patiently. "Adelita and her kids sleep in one of them; Pilar and Jonas sleep in here. Tonight Pilar is doubling up with Adelita and the kids, and Jonas is sleeping on a mat in the kitchen. They don't know why I've brought you here, but they seem to find it perfectly natural that we would share a room."

"Well we're not going to share a room!" Elizabeth snapped.

Dan threw his sweater on the bedpost. She saw the money belt strapped around his waist.

"Are the jewels in there?" she asked nervously.

He nodded, and with a weary sigh, he said, "I've been on the run for three days. I've had maybe five hours of sleep, and I'm so tired my teeth ache. I wouldn't be interested in you tonight if you looked like Marilyn Monroe." He sat down on the bed and began to remove his boots. "Believe me," he said, "I don't plan on attacking you."

Then he turned the lamp off and lay back on the bed.

The room was absolutely pitch dark. Elizabeth, sitting straight up, pulled the quilt up to her chin.

The bed moved and she knew he was taking his trousers off. Then with another sigh he turned on his side away from her. In two minutes his breathing evened and he slept.

But Elizabeth didn't. The minutes passed. Dan began a slow, low snore, and at last Elizabeth lay down, as far away from Dan Thornton as she could get. Finally, worn out by all that had happened, her eyes closed.

She awakened once in the night, frightened, unsure for a moment where she was, closed in by a darkness unlike any she'd ever known. She reached out, trying to find a lamp, and when she touched a warm shoulder, she cried out in alarm and shrank back against the headboard. Her heart pounded a tom-tom of fear, and she couldn't get her breath. Then she remembered that she was locked in this cavelike room with a stranger whose name was Dan Thornton and that he'd crawled under the blanket beside her.

It was a strange feeling to be lying here next to him. Very cautiously she lay back down again. He turned on his side, and he was so close to her that she could feel his breath on her face. She edged away until she was half-hanging off the narrow bed.

He moved restlessly in his sleep. She froze and lay still. Finally the darkness of the room closed in upon her, and she slept again.

She awakened with her face against Dan's shoulder, his arm around her waist.

She moved quickly away, and he said, "Whazzat?" before he opened his eyes and stared at her. Still half-asleep, he mumbled, "Hello there," in a low, sexy voice and reached for her.

Elizabeth yelped and leaped from the bed, pulling the quilt with her.

Dan came fully awake. He rubbed a hand over his stubble of beard. "Who. . . ?" he started to say. Then he remembered that this was the woman he'd run into yesterday in the gardens of the Alhambra, the woman he'd brought here last night.

She looked different in the half-light of the room. Her rich brown hair, tousled from sleep, hung down over her shoulders. Her cheeks were rosy and her mouth looked soft and vulnerable.

Dan sat up and shook his head to clear it. "Good morning," he said. "I'll get out of the way and let you dress."

"I'd appreciate that."

He swung his bare feet onto the floor. He was wearing dark blue bikini briefs. His tanned legs were strong and muscular, his hips were narrow and his stomach was flat.

Elizabeth looked away.

He reached for his pants and put them on. "I'm going to wash up," he said, then after a moment's hesitation added, "I don't want to keep you locked up in here all day, Miss Kensington. I'd like your promise that you won't try to run away."

Elizabeth hesitated. She didn't want to promise Dan Thornton anything, but the thought of being confined in this small, windowless room all day was unbearable. She nodded and said, "Yes, all right, I promise."

"Good." Dan grabbed his sweater off the bedpost where he'd hung it the night before. He looked at her again and shook his head. "I'm sorry about this," he said.

Before Elizabeth could answer, he went out and closed the door.

But this time he did not lock it.

Chapter 3

Elizabeth borrowed thread from Pilar to mend her torn skirt. The jacket was ruined so all she had was the skirt and the white blouse. Everything else had been left on the bus.

As the morning passed, it became obvious that Thornton had told Jonas and Pilar who Elizabeth was and why he thought it necessary to keep her with him. Not only did Dan and Pilar keep their eyes on her, so did other Gypsies who came to visit during the day. Every time she ventured toward the open door, either Dan or one of the Gypsies was immediately beside her.

Rosalia, who had stayed home from school to take care of her younger brother, was also a constant but friendly shadow. She was a thin girl and small for her age. Her long, delicate fingers were festooned with cheap, glittery rings, and she wore tarnished gold loop earrings in her ears.

Her dark hair was parted in the middle and worn in two skinny braids that came down past her shoulders. Last night she had worn a dress in a dreadful shade of green. Today she had on a mustard-yellow blouse and red plaid pants that hung from her thin frame like worn and comic scarecrow trousers.

Rosalia hadn't gone to school because Paquito had a cold, she told Elizabeth, and since her mother had to entertain the tourists who passed through the Sacromonte, Rosalia had to stay home to take care of her brother.

As soon as a tour bus arrived in the barrio, one or two of the men would reach for their guitars and position themselves outside the Gypsy houses, while the women, dressed in bright flamenco dresses, would begin to dance.

It seemed to Elizabeth, who watched from the open doorway, that the performance was lackluster and the smiles of the entertainers were forced. As soon as the tourists departed, they slumped down in their straight-backed chairs and began to smoke while they waited for another group to arrive.

Elizabeth admitted to herself that part of the reason she hadn't enjoyed the performance had something to do with Adelita, supposedly the star of the company.

There was no mistaking the fact that Pilar's daughter was pretty. Even now, slumped in the cane chair, legs akimbo, a cigarette dangling from her lips, she was attractive in a way that seemed to Elizabeth as obviously sexual and cheap as the perfume she wore. When she had danced just now, there'd been a look of utter boredom on her face. Then she had noticed Dan watching her and her movements had changed, become slower, more seductive. She had moistened her parted lips as she'd looked directly, provocatively, at Dan, and there had been an expression that said, I'm yours if you're man enough to take me.

Adelita paid little or no attention to her children, and when she did it was to yell at Rosalia, "What in the hell is wrong with you? Wipe Paquito's nose."

Elizabeth turned away from the door. "I don't have anything to do," she said to Rosalia. "Let me help you with him."

"Gracias, señorita," Rosalia said shyly. "Poor Paquito is always sick."

"Do you stay home from school every time he is?"

"Of course. Grandma Pilar and Mama are busy with the tourists. It's my job to take care of him."

"Where's your father?"

"¿Quién sabe?" Rosalia answered. "Who knows? Mama said this time he's not coming back. She said she would get us another father, though."

Wonderful, Elizabeth thought. And another baby for either Pilar or Rosalia to take care of.

When she had given Paquito some juice, Elizabeth told Rosalia to go outside and play, that she would watch over the sick boy. She had just settled into a wicker rocker with him when Dan came in with a newspaper.

"What's the matter with Paquito?" he asked.

"He has a cold and a fever."

"Why are you taking care of him?"

"Because his mother is otherwise occupied."

"Adelita has to earn a living."

"I'm sure she does," Elizabeth said sarcastically.

Dan frowned. "Entertaining tourists."

"Uh-huh."

"You don't understand these people."

"Probably not." She looked up at him. "How long have you known them?"

"For years." Dan pulled up a chair and sat down facing her. "I met Jonas when I was a student at the university here. I used to come down to the Gypsy quarter to hear the music, and one night I got into trouble. A bunch of ruffians decided I had no business in the barrio, and they lit into me. I was outnumbered and fading fast when Jonas and one of his cousins appeared and decided to even things up. When the fight ended, Jonas took me home and Pilar patched me up. We've been friends ever since." He hesitated. "There's something in the paper about you today."

The rocker stilled. "What? What is it?"

Dan handed her the newspaper, and she took it with her free hand. It was folded to an inside page. There was a snapshot of her that one of the teachers had taken while they were on the tour, and under it a caption that read: "Señorita Elizabeth Kellington."

"They spelled my name wrong," she said, then went on to read a two-paragraph story about the possibility of her having been kidnapped by an American terrorist who was suspected of working with one of the separatist groups.

> However it is not certain whether Señorita Kellington is a victim or an accomplice. Until more information is obtained, she and the man, Daniel Thornton, who may or may not be her partner, are to be considered dangerous.

Elizabeth looked up at him. "My God," she gasped. "They think I'm a terrorist, too."

"I'm not a terrorist any more than you are," Dan snapped. "I'm an insurance investigator. I go after the thieves or insurance frauds, and I get a cut of whatever I bring back." He took a black leather billfold out of his back pocket, sifted through it and handed her a card. Hultinius, Ettles and Honningsberg Insurance, she read. There was a New York address, then, Dan Thornton, Investigator.

"But this is an American company," Elizabeth said. "What are you doing in Europe?"

"The jewels were stolen in the States." Dan drew up a chair so that he could sit down and face her. "A Spanish diplomat by the name of Enrique Calderon brought $6.5 million in jewels to Washington. They were to be on loan to the Smithsonian from the Spanish government. But the day Calderon arrived, they were taken from his hotel suite."

"But weren't there guards? An escort of some sort?"

"Sure, but two of the guards had been planted by Castro, one of the men shooting at us yesterday. They took care of the three other guards, and Castro was on a plane back to Spain before an alarm went out. My boss got hold of me in Puerto Vallarta...." Dan paused long enough to wonder what had happened to the blonde, then said, "I flew into Mexico City and on from there to Madrid. I caught up with Castro and his pal, Paco Sanchez, in Córdoba, grabbed the jewels and headed here to Granada. I was supposed to meet somebody from Interpol at the Alhambra yesterday, but he didn't show."

"But I was there and so were the men shooting at us." Elizabeth raised an eyebrow. "If what you've told me is true."

"Dammit, woman, I'm telling you the truth."

"Then why don't you go to the police? Why is the Guardia Civil involved?"

"I don't know that they are. Probably there are only one or two of them who've been bribed by Castro." Dan ran a hand through his dark brown hair. "As far as the police are concerned, I've been told not to contact them, because there's to be no publicity about the jewels."

He studied Elizabeth, wondering just how much more he should tell her. She was obviously intelligent, and she seemed sensible enough. It would make things easier if he could get her to trust him.

She didn't look quite as drab in the white blouse as she had yesterday with the gray suit jacket buttoned up around her neck. Her skin, without makeup, was smooth and flawless. She had a light sparkling of freckles across her nose and her cheeks, and her pale green eyes were bright and clear. Her features were good, and he wondered how her mouth would look if it wasn't always drawn into a thin line. Just then the child whimpered. She leaned close to Paquito and spoke to him. Her mouth softened and Dan saw how it would look.

When the child quieted, she said, "Why not?"

"Why not what?" He shifted his gaze from her mouth to her eyes.

"Why wasn't there supposed to be any publicity? Why didn't you notify the police?"

"I had orders not to. I was supposed to find the jewels and either turn them over to Interpol or get them back into the States myself. They're important, more than monetarily. They mean something special to the Spanish people, and they were loaned to the United States as a very special favor. If it was generally known that we had been careless enough to allow the jewels to be stolen, it might seem as though we hadn't put the importance on them that they deserve."

"I see."

But Elizabeth wasn't sure she believed him, because it didn't make sense to her that he wouldn't go to the police. Orders or not, bad publicity or not, he was accused of being a terrorist, and so was she. That scared her a lot more than having been shot at yesterday.

Dan stood up. He smoothed the hair back from Paquito's forehead and said, "I'm sorry you're involved in this, Miss Kensington. I'm going to do my best to protect you and to get you out of here just as soon as I can."

Elizabeth looked up at him. Carefully she studied his unsmiling face, trying to see what lay behind his eyes. He had a small scar near the cleft in his chin, another over his right eyebrow, which gave him a rakish look. She could see that a certain type of woman—someone like Adelita—would find him terribly attractive.

His type would never appeal to her, of course. She had more sense than that.

That night, when the moon came out full and fat and yellow, some of the Gypsies gathered outside of Jonas and Pilar's house. The talk began; the Manzanilla flowed. Soon one of the men went to get his guitar, then another got his, and another.

A man began to sing the eerie song of a *cante hondo*. "The deep song," the Spanish called it, a lament of love and sadness, of loss and forgiveness.

Elizabeth, in a straight-backed chair beside Dan, felt a chill run down her spine as the sliding, fragmented notes struck through the darkness of the night. The sharp quaver, the piercing cry that was part African, part Moorish, and the staccato accompaniment of the guitars told of a passion, a rhythm of life that was as old as time.

The singer's eyes closed in a kind of agonizing ecstasy. "Ay...eee..." he sang in a tone that held an everlasting pessimism, a deep and abiding sense of the tragedy of life.

Abruptly the guitarist stopped and rapped with his fingers on his instrument. The singer's voice went higher, still higher in frenzied emotion.

Elizabeth, breathless with excitement, her heart pounding with the drama of the song, looked at the others seated around her. The Gypsies' heads were bowed; their eyes were closed. The palms of their hands came together in time to the rhythm. The claps became louder, the voice higher, the guitars faster.

Pilar stood up. She listened for a moment, then she lifted her arms above her head and began to dance. There were no formal steps, no practiced movements. This was a dance that spoke of hundreds of years of the heritage of her people, of the rhythm, the mystery of who and what, of everything she was. It came from somewhere deep down in her soul.

Pilar was neither young nor beautiful. She was fifty pounds overweight. And yet, now, dancing here beneath the moon, she seemed to Elizabeth the embodiment of the eternal female.

The guitars played. The singer sang. The music, the singer and the dancer were all woven together, in and out, beautifully, magically.

Cries of *"¡Olé! ¡Olé!"* echoed softly in the night.

Elizabeth turned to look at Dan. His face, in the glow of moonlight, was transfixed. He looked at her and their glances locked and held. And suddenly, clearly, Elizabeth remembered the heat of his body next to hers last night, the warm man scent of him, the hush of his breath against her face.

As he looked at her now, there was a sudden awareness in his eyes. His body tensed. His lips formed her name, and she looked quickly away.

The music came faster. The combs that held Pilar's long dark hair in place flew to the ground. Her hair moved with her body now—swayed as she swayed—a dark veil that hid her face.

The music reached a frenzied crescendo, then abruptly, as sudden as death, it quivered and stopped. For a moment there was only silence, then muted cries of *"¡Mucho! ¡Mucho!"* And finally the pounding of hands, the shouted, "*¡Olé*'s."

Elizabeth let out the breath she hadn't even known she'd been holding. She wet her lips, and in a voice trembling with emotion, she whispered, "I've never seen anything quite... quite like that before. She's magnificent, isn't she?"

Dan smiled. "She's a Gypsy," he said.

The hour had grown late. Jonas and Dan, together with an elderly uncle, were seated around the kitchen table drinking wine and exchanging stories.

The guitarists and the singers, with a soft *"Adiós,"* had drifted away to their homes or down to the city, where they would find a club and play till morning. Pilar and Elizabeth sat side by side in their cane chairs outside the still open door.

"You're a wonderful dancer," Elizabeth said. "I've never seen anything like that before."

"You've never seen flamenco?"

"Not the way you dance it."

"I am Gypsy." Pilar said. "The flamenco is part of me. It is in my blood."

Elizabeth, her face solemn, nodded. She leaned her head back and looked up at the sky. "I don't think I've ever seen the moon so bright," she murmured.

"It is a Capricorn moon." Pilar looked at her more closely. "The Gypsies say that strange things happen under a Capricorn moon."

And again Elizabeth nodded, for it was true. Tonight she had felt something—an emotion she'd never felt before. Perhaps it was a sense of timelessness, of mystery, passion and a deep, almost overwhelming sensuality that emanated from the music of the guitars, from the voice of the man who sang the *cante hondo* and from the woman who had danced.

Pilar stood up. "Come inside," she said. "I want to read your palm."

"Oh, I don't think..."

But Pilar took her arm. "Come," she said. "It is a Gypsy tradition to read the palm of a guest."

Once inside, she seated Elizabeth on a stool beside a gaudily fringed lamp, sat down next to her, and took her hand. She bent the fingers back a bit, forcing the palm upward and closer to the light.

For a long moment she didn't speak. Then she said, "Your life is going to change. You yourself know that the change has already begun." She raised her dark eyes and looked at Elizabeth. "You will travel," she said.

"The only place I want to travel is away from here."

"But why?" Pilar looked down at Elizabeth's palm again. She traced a finger down a crisscross line. "There will be adventure," she whispered, "and danger. But the danger will free you."

"What... what do you mean?"

"You are afraid." Pilar looked at her again. "Not of life, but of living. You shouldn't be, you know, for life is an adventure, and you must live every moment of it." Her hand closed around Elizabeth's. "Close your eyes. Feel the beat of life; feel it all around you."

Pilar closed her eyes and for a moment was silent. When she opened them she smiled a slow, secret smile and said, "I place a Gypsy curse on you, Señorita Eleezabet. The curse of love. May its wings enfold you, bind and hold you, break and shatter you. This love will strip you of your defenses and render you naked. You will do things you've never thought of doing. You—"

Elizabeth pulled her hand away.

Pilar hesitated, then with a mocking smile said, "And, of course, I see a long life, a handsome husband and many children."

Elizabeth took a deep, shaking breath. "I don't want to hear any more of this nonsense," she said. Then, lowering her voice, she whispered, "Please, won't you help me get away?"

"But why do you want to get away? Thornton is a good man. He is handsome, and more than that, he has the look of a skillful lover—of a man who knows how to please a woman."

Elizabeth's mouth tightened. "Really!" she said.

Pilar laughed, a belly laugh that shook her whole body.

"What's so funny?" Dan called out.

"Nothing." Elizabeth stood up. "I'm going to bed. I'm tired." She went to the room she'd slept in the night before.

Too much had happened to her these past two days. She'd been knocked down, shot at, kidnapped and thrust in among a band of Gypsies. Suddenly her well-ordered life wasn't so well-ordered. She'd lost control. She couldn't come and go as she wanted to, for although she hadn't been mistreated, she was a prisoner. And worst of all, she was being forced to share a room—a *bed*—with a man who was a total stranger.

She still wasn't sure whether or not he was a terrorist, but whatever or whoever he was, the minute he turned his back, she'd make a run for it. She— There was a knock on the door. Since Elizabeth was in only her slip now, she grabbed the blouse she'd just taken off and held it in front of her before she said, "Yes? What is it?"

"May I come in?"

"If you have to," she said testily, and frowned when Dan opened the door. "What do you want?" she asked.

"To go to bed."

Her frowned deepened. "If you were a gentleman, you'd sleep on the floor."

"Then I guess I'm not a gentleman." He yawned and flexed his shoulders. "Look," he said patiently, "it's been a long day. We're both tired. I'll sleep on top of the quilt like I did last night."

"You crawled under it during the night."

Dan grinned. "Oh yeah, that's right. I did, didn't I? I won't tonight, I promise. I'll put my jacket over me. Okay?" And when Elizabeth didn't answer, he said, "I'm too tired to argue. Get into bed."

She glared at him. He took a step toward her, and she got into bed and pulled the quilt over her before she tossed her blouse out. Between clenched teeth, she said, "How long is this going to go on?"

"With any luck we'll be out of here tomorrow."

"Tomorrow? Thank God! I'll take a bus into Málaga. From there—"

Dan shook his head. "You're sticking with me."

"No, I'm not!"

He sat down on the bed and pulled his boots off. When he saw that she'd edged as far away from him as she could get, he said, this time not so patiently, "I don't plan on making a move on you, not tonight and not tomorrow. All I want to do is keep both of us alive."

Elizabeth opened her mouth to speak, but Dan held up his hand. "Castro and Sanchez have friends all over Spain. Your picture has been in the paper, and by now they've spread the word to be on the lookout for you." He lay back on the quilt, hands behind his head. "You've got no choice—you have to stay with me until this is over. We'll head for Seville tomorrow. That's where Al Thomason, the guy who was supposed to meet me in the Alhambra, is. Once I turn the jewels over to him, you and I are out of the country."

"But I'm on a sabbatical leave," she protested. "I'm going to do my dissertation on Spanish culture and ethnic dances. I *have* to stay in Spain. I—"

"You can come back next year." Dan snapped the light off, and the room was plunged into darkness.

"I haven't finished. I—"

Dan rolled over. "Good night, Elizabeth," he said firmly.

Chapter 4

The night before, Dan had been too tired to have been aware of the woman in bed next to him. She'd only been someone who'd gotten in his way, an unnecessary burden that he wanted to get rid of just as soon as he could.

He still wanted to get rid of her, but the difference now was that he saw her as a person. Tonight when Pilar had danced, he had looked at Elizabeth. Her face had been partly shadowed by the moon, and there had been something about her, an expression of breathless excitement that had made him want to reach out to her. Her lips had been parted, and when she'd looked at him, her eyes had been luminous. He'd seen the rapid rise and fall of her breasts, and his body had stirred and tightened. It had excited him to know that she was as deeply affected as he was by the raw emotion of Pilar's dancing.

He was sorry he'd brought her into this, but he knew even now that he'd had no choice. If he'd left her behind, she'd either have been killed on the spot or Castro would have turned her over to Sanchez, which just about amounted to the same thing. He had to keep her with him until he reached Seville and turned the jewels over to Thomason. He cursed silently, wondering what the hell had happened to Thomason and why he hadn't shown up.

It would be dangerous traveling, especially since Elizabeth's picture had been in the newspaper. But he had no choice. He couldn't stay here forever; he had to get to Seville.

Elizabeth turned on her side, and in spite of the seriousness of his thoughts, Dan grinned, because he knew that when he'd turned out the light, she had gotten as far over on her side of the bed as she could get. But now, in her sleep, and in the chill of the night, she had unconsciously moved closer to him.

He tried to conjure up a picture of the blonde he'd met in Puerto Vallarta. He couldn't. He thought about Adelita, a young woman of obvious charms and a deep reluctance to ever say no. Before she had gone into the city with the others tonight, she had said, "Come with me, Danny."

"I can't, Adelita, I'm sorry," he said.

Her bright red lips had come together in a pout. "But I want to dance for you, Danny."

"Another time."

"Then I will stay here with you. We will take a walk in the moonlight, and afterward—" she tucked her arm through his "—afterward we will make love on the sofa. Yes."

Dan had shaken his head. "The sofa's too lumpy," he'd told her with a grin.

Adelita moved away from him. Hands on her hips, her eyes narrowed, she'd said, "If you don't want me, then you are doing it with the American woman. *¡Hijole!* That must be as exciting as making love to a dead fish."

"Mind your manners, Adelita."

"I thought you had better taste, Dan," she taunted. "But I see you don't. So go to your dead fish, and while you are making love with her, think about what it would be like making love with me."

He didn't want to make love to Adelita. It wasn't just because he didn't go for women who were so blatantly obvious, it was also because he was Jonas and Pilar's friend. As for the schoolteacher... He was suddenly, uncomfortably, more than a little aware of Elizabeth beside him in the bed. He remembered then that when he had awakened this morning, her head had rested against his shoulder and his arm had been around her waist. He remembered the softness of her skin, the scent of her hair.

He wanted to touch her and wondered what she would do if he did. Would she scream if he put his arms around her, or would she move willingly, warmly, into his embrace?

Once again, as he had earlier tonight, Dan felt his body tighten. He moved as closely to his side of the bed as Elizabeth had moved to hers.

To get his mind off her, he touched the pouch that held the jewels. He'd snatched them and gotten out of Córdoba without ever having taken the time to look at them. He was curious to see what $6.5 million worth of jewels looked like, and he decided that maybe on the long ride to Seville, he'd stop and take a look at them.

He thought about the trip he'd arranged and barely managed to suppress a chuckle. Wait till the schoolteacher gets a look at our transportation, he thought. Then, with a smile, Dan closed his eyes and went to sleep.

* * *

"A wagon! You expect me to ride in a Gypsy wagon!"

Scarcely daring to believe her eyes, Elizabeth looked out the door at the bright green, red and gold-trimmed wagon. The door in the back was decorated with orange-and-blue flowers, the wheels and undercarriage were painted black and gold. Two horses were hitched to the front of it.

She hadn't expected a Mercedes to be waiting at the door when Dan told her this morning at dawn that he'd arranged transportation and that they'd be leaving as soon as she was ready. But this . . . this *thing*! It belonged in a carnival!

"You'll have to change your clothes," he said.

"Change my clothes!" So upset she could barely speak, Elizabeth faced him. "My clothes were on the bus, you idiot. God only knows where they are now."

"Not *your* clothes," Dan said impatiently. "You couldn't ride around Spain in a Gypsy wagon wearing your clothes."

"Then whose clothes am I supposed to wear?"

"Adelita's."

"Over my dead body," she spat out.

"Anyway you want it." Dan reached behind him and thrust a small bundle into her arms. "Put 'em on," he said, "or I'll do it for you." He turned to Pilar, who watched from the beaded curtains that separated the living room from the kitchen. "Will you help her?" he asked. "If she gives you any trouble, call me."

"I'm not going with you," Elizabeth protested. "I'll take my chances on a bus. I'll—"

Pilar gripped her arm. Pleasantly but firmly she said, "Come along, Señorita Eleezabet. This will be fun for you, like a game, yes?"

No, Elizabeth thought while Pilar propelled her through the narrow cave-house. This isn't a game and I don't want to play.

But she didn't have any choice. Pilar stood in front of the bedroom door watching while Elizabeth changed from her white blouse and gray skirt into the clothes that Dan had given her.

The bright red off-the-shoulder blouse had short puffed sleeves and laced provocatively up the front. Because Elizabeth was more richly endowed than Adelita, it hugged and accentuated her breasts and made her look, she thought with a scowl, like a two-bit hooker.

Pilar handed her a long flowered skirt and a pair of high-heeled black patent-leather shoes. "Put these on," she ordered.

"Can't I at least wear my own shoes?"

"Yours are old-lady shoes," Pilar said disdainfully. "I will give them to Jonas's old aunt. You can keep that awful gray thing you wear, but hide it out of sight. If anybody stopped you they would know that no Gypsy would wear such a drab outfit. Now sit in the chair and let me do something about your hair."

"My hair is perfectly all right."

"Hah! You look like a nun. Gypsies do not look like nuns."

Pilar took the clasp out of Elizabeth's hair and threw it on the bed. She ran her fingers through the dark brown waves, then took a hairbrush out of her pocket. "We will brush it," she said. "Then we must do something about your face."

"My face is—"

"Perfectly all right," Pilar finished for her. "We just embellish it a little, yes?"

No! Elizabeth wanted to shout out in protest, but she knew it wouldn't do any good. Pilar was in charge, and Pilar would have things her own way.

Twenty minutes later the Gypsy declared that Elizabeth was ready and allowed her to look in the mirror that hung behind the door.

Elizabeth gasped when she did. Pilar had outlined her eyes and coated her lashes with mascara. There was a blush of color high on her cheeks, and her lips were bright poppy red. As for her hair, Pilar had brushed it loose down around her shoulders and cut a wisp of bangs across her forehead. She'd snapped gold loop earrings on Elizabeth's ears and half a dozen bracelets around her wrists.

"It's too much," Elizabeth gasped.

"Too much? What are you saying? You're perfect, Eleezabet. With your dark hair and green eyes, you could be a real Gypsy. A beautiful Gypsy." Pilar rested a hand on Elizabeth's shoulder. "I told you last night that I saw adventure in your palm. There is danger, too, but I think that whatever danger you suffer will be balanced by new and exciting experiences if you allow yourself the freedom to release the passion that is inside you."

"Passion?" A self-mocking smile formed, then faded. Elizabeth shook her head. "I'm not a passionate woman, Pilar. Nor am I beautiful. I'm intelligent and realistic and always practical. You're wrong about these clothes and about me. I'm not the kind of woman who wears red. I'm the kind who wears gray."

But Pilar shook her head. "My poor, intelligent Eleezabet," she said sadly. "You know so little of life and almost nothing of yourself." She handed Elizabeth a shawl, then opened the door and motioned her out. "But perhaps on this trip you will learn," she murmured too quietly for Elizabeth to hear.

They went out to find Dan, who looked only a little self-conscious in old black pants that fit tightly around his muscular legs, a belt with a brass buckle and a white shirt with rolled-up sleeves. He had a red kerchief around his neck and a checked cap pulled on over his brown hair.

"Are you ready?" he said, then stopped and stared at Elizabeth. For a moment he didn't say anything, then he took a deep breath and with a nod said, "Yes, you'll do."

She gave him a dirty look, but before she could answer him, Jonas came out with Rosalia and Paquito. The two-year-old made a beeline for the wagon, but the little girl grabbed him before he could hop up onto the steps.

"It's okay," Dan said. "He can look inside, but you'd better hold his hand, Rosalia, so that he doesn't get into anything." He turned to Elizabeth. "Would you like to have a look?" he asked.

She clutched her purse and a paper bag that held the gray suit and white blouse, and with a nod followed Rosalia and Paquito.

The inside of the wagon was small. A dozen or so copper pans hung from every available bit of wall space. There was a fold-up table on one side next to two camp chairs with boxes and baskets of food stowed under them. There was hardly any space to move around, because most of the wagon was taken up with a brass bed canopied with tasseled red curtains that were held in place by shiny yellow bows. A small window above the bed was draped in the same tasseled red material as the canopy.

Elizabeth's eyes widened in disbelief. She felt as though she'd been asleep and had awakened in the middle of a technicolor nightmare.

"It's so beautiful!" Rosalia said in a breathless little voice. "It's the most beautiful place I've ever seen." She touched the worn pink satin comforter. "Isn't it beautiful, *señorita*?"

"Yes, well it certainly is something."

"I wish I was going with you," Rosalia whispered so that Paquito, who was already climbing out of the wagon, wouldn't overhear.

"Yes, so do I," Elizabeth said, and meant it. She liked the child, even though she didn't like the mother, and so she gave Rosalia a hug. "I'm going to come back," she promised, "and when I do we'll do something special, like maybe go to a restaurant or to a movie. Would you like that?"

"Oh, yes!"

Dan stuck his head in the doorway. "Sorry, honey," he said to Rosalia. "The *señorita* and I have to leave now."

Elizabeth went back outside with Rosalia. Pilar and Jonas were there, together with some of the relatives and neighbors. Thc men, outshouting one another, gave Dan directions.

"Take only the country roads."

"Watch out for the Guardia."

"Don't talk too much. Your Spanish is good, but you have an accent."

"Be careful when you're near a city."

"Do you have enough wine?"

Dan assured them that he'd be careful and that he had enough wine before he turned to Jonas and Pilar. "There's no way I can ever thank you," he said.

"You'll come back when this is over?" Jonas asked him.

"Yes, my friend. I will come back."

Pilar kissed both his cheeks. Then, before Elizabeth could step back, she kissed her, too. "You come back, too, Eleezabet." And it was a statement, not a question.

"Thank you for..." For what? Elizabeth wondered. For keeping me a prisoner? For dressing me up in this ridiculous outfit? Nevertheless, Pilar and Jonas had both been kind to her, so she said, "Thank you for your kindness and your hospitality," and meant it.

Dan took her arm. "You can sit up front with me for a while, if you'd like to."

Elizabeth looked around for Rosalia. She wanted to tell her goodbye, but Rosalia was nowhere to be seen.

As the *adióses* were said, Dan led Elizabeth around to the front of the wagon. He had just taken her arm to help her up when Rosalia came running toward them, clutching a bunch of wildflowers in her hand.

"These are for you," she said as she thrust them into Elizabeth's hands.

Then, before Elizabeth could thank her, she turned and ran into the house.

Dan liked riding through the Spanish countryside this way, past fields where sheep still grazed on the late grass of autumn. It gave him pleasure to watch the shepherds, old and gnarled, most of them, leaning on their walking sticks as they paused to wave, then to shout to their dogs. Unlike some farmers in the States who wore broad-brimmed straw hats to protect their faces from the sun, the shepherds of Spain wore only the *boina*, the small felt beret, to protect them.

They were as ageless as the whitewashed mountain villages, Dan thought as he flicked the whip idly across the backs of the horses. Kings came and went, as did dictators, but Spain remained eternal. Always and forever there would be good red wine and the strum of guitars. And shepherds tending their flocks in fields made golden in the hot Spanish sun.

He glanced at the woman sitting next to him on the narrow seat and knew by the expression on her face that she, too, was enjoying the countryside.

Elizabeth Kensington, Ohio schoolteacher. He wondered if she knew how different she looked dressed the way she was today. For a moment when she'd come out of the house with Pilar, he'd thought she was Adelita. Then he'd realized that her figure was fuller, more womanly than Pilar's daughter's.

He was glad that he hadn't realized it last night. God knows he'd been too much aware of her as it was.

A little after noon, Dan pulled the wagon off the road and under some overhanging trees. "Lunchtime," he announced. "Are you hungry?"

Elizabeth nodded as Dan jumped down off the wagon, then held a hand up to help her off.

"We'll just have some bread and cheese now," he told her. "When we stop tonight, we'll build a camp fire and have a hot meal."

"I don't know how to cook over a camp fire."

"You'll learn."

"I have no intention of learning."

Dan reached into the back of the wagon and pulled out a basket of food. "You will if you want to eat." He moved toward the trees. "Seville is over 150 miles from here. If we do twenty-five miles a day, it'll take us six days to get there, if we don't run into any trouble." He looked at her. "So you'll do your share, Elizabeth." He stopped and opened the basket, then handed her a roll of salami and a knife. "Slice it while I unwrap the cheese," he ordered.

They spread the lunch out on the clean white cloth that had covered the basket. Elizabeth put Rosalia's flowers in a cup on the white cloth next to the bottle of red wine. She didn't notice the smile on Dan's face while he watched her. She only nodded when he said, "Rosalia's a nice little girl, isn't she?"

The salami and cheese tasted good, and when they had eaten their fill, Dan said, "It's nice here. I wish we could stay awhile."

Elizabeth looked around her. The landscape stretched out before them, amber and golden in the sunlight. In the distance there was a church made of stone the same color as the land and a cluster of red-roofed houses. Beyond, the mountains rose toward a sky as blue as any Elizabeth had ever seen. The sun streaked through the branches of the trees, and meadowlarks sang their way across the field. "Yes," she said, "it's nice here."

Dan leaned back against the trunk of a tree and stretched his legs out in front of him. "Tell me about yourself. I've forgotten the name of the place you're from."

"Rocky River. It's a suburb of Cleveland."

"And you teach school?"

"High school Spanish."

"And you're in Spain because . . ."

"I'm working toward a Ph.D. on Spanish culture and dance."

Dan's eyebrows went up. "Are you a dancer?"

"I teach folk dancing."

"But do you dance?"

"I *teach*."

"Oh." He plucked a blade of grass and rolled it between his fingers. "What else do you do? I mean, what do you do for fun?"

Elizabeth shrugged. "The same things anybody else does, I suppose."

"Do you have a family?"

"My sister Paula and my mother. My father died when I was fifteen."

"Are you and your sister close?"

"Yes." A smile softened Elizabeth's mouth. "We weren't for a long time. I resented her when I was younger because she was pretty and I wasn't. My mother always said that Paula had the looks and I had the brains. That wasn't fair to Paula—she's got plenty of brains. She's married now and has three little boys."

Dan studied her face. She'd said she wasn't pretty as though it were a matter of actual fact, and perhaps in her mind it was. Certainly if she'd heard it often enough, she would have come to believe it. And it was true, she wasn't pretty—she was more than that. Her face, if one had the sense to really look at her, was quietly, classically beautiful.

Dressed as she was now in the red off-the-shoulder blouse, he could see how lean and lovely her body was, how womanly. He gazed at the string that fastened the front of the blouse and thought, with only a tug, it would open to reveal her breasts.

Abruptly Dan got to his feet. "Time to go," he said almost roughly. "I'd like to be on the road to Loja before dark."

There was little conversation after that. When the air grew cooler, Elizabeth moved back into the wagon and stayed there until Dan left the small road they'd been traveling. She poked her head between the curtains and saw that he had taken what was little more than a cow path down a country lane.

"We'll stop here," he said. "It's not a good idea to be on the road at night."

He jumped from the wagon, unharnessed the horses and led them to a brook. After they'd drunk their fill, he tied them under one of the trees.

Elizabeth climbed down from the wagon and looked around. The spot was nice enough, but it was so completely away from the road, so far from anything that for a moment she felt a chill of fear. She'd been alone with Dan all day, but there'd been houses in the distance and the occasional shepherd. Here in this desolate spot, there was no sign of civilization. She didn't know if Dan Thornton was who he said he was. For all she knew *he* was the criminal, not the men who'd been shooting at him.

"There should be coffee in one of the boxes," he said, breaking in on her thoughts. "Drag out what we need for supper while I get a fire started."

Restraining the urge to salute, Elizabeth reached back up into the wagon and took out the same salami and cheese they'd had for lunch. That would have to do tonight, because she had no intention of trying to cook on a skewer over a camp fire.

It was dark by the time Dan got a fire going and put a pot of coffee on. He eyed the cold supper that Elizabeth had laid out and said, "We'll buy a chicken for tomorrow. You do know how to cook chicken, don't you?"

"In a microwave," she said.

"I don't think we brought one along."

Her brow puckered in a frown. She tore off a piece of bread and put a slice of cheese on it.

Because Dan knew she was angry, he grinned at her and said, "If anybody saw you now, they'd swear you were a Gypsy."

And it was true. She sat cross-legged on a blanket he'd spread over the ground. In the Gypsy skirt and blouse, with her dark hair down over her bare shoulders and the firelight dancing against her face, she did look like a Gypsy.

"Your mother was wrong," he said.

"What?" Her green eyes widened. "What are you talking about?"

"You're really a very beautiful woman."

She stilled. For a moment she didn't say anything. Then, in a voice that trembled, she said, "Don't...don't say that."

"Why not? Hasn't anybody told you that before?"

Her hand came up to her throat. She took a deep, shaking breath. "Don't make fun of me."

"I'm not making fun of you," he said quietly.

For a moment Elizabeth didn't answer him. Then she said, "I'm tired. I think I'll rest now."

Dan nodded. "Just let me get my bedroll."

He wanted to say something else to her, something to reassure her that when he'd told her she was beautiful, he hadn't been making an advance, he'd simply been stating what seemed obvious to him.

He stood up and went to the wagon and took down the bedroll that Jonas had packed.

"I'll be sleeping under the wagon," he told Elizabeth.

She nodded without looking at him, then pulled the shawl around her shoulders as though for protection. "Good night, Mr. Thornton."

"Dan. Please call me Dan."

"Elizabeth," she said with the slightest of smiles.

When she went into the wagon and closed the door behind her, he poured himself another cup of coffee. Then he moved closer to the fire and sat for a long time, watching the flames.

Chapter 5

Dan Thornton had had only one serious love affair in his thirty-five years. Her name was Annabel and she had lived in the house next door to him on Briarwood Avenue in Laurel, Mississippi, where his parents had moved when he was fourteen.

He hadn't wanted to move, and he'd vowed that he'd hate living in Laurel. He'd been sulky and mean the first few days there. Then he'd gotten a look at the girl next door.

Annabel had been blond and beautiful, a fourteen-year-old nymphet in bright blue shorts and a skimpy little halter that barely covered her already developed breasts.

Dan and Annabel went steady all through high school. Sometimes she was as sweet as the molasses cake her mother made for all the church socials; sometimes she wasn't. She was as seductive as a cat, deliberately teasing and provocative. She'd lure him on, then push him away and drive him right out of his adolescent mind.

They became lovers the night before he left for Tulane.

Annabel, who had decided not to waste her time going to college, visited him in New Orleans as often as she could, and, of course, Dan had gone home every summer.

He'd never been able to figure out why his mother's face grew stiff and cold whenever Annabel was around or why his father told him he was too young to be so serious. And he'd knocked Sam Detweiler down when Sam said, "Wise up, pal, your lady's got round heels."

Dan's graduation was in June; he and Annabel planned a July wedding. She came to New Orleans a few days ahead of graduation, and they'd had a wonderful time together, right up until the afternoon of the big dance.

Because he had a lot of things to do, Dan had asked his roommate, Artie Schofield, to take care of Annabel.

Artie had—he'd taken Annabel to bed. And Dan had walked in on them.

He didn't go to the dance or to the graduation ceremonies. Instead, he'd enlisted in the air force.

There'd been a lot of women since Annabel, and most of them, like her, had been beautiful and blond. But he'd never had a serious relationship with any of them, and he'd vowed he never would.

Dan got up and put some wood on the fire before he stretched the bedroll out under the wagon and lay down. He closed his eyes, but when he did he thought about Elizabeth, who lay just a few feet above him.

He wondered if she was wearing the same white slip she'd worn to bed the past two nights. What did she usually sleep in? Tailored pajamas, probably. Or maybe not. Maybe that was the one time she allowed herself to be frivolous. Maybe she wore slinky-soft gowns. Maybe she even slept in the nude.

He had a sudden and vivid picture of her curled up above him under the pink satin comforter. Behind his closed eyelids he could see the outline of her breasts, the curve of her hips.

He cursed and without thinking sat up and banged his head hard against the underside of the wagon. He cursed again, then lay down on his side. He would not—he absolutely, by damn, would not—think about Elizabeth Kensington.

She felt the bump when Dan hit his head and knew that he lay just beneath her.

That gave her a peculiar feeling.

They were strangers, yet she had experienced things with Dan Thornton that she'd never experienced with any other man. She'd slept with him. She'd listened to his quiet breathing and felt the warmth of his body next to hers. Today, riding up on the wagon beside him, she'd been more aware of the world around her than she'd ever been before. The air had smelled sweeter, the colors of the landscape and the sky had seemed more vivid.

Elizabeth pulled the comforter up over her head, furious with Dan Thornton and with herself for thinking about him. He'd said it would take six days to reach Seville. Six days! She had to get away from him, to get to a town, a village, anywhere there might be a bus passing through. She didn't believe she was in the danger he'd said she was in. And in spite of what he'd said about keeping her with him, he'd be relieved to have her out of his way.

A trembling sigh escaped her lips, because she'd made her mind up; she was going to get away from Dan Thornton.

Dan wasn't sure what had awakened him. He lay for a few minutes with his eyes closed, listening to the morning songs of the birds in the trees and the soft whinny of the horses.

The wagon above him was quiet, and he wondered if Elizabeth was awake.

He lifted his foot and rapped against the bottom of the wagon. "Hey," he called out. "Time to move it. Let's get the coffee going."

There wasn't any answer, so he eased his way out of the bedroll, then out from beneath the wagon. The air was cold, and he wondered if she'd been warm enough during the night.

He stood up and stretched, then rapped on the wagon door and said, "Up and at 'em, Elizabeth."

When she didn't answer, a frown creased his forehead and he opened the door. She wasn't there.

He told himself she was probably answering the call of nature and that she'd be back in a minute. He went over to the fire, stirred up the few embers that remained and added some of the kindling he'd picked up last night. Then, instead of taking care of the horses, he went back to the wagon and stood looking out toward the distant stand of trees. A flash of red caught his eye. Then he swore out loud and began to run, because he knew it was Elizabeth and that she was running away.

She'd been moving quickly, but she didn't start to run until she turned to look back at the wagon and saw him coming after her.

"Come back!" he cried. "Stop! Elizabeth, wait!"

She ran then, ran with her heart clamoring in her chest, past stunted trees and scraggly brush, over fallen leaves and moss-covered ground. Once she fell and scraped her ankle. She cried out in pain, but when she heard the slash of branches behind her, she scrambled to her feet. The breath rasped hard in her throat. Her ankle hurt and a pain ripped through her side, but she made herself go on.

He gained on her, reached out to grab her. She shook his hand off. He grabbed her again and spun her around. She yanked away from him. He fastened his hand around her arm. She staggered, then fell, dragging him down with her.

Weeping in frustration, flailing with her arms, she tried to squirm away from him. He grabbed her hands and held her pinned with his body.

"Stop it!" he gasped. "Dammit, Elizabeth...."

Her body surged under his, and she skittered away from him on her hands and knees. Dan lunged for her, caught the ankle she'd hurt and yanked.

She cried out in pain and tried to kick him. But he had her now, flat on her back, holding her body with his.

"Take it easy," he panted. "I don't want to hurt you."

"Let me go!"

"Not till you quiet down."

"Damn you!" She swung at him but he caught her hand, then pinned both hands together. Beside herself now at having been caught, Elizabeth's body writhed under his as she tried helplessly to get away from him.

The red blouse slipped low on her shoulders. Her skirt was halfway up her hips. Her hair was in wild disarray, and her face was scratched and dirty. And she moved so frantically, so hotly under him.

Dan looked down at her, and the breath caught in his throat. He said her name in a voice grown husky and raw with need.

Her movements stilled. Her eyes widened. "Let me go," she whispered.

He smoothed the tousled hair back from her face. He cupped her chin and leaned to take her lips.

She tried to move her hands, but he held her still with his two hands now while he tasted her.

Elizabeth fought to push him away. She struck out against him, and a sob rose in her throat because she was so helpless and because suddenly, traitorously, her body was on fire.

He knew, oh damn him, he knew. He lifted his mouth from hers. "Elizabeth?" he whispered, then he kissed her again, deeply, thoroughly, and when she trembled against him, his arms tightened around her.

He kissed her until her lips parted and her body softened under his, until her arms crept up to his shoulders and a small, pleasured sigh escaped her trembling lips.

She whispered, "No, no," but even as she did, her hands pressed him closer.

His mouth gentled on hers. "Sweet, sweet," he murmured. He kissed the side of her face, her closed eyes, her ears, her throat. But when he reached down and pulled at her skirt to hike it higher, Elizabeth stiffened.

"Don't," she whispered. "Please don't do that."

He hesitated.

"Please," she said again.

He nodded, unable for a moment to speak. He rested his head against her breasts, then shifted away from her.

"I'm sorry. I didn't mean for that to happen." He reached out and pulled the blouse up around her shoulders. He looked at the string that held the blouse together. With one tug he could...

"Come on," he said gruffly, and stood up.

It wasn't until they were almost back to where they had camped that Dan realized she'd hurt her ankle. "Why didn't you tell me you were hurt?" he said, and in spite of her protests picked her up and carried her the rest of the way.

"Where are your shoes?" he asked when he placed her on the back doorstep.

"I was carrying them. I guess I lost them when you came running after me."

"You'll have to wear your old ones."

"I don't have them. Pilar said they were old women's shoes. She gave them to Jonas's aunt."

"Then until we can buy you a new pair, you'll have to go barefoot." He looked at her and grinned, feeling some of the tension ease out of his body. "You've come a long way from Rocky River, Ohio," he said.

He bathed her scraped ankle. It was delicate and so slender he could circle it with his thumb and third finger. Touching her this way made his body tighten again, so he quickly bound the ankle in one of the white cloths Pilar had put in the wagon. Then he left her to go put a pot of coffee over the fire, and while it heated he took care of the horses.

When he went back to her, carrying a cup of coffee for her and one for himself, he said, "We have to talk, Elizabeth."

She avoided his gaze. Her mind was a jumble of thoughts; her body still trembling from his touch. She'd never experienced the kind of feeling she had when Dan Thornton kissed her. The crush of his body over hers, the feel of his lips... He'd been rough, then he'd been tender. And though his body had been hard against hers, he had stopped when she asked him to. She wasn't sure, even now, whether she'd been relieved or sorry.

"I know that all you want in this world is to get away from me," he said. "I'm a stranger who has come charging into your life, turning everything around. You've been shot at and kidnapped. You've been made to feel like a prisoner, and I'm sorry. I've forced you to come along with me in this ridiculous wagon, but honest to God, Elizabeth, I've only been trying to protect you."

He took her hand. "Look at me," he said.

And when she did, he went on. "I swear on all that I hold holy that I've told you the truth. I'm an insurance investigator. Ernesto Castro and Paco Sanchez took the jewels in Washington, and I took them back in Córdoba. I contacted Thomason as soon as I had them, and he promised to meet me in Granada. I don't know why he didn't. As soon as I can, I'll call him and let him know I'm coming to meet with him."

Dan's hand tightened around hers. "You've got to promise me you won't try to run away from me again. If Castro and Sanchez got hold of you—"

"Maybe I'd be safer with them than I am with you," she said huskily.

Dan shook his head. "I'm going to tell you about the kind of man Paco Sanchez is." He let go of her hand and sat down beside her. He took a sip of his coffee before he said, "I met him seven years ago. He was working in Tangier, and I was on a case. I didn't like him, but he knew somebody I needed to know, so we spent some time together. For a month or two I hung around with him and the woman he was living with."

Dan looked out at the trees. "She was a small woman. She was young and she was beautiful. One night Paco took me to their place for dinner. He got a call and he had to leave, but he told me to stay, that Yolanda—that was her name—would entertain me until he returned.

"He'd been gone maybe five minutes when she made her play, and it wasn't subtle. She looked at me and smiled, and then she pulled the gold satin caftan she'd been wearing over her head. She walked over to the bar, naked as a seal, and began making a couple of drinks. I remember her asking me if I liked my martinis dry as I headed for the door."

"You didn't stay?"

"Elizabeth, my dear, I know danger when I see it. She was a dangerous woman, and Paco was a dangerous man. I wanted no part of that scene. I was out of there as fast as my legs could carry me."

"Did you ever see Paco again?"

"No, but I've heard stories about him off and on through the years, about what he did to Yolanda." Dan put his coffee cup down and took one of Elizabeth's hands in his again. "A few months after I'd left Tangier, Paco got off work early one night. He went back to the apartment, and he found Yolanda with another man. He killed the man, but he didn't kill Yolanda—he cut her face and slashed her breasts."

Elizabeth paled. "He . . . ?" She swallowed, unable to go on.

"Your picture's been in the paper. If Paco or Castro spotted you, if they caught you..." He squeezed her hand hard enough to make her wince. "I want you with me until this is over. If I have to tie you to the bed, I will, but I'm going to make sure you're safe."

Elizabeth looked at him. For a moment she didn't say anything, then she said, "You won't have to tie me to the bed. I believe you. I'll stay with you till this is over, Dan."

He liked the way she said his name.

"I won't try to run away, but..." She hesitated and hot color rose in her cheeks. "But what happened a little while ago...between us, I mean, that can't happen again."

"It won't," he said, "not unless you want it to."

Then he went to get the horses so that he could hitch them to the wagon.

A little before noon they came to a village, where Dan bought a chicken, some fresh vegetables and a pair of sandals for Elizabeth. He asked if there was a telephone he could use, and the farmer he'd bought the chicken from told him there was a phone in the post office.

He tried to call Al Thomason in Seville, and when he couldn't get him, he called Al's fiancée in Madrid.

"I'm trying to get in touch with Al," he told Maria Cortez. "He was supposed to meet me in Granada four days ago, but he didn't show up. I've just tried to call him at the Seville office. There was no answer."

"I know, Dan." Maria sounded worried. "I haven't heard from him, either."

"Did he say anything about going to Granada?"

"*Sí*, Dan, but he said there were a couple of problems that he had to deal with first."

"He didn't mention what the problems were?"

"No," she said, and he heard the tremble in her voice.

"I'll be in Seville in a few days, Maria. I'll check on him and let you know." Dan paused, then said, "Have you seen anything in the newspapers about the kidnapping of an American woman?"

"A kidnapping? Yes, I think so. Wait a minute, I have today's paper here." Dan heard the rustle of paper, then Maria said, "It's on an inside page. A Miss Elizabeth Kensington. Is that what you mean?"

"Yes, what does it say?"

"That she is a teacher from the United States and that they think in some way her kidnapping is connected to the separatists. Wait.... It also says that the Guardia Civil has set up roadblocks. They're watching all of the exits out of the country. What's this all about, Dan? Does it have something to do with Al?"

"I can't tell you that now, Maria. I've got to go. I'll call you as soon as I've seen Al."

He put the phone down. Roadblocks! What in the hell was he going to do now? He'd been sticking to the country roads, but there were towns he couldn't avoid going through. The Guardia would be watching the main roads, but there was always the chance they'd also set up a block on the smaller roads.

He was frowning when he went back to where he'd told Elizabeth to wait and found her surrounded by a group of teenage girls. As he approached, he heard her say, "No, I can't. Really, I..."

"But all Gypsies read fortunes," one of the girls said. "Please read ours."

"What's going on?" Dan asked.

"We want your wife to read our palms," a girl said.

"Oh?" Dan raised an amused eyebrow. Then he scowled at Elizabeth. "Don't be lazy, woman," he said. "Are we so rich you can scoff at money?" He turned to the girls. "Will you cross her palm with silver?"

"Yes, of course. We already said we would."

"Then read their fortunes, *vieja*, or I will drag you off to our wagon and beat you."

Elizabeth, mortified, glared at Dan.

"Do me first." A girl of about sixteen pushed forward and thrust her hand toward Elizabeth. "Tell me everything you see."

Elizabeth bent her head. "You will meet a handsome young man," she said.

Fifteen minutes and hundreds of pesetas later, Elizabeth let Dan lead her back to the wagon.

"You did all right," he said with a laugh. "I know what to do now if we run out of money."

Surprisingly she laughed with him. Her face softened and he felt a glow of warmth flow through his body.

"I felt like a Gypsy just now," she said with a chuckle. "I told them exactly what they wanted to hear, and they loved it."

"Didn't Pilar read your palm the other night? What did she tell you?"

"She said I'd travel, that there would be adventure and danger..." Elizabeth looked at him, then quickly looked away.

"What else?" Dan prompted.

"I don't remember."

But she did, of course. She remembered all too well. "Life is an adventure," Pilar had said. "You must live every moment of it." And she'd said, "Thornton is a good man. He is handsome, and more than that he has the look of a skillful lover."

Elizabeth felt the flutter of pulse in her throat. She looked at Dan, then away. "I don't remember," she said again.

But that night as she lay in her bed in the wagon, every word that Pilar had said came back to her.... "He has the look of a skillful lover—of a man who knows how to please a woman."

A sigh shuddered through Elizabeth. She touched her tongue to her lips as though the taste of his lips still lingered. She moved restlessly in the bed, then suddenly lay still, wondering if he could feel her move above him. Her heart beat hard in her chest, and her body felt tense with longing as she gazed up at the tasseled red canopy above her bed.

"Dan," she whispered, and with his name on her lips, she finally slept.

Chapter 6

The weather turned bad. The skies were heavy and gray; dark clouds scudded low over the horizon. A little after noon, a slow, bitingly cold drizzle began. Dan turned to Elizabeth, who had been sitting up on the wagon with him, and said, "You'd better get inside."

"What about you?" She pulled the woolen shawl closer around her shoulders. "It's getting colder."

"You can hand me my jacket. That'll help."

He drove the team for another hour, the checked cap pulled down over his hair, his shoulders hunched against the cold. When the wind picked up, he swore under his breath, because he knew it would bring a hard rain. And it did. The sky darkened even more, and in a little while the rain came hard and fierce, making it almost impossible to see where he was going.

Dan slowed the horses, and when he spotted what was little more than a path leading off the road into the trees, he took it. He found a place to stop, then jumped off the wagon to unhitch the horses. After leading them a little distance away, he tied them under a tree, then made a dash for the wagon.

"You're soaked." Elizabeth sounded dismayed. "You've got to get out of your clothes."

Dan, shaking with cold, managed a grin. "I've been waiting for an invitation like that," he said.

Elizabeth frowned at him, then turned her back and began searching through a bundle of things Pilar had packed. At last she pulled out a worn black turtleneck sweater and a pair of jeans and handed them to Dan along with a towel.

He looked around. The inside of the wagon was small, no more than five feet by seven feet, and the bed took up most of the space. One eyebrow raised in question, he asked, "Where's the dressing room?"

"I'll turn my back," Elizabeth said in a no-nonsense voice.

She was very conscious of him only a few feet away from her as she rummaged through one of the baskets for a bottle of red wine. When she found it she poured some into two glasses, and when Dan said, "Ready," she turned around and handed him one.

"Perhaps this will help," she said.

"I'd prefer a hot cup of coffee, but wine will do. Thanks."

They drank in an uncomfortable silence, both of them terribly aware of having to share this small, crowded space. Elizabeth knew that even if the rain stopped, the ground would be too wet for Dan to sleep outside tonight. He'd have to sleep in here with her.

When darkness came he lighted the lantern that hung in one corner. It cast a dim, dusky glow that made everything look cozier, more intimate. Elizabeth sat on the edge of the bed. Dan sat on a camp stool only inches away.

He had never been so aware of a woman as he was of Elizabeth. He liked the way the light of the lantern brought out the auburn tints of her hair and the way the shadows played across her face. She looked beautiful, mysterious and infinitely desirable, and he thought he'd go crazy if he didn't touch her. He'd have moved away if he could, but there was nowhere to go. He had to think about something else, and so he said, "I telephoned Al Thomason's fiancée today to find out if she'd heard from Al, if she knew why he hadn't met me in Granada."

He took a sip of his wine. "She read me a piece out of the newspaper." He hesitated, then looked at Elizabeth. "The Guardia has set up roadblocks. The paper said they were looking for you. It's me they're really after, but if they find us together..." He drained his glass and reached for the bottle. When he'd poured more wine, he said, "Probably the one or two of the Guardia who are involved with Castro and Sanchez have arranged it so that if we're captured, we'll be turned over to them." He shook his head. "We've got to avoid the roadblocks."

"But how?" A pale hand fluttered at her throat. "We're using the country roads. Surely those won't be guarded."

"We can't be sure. We'll have to be careful. If we see any sign of them ahead, we'll abandon the wagon."

"And go on foot?"

"Or grab a local bus." Dan wanted to reassure her. He wanted to tell her that maybe things weren't as bad as he thought they were, but he couldn't. She had to be as aware of the danger as he was. That was the only way he could protect her.

The hour grew late. The rain beat hard against the roof. They ate some bread and cheese and had another glass of wine. Elizabeth stifled a yawn.

"We'd better get some sleep," Dan said.

"I'm not tired.

She yawned again and Dan wanted to put his arms around her. He wanted to say, It's okay. I'm not going to do anything you don't want me to do.

Instead, he got up and pulled the bedroll out from under the bed, where it was stored. "If I move a couple of boxes, there'll be room for this on the floor," he told her. And when he had stacked them, he unrolled the bag. It barely fit between the wall and her bed. "This'll do fine," he said in too hearty a voice.

He looked up at her. She was still sitting on the edge of the bed, the shawl pulled tightly around her shoulders as though for protection. Dan thought how vulnerable she looked, and suddenly his desire muted, because more than anything in the world, he wanted to keep her safe. He thought about what Paco Sanchez had done to Yolanda, and his stomach tightened with fear. He'd do anything, anything he had to, to keep Sanchez from ever laying a hand on Elizabeth.

He looked at her again, then he reached up and turned down the lantern. "Good night, Elizabeth," he said.

He felt the bed move and knew that she was taking off the red blouse and the skirt. Then he felt the mattress give and thought of what it would be like to be under the soft down comforter with her, how warm it would be there, how her body would feel curled next to his.

He rolled over onto his other side and tried to conjure up the faces of all the women who had come and gone in his life. But he couldn't. There was only one face, Elizabeth's face, and it refused to go away.

He was asleep when thunder roared across the sky. He felt the terrible force of the wind rock the wagon and opened his eyes just as lightning shattered the room.

Elizabeth, still half-asleep, cried out, "What's happening? What is it?"

"It's only a storm." Dan reached up and felt around on the bed until he found her hand, and when he did, he reached under the comforter and took it. "It's all right, honey. Go back to sleep."

Lightning struck again and her hand tightened on his. "Don't let go," she whispered.

"I won't. I'm right here. I won't let go." And he didn't; he held her hand all through the long night, till morning came and the wind stopped.

The rain stopped toward morning, too. The sun came out, and by noon they were able to build a fire and cook the chicken and the vegetables that Dan had bought the day before.

Dan watched Elizabeth lick a scrap of chicken off her fingers and tried not to smile. She'd changed a lot in the short time he'd known her. It wasn't just the clothes or her hair or that her face was tan from the sun and the sprinkle of freckles across her cheeks looked infinitely kissable—it was everything about her. She smiled more readily; she seemed more confident, more at ease with herself.

Last night her hand had felt very small in his, and a feeling he'd never before experienced had gripped him. He'd lain awake for a long time trying to figure out a way to get her out of Spain. But he couldn't come up with anything. Maria had said the Guardia was watching all exits out of the country. Until this thing was settled, Elizabeth would be safer with him.

Safer with him? That was a laugh. He wanted her so much every muscle in his body throbbed with it.

He glanced at her now, sitting up on the wagon seat beside him, clinging to the edge as the wheels rocked from side to side over the muddy ruts. She'd changed into another blouse this morning, a blue one that was too small and too tight across her breasts. He tore his gaze away. He called himself a fool and tried to tell himself that he'd be glad to get rid of her. As soon as this was over, he'd put her on a plane, and that would be the end of Miss Elizabeth— "There's something up ahead," she said, breaking in on his thoughts.

Dan reined the horses in. In the distance he saw a line of brightly decorated wagons. "What the hell!" he muttered, angry because he'd never be able to pass the whole line of them on this narrow country road.

"Gypsies," he told Elizabeth. "A whole caravan of them. Probably on their way to some kind of fiesta. We'll have to follow them until they turn off." He pushed the checked cap back on his head and smiled. "Or we could go with them."

"'Go with them'? What are you talking about?"

"The Guardia is looking for us. They might think to stop one Gypsy wagon, and maybe if they did, we'd pass for Gypsies and be all right. But I don't think they'd stop a whole caravan, and even if they did, I doubt they'd check every wagon thoroughly." He flicked the whip across the horses' backs. "If they're headed anywhere near Seville, we're going with them. Tousle your hair, Elizabeth. You're about to become a full-fledged Gypsy." Then, with a grin, he said, "But I can't call you Elizabeth, can I? That's not a Gypsy name. What'll it be—Isabela or Elisia?" And without giving her a chance to answer, he said, "Isabela. Yes, that suits you."

Elizabeth clung to the side of the wagon as the horses moved toward the caravan. The way things were going, she didn't know who she was. She looked down at the too-tight blouse that stretched across her breasts. I don't even look like me, she thought frantically. What's happening? Where's the *me* I started out with?

Then there was no more time for her scattered thoughts, because they'd caught up with the caravan.

The Gypsies accepted them without question. "We're on our way to the village of Cuevarubia, near the town of Estepa," they told Dan. "There we will celebrate the feast day of Santa Martina, the saint of all the Gypsies."

Dan nodded. He'd never heard of Cuevarubia, but he knew of Estepa and that was on the way to Seville. "My name is Daniel," he said. "My woman and I are going there, too. We were hoping to join a caravan."

"Then you are welcome to join ours." The leader, a man in his early forties, held out his hand. "I am Antonio Cortes." He turned and snapped his fingers, and a young woman of no more than sixteen hurried over. "This is my wife, Lupe." He draped one arm over her shoulder. "She is pretty, yes?"

A Gypsy dandy, Elizabeth thought. He wore a black felt hat tilted to one side of his shoulder-length wavy hair. He had on a flowered shirt with a white collar, a bright red tie with diamond-shaped black dots running through it, and a blue-and-silver silk jacket. There were rings on his fingers, and a cigarette dangled from his lips.

He let his young wife go, slapped her bottom and said, "Bring wine, Lupe, while I introduce our new friends to the others."

There were fifty or sixty in the group, people of all ages, boys and girls and babies, young couples and old couples. Some of the men were as flashy as Antonio; others were dressed like Dan, who'd changed back into the white shirt this morning. With the sleeves rolled up and a kerchief around his neck, he didn't look any different than they did.

Some of the women wore pants; some wore bright polka-dot flounced dresses. But most of them wore the same type of skirt and blouse that Elizabeth wore.

We fit in, she thought. We really don't look that much different.

That night, after everyone had eaten the evening meal, they sat together around a big camp fire. The air smelled sweet after the storm; the night was softly scented. One of the men brought out his guitar. He strummed as though unaware of the others and began to improvise. The music he played was his own, something that came from within. The melody was Moorish and sad, and the Gypsies murmured, *"Mucho, hombre, mucho."*

He began to sing softly to himself, songs of abandonment, of traitorous loves, of passion and infinite melancholy.

Elizabeth felt something stir deeply within her. Warmth spread through her body, but at the same time a chill, like a cold naked finger, ran up her spine. She felt hot tears sting her eyelids and a longing, a hunger unlike anything she'd ever known, crushed heavily against her heart. She raised her head and looked across the flames at Dan, looked into his face until the face was lost and there were only his eyes, amber in the firelight, gazing into hers.

She felt the beat of pulse in her throat, and the warmth she had known earlier turned into a fever that singed those secret places of her body. She tried to look away and could not, for she was caught, as he was, by a sudden bond, and by the music of the guitar and the sobbing voice of the man who sang.

Only when the music changed was Elizabeth able to look away.

Another man got his guitar, followed by another and another. They matched the rhythm of the first man, then little by little the music changed. They played *Sevillanas* and fandangos. *Malangueñas* gave way to, "Corners of the Albacín," and so many more. But all of them were songs of love, laments of a passion too deep to bear.

Elizabeth listened, watching through half-closed eyes. She had surrendered to the music now; she had become one with it and the night and the vibrant, rhythmic pulse of life all around her.

The hour grew late. A few of the Gypsies drifted away, but still the guitarists played on.

She stirred when she felt a hand on her shoulder and looked up when Dan said, "Come, Isabela, it's late."

He helped her to her feet, then nodded good night to the others, and with an arm around her waist, led her to their wagon.

They walked silently through the darkness. And because he knew that if he didn't say something he was going to pull her into his arms, he said, "We were lucky to find these people. We'll stay with them until Cuevarubia. They'll protect us if there's a roadblock."

Elizabeth nodded, but she didn't answer.

Dan opened the back of the wagon. He took her hand to help her in, then quickly let it go. "The ground is dry." His voice sounded too loud in the darkness of the wagon. "I can sleep outside tonight." He reached for the lantern. "Just let me light this for you—"

"No." Her voice was husky. "No, Dan, don't light the lantern."

"Elizabeth?" He held his breath. "Elizabeth," he said again, and reached for her.

She came to him, trembling in his arms, and raised her face for his kiss.

His kiss. Had anything ever been so good as this?

They stood together in the darkness, clinging, close. Her lips parted under his. He tasted her, slowly, deeply. His body grew hard with need, but he knew he must go slowly.

Elizabeth rested her hands against his chest. She could feel the accelerated beat of his heart, and the need to touch him, to be close to him, almost overwhelmed her. She pulled at the buttons of his shirt and when she laid her hand on his skin, she felt him shudder with pleasure.

He rubbed his face against her hair. "Elizabeth," he murmured. "Oh, Elizabeth."

He sought her mouth again. He kissed the corners and nibbled her full lower lip, excited by her softness, her taste. He eased his tongue past her parted lips, and the breath caught in his throat when she met him in a silken duel.

Their mouths still clinging, Dan reached for the string that fastened her blouse, and when it fell open, he slipped it off her shoulders and cupped her breasts.

And she was lost.

The kiss deepened, heated and grew until they were both frantic with need. He let her go long enough to pull her skirt and panties down, and when she stepped out of them, he sat on the edge of the bed and took off the rest of his clothes.

When he stood up, Elizabeth threw back the comforter. He put his arms around her, and they stood that way for a moment, naked bodies pressed together, and gently kissed.

She began to tremble again, from the cold and from an edge of fear of the unknown, but when Dan took her hand, the fear and the cold disappeared. Wrapped in each other's arms, they snuggled together under the satin comforter.

They kissed a thousand kisses. Dan ran his hands down her body as though memorizing her generous curves, her smooth planes, her swelling breasts. When he cupped them in his hands, he kissed each one in turn, gently, tenderly, and took one peak between his teeth to tug and tease. Elizabeth moaned with pleasure and his body flooded with joy.

Then she said, "Oh, please, Dan. Please," and he came up over her. He kissed her mouth. He felt the whole soft, womanly length of her beneath him.

"Elizabeth," he whispered, and joining his body to hers, he began to move against her, slowly at first, relishing the feel of her softness closing around him. And when she lifted her body to his he gasped with pleasure and drove himself deeper, harder into her moist warmth.

She pressed her hands against the small of his back to urge him closer. Her body on fire, she strained against him, wanting more and still more.

From outside she could still hear the slow, sensuous strum of the guitars. Their rhythm became her rhythm, and the woman who had been Elizabeth Kensington became Isabela the Gypsy, Daniel's woman.

She was fire and ice, a woman of passion, a woman who gladly gave and as gladly received. Her body was pulsing quicksilver. She kissed Dan's shoulder and tasted his skin. She raised her body close to his, murmuring, "Yes, like that. Yes."

His heart beat fast and his body shook with pleasure. He caressed her skin. He sought her lips and whispered frantic words of desire against them. He told her how she made him feel, how smooth and soft her body was, how sweet her lips.

Suddenly it was too much. Dan couldn't hold back. He plunged against her, driving, forceful, and groaned aloud when she told him she loved what he was doing to her.

"Yes," she said, "like that. Yes." Then, "Dan, oh, Dan..." as her body soared to a place she'd never known. And she shook with pleasure when she heard his answering cry.

He clasped her closely in his arms. He murmured her name against the dark cloud of her hair. She was warm and soft against him, her body still trembling with the reaction of what they had shared. He kissed her eyes, her nose, her mouth. He soothed her to calmness and knew that he had never felt this way before.

Morning came gently. Birds sang in the trees above them. A dog barked; a child laughed. The first soft rays of sun filtered in through the curtained window above the bed.

Elizabeth sighed and moved closer to Dan. She had an arm around his waist. Her head was against his shoulder, and their legs were intertwined. Without opening her eyes, she breathed in the good man-scent of his skin and touched her tongue to his shoulder, needing to taste him.

"'Lizbeth?" He kissed the top of her head and pulled the comforter up over her shoulders. "Good morning."

Her "good morning" sounded muffled. She snuggled closer but she didn't look at him.

He put a hand under her chin and lifted her face to his so that he could kiss her. Her lips were uncertain under his, and he knew that she was shy and that she felt awkward about what had happened between them.

In the clear light of day it seemed impossible that the woman in his arms was Elizabeth Kensington. Elizabeth the schoolteacher. Elizabeth the proper. She'd been like a brightly burning flame last night. Her mouth had been as hungry as his, her body as eager.

He didn't know what had brought her into his arms. He only knew that it had been heaven to hold her, and that when he'd joined his body to hers, it had been like no other joining he'd ever experienced.

"Open your eyes," he said. "Look at me."

Her long sooty lashes slowly raised to reveal her pale green eyes, eyes that looked shyly into his.

"Don't be sorry about what happened between us last night," Dan said.

She took a breath. "I'm not."

Dan kissed her nose. "I like the way you look," he said. "Are you cold?"

Elizabeth shook her head.

"I'd like to look at all of you. Is it all right?"

She caught her lower lip between her teeth, and her eyes widened as she nodded slowly.

Dan pushed the pink comforter back. He looked at her without speaking, and the breath caught in his throat because she was so perfect, so unbelievably lovely. Her breasts were high and full, and there was the same sprinkling of freckles across them as on her nose and cheeks. Her waist was narrow and her hips flared, just enough, before they tapered to her shapely legs.

He nuzzled her ear. "You're beautiful," he whispered. "I told you that before, and you didn't believe me." He raised his head and looked at her. "But believe me now, Elizabeth. You really are beautiful."

She threaded her fingers through his hair. "Thank you for saying that."

He looked at her. "I want to make love to you again."

She raised her arms and embraced him. Their lips met and it began again, that lovely warmth, that liquid fire that melted all the way through to her bones.

"I have to kiss your freckles," Dan said, and when she offered her nose, he said, "not there, love," and rested his face against her breasts. "These," he told her. "All of them, one by one."

His lips were soft and moist and hot against her skin. He kissed her while she threaded her fingers through his hair and kneaded his back. He kissed her until she thought her body would explode and she said, "Dan, oh Dan," and her body arched and small whimpers of pleasure tumbled from her lips.

When he came up over her, her arms encircled his back and her hungry mouth sought his mouth. He entered her quickly, and when he did, she buried her face against his shoulder so she would not cry aloud with the joy of having him inside her.

It was as it had been last night. They moved urgently together. Kissing, touching, their bodies yearning closer and still closer until it was so much more than either of them could stand.

"Now, love?" Dan managed to choke out. "Now?"

"Oh, yes. Please yes. Now yes."

Clinging, kissing, holding each other close, they climbed higher and higher until, with that final blissful, painful cry, they reached that almost impossible peak of ecstasy. And with trembling sighs settled gently back to the comfort of each other's arms.

Chapter 7

They came to a roadblock just before dusk that evening. Dan said, "There they are," and Elizabeth looked up the road to where the other wagons had stopped.

"Should I get in the back?" she asked nervously.

Dan shook his head. "No, stay where you are and try to look relaxed. It's going to be all right." He covered her hand with his and said, "You look like a Gypsy, but you'd better not say too much. Your Spanish accent is more Ohio than *Gitana*. I've been around Pilar and Jonas and their friends so often that I can get by, and I know enough Gypsy expressions to sound authentic."

His hand tightened on hers. "Don't worry," he said, "it's going to be all right. My name is Daniel and you're Isabela, *mi mujer*, my woman."

"Yes," Elizabeth said.

And yes, she thought, I *am* your woman, Dan. For as long as this lasts and for as long after that as you want me.

She had not known that falling in love would be like this. She had assumed that someday she would marry, probably someone like herself—a teacher—or perhaps a lawyer or an accountant, someone steady and reliable, a nine-to-five man. They would live a well-ordered life, and when he retired they would move to Florida.

That had been her somewhat sketchy dream of the path her life might take. Now she knew that dream would never be enough, that she would rather ride forever in a Gypsy wagon like this one, just as long as Daniel Thornton rode by her side.

This morning Elizabeth had tried to tell herself that what had happened last night had been because of the tension she'd been under since the first insane day in the gardens of the Alhambra. Pilar had told her that her life was going to change, and it had, it had done a complete turnaround from the moment she'd met Dan.

Last night sitting around the camp fire, listening to the vibrant music of the guitars and the passionate voice of the man who sang, she had felt something awaken within her. She had looked at Dan, and suddenly desire unlike anything she had ever known had gripped her. She'd wanted Dan to make love to her, and he had. Oh yes, he had.

She had awakened sometime during the night, overcome with shame. But before she could move out of Dan's embrace, his arms had tightened around her, and he'd nuzzled his face against her throat and murmured, "Sweet 'Lizbeth," and slept again.

This morning when she awakened, she'd half expected the madness of the night before to have subsided and that she would go right back to being sensible, proper Elizabeth again. But the madness hadn't gone away. Dan looked at her and touched her, and everything, all of the wonderful, tumultuous feelings of the night before had returned.

He had been tender and loving, and he'd carried her to heights she hadn't even known existed.

With a smothered sigh Elizabeth looked ahead and saw that a few of the wagons had passed the barricade and pulled up on the other side of the road. The wagon in front of them stopped. Three men in dark green uniforms, their patent-leather hats shining in the sun, stepped up to the wagon. Elizabeth put her hand on Dan's knee.

"Easy," he murmured. "Easy."

The wagon ahead moved on; it was their turn.

"Hola," Dan said. *"¿Buenas tardes, qué pasa?"*

"We're looking for a woman," one of them said.

Dan slapped Elizabeth's leg and with a chuckle said, "Well you can't have mine."

They laughed, and one of them remarked, "Your woman is *muy guapa*, Gypsy," He came closer to the wagon. "Very good looking, indeed."

Elizabeth tossed her dark hair over one bare shoulder and gave him a sloe-eyed smile.

"Enough of that." Dan pretended to scowl. Then, he asked, "Are we free to go?"

"Yes, you may go now." He winked at Dan. "But be careful of that woman of yours, Gypsy. She is *mucho mujer*, a lot of woman."

Dan saluted the men, then chucked to the horses. When they were out of earshot, he grinned at Elizabeth. "A lot of woman!" he said.

Elizabeth blushed. But she was pleased. Although last night had been wonderful beyond her expectations, she still felt shy about what had passed between them. She was pretty sure that Dan was a man of the world in more ways than one, that his experience with women far outweighed her one brief affair. She had wanted to please him, but last night there'd been no time to think about what she should do or how she should do it. Everything had been spontaneous because she'd been overwhelmed by her need to be close to Dan, to become a part of him and have him become a part of her. In the cool, clear light of day it seemed impossible that she had abandoned herself so completely to her feelings. She couldn't believe she had whispered his name in the quiet of the night and pleaded for more as she lifted her body to his like some wild creature out of control, spinning higher and higher on a crest of ecstatic feeling such as she had never known.

She glanced sideways at Dan. She had been wrong in her assessment of him before. Certainly he was masculine, but he was more, much more than that. He was probably the most attractive man she'd ever seen. His dark brown hair formed a perfect widow's peak above his broad forehead. His heavy brows were boldly shaped, and his eyes were the color of warm, dark cinnamon. She loved the cleft in his chin, and his lips . . . his lips . . .

He looked at her. "Elizabeth...?" She heard the catch of his breath and saw his eyes widen. "Don't look at me like that," he said huskily.

"Dan..." The same flame of desire she'd felt last night ignited and spread through her body. She tried to look away and couldn't.

Dan tightened his hands on the reins, and his body went so taut with longing that it was all he could do not to pull the wagon off the road. He wanted her now, wanted her on that Gypsy bed whispering his name, her mouth gone soft and trembling, her body pliant and warm under his.

"Soon," he said, his voice clogged with all that he was feeling. "Soon, my Isabela."

The caravan stopped an hour later. Elizabeth cooked their dinner over the fire Dan had made while he talked to the other men about the Guardia Civil and the events of the day.

For the first time since they had joined the caravan, their leader, Antonio, questioned Dan.

"Where do you and your woman come from?"

"From the Sacromonte," Dan said.

"Then it is the first time that any of the Gypsies of the Sacromonte have ever joined us. It's too far—they have their own special saint."

"My woman loves Santa Martina. She insisted we come."

"She has a strange accent."

"She comes from a family of French Gypsies." Dan raised a questioning eyebrow. "Why so many questions, *amigo*?"

Antonio scratched his ear. "I'm curious, Daniel. There is something about you, about your woman..." He shook his head. "I don't think you're who you say you are."

"My name is Daniel, she is Isabela. That is who we are," Dan said flatly. "We are on our way to Cuevarubia, just like the rest of you."

Antonio's dark eyes were suspicious. "We Gypsies are a close lot. We don't like outsiders."

Dan waited. He wanted to say, Then we will go our own way. But that wasn't what he wanted to do. He and Elizabeth needed the protection of the caravan.

Antonio shrugged. "But we're almost there. Tomorrow we will reach Cuevarubia. You will stay with us until then."

Lupe called him to dinner and Dan went back to Elizabeth. But he didn't tell her about his conversation with Antonio.

They ate the dinner she had prepared, and the feeling that had been between them for most of the day—a tension that was like a live electric wire drawn tight—vibrated now.

"We have to join the others for a little while tonight."

"I know."

He closed his hands around hers. "Think about later," he said.

Elizabeth moved as though in a dream that night. She sat with the other women around the camp fire and listened to them talk. Again and again her gaze met Dan's. When the guitarists began to play, he came to sit beside her. He put his arm around her and pulled her closer. They didn't speak because words weren't necessary; each knew how the other felt, each longed for the other's touch.

The Gypsies were in a gay mood tonight. Excited at the prospect that tomorrow they would be in Cuevarubia, they had dressed for a party. The older women wore their most colorful flowered skirts and brightest blouses. They had ribbons in their hair and bangles on their arms. The younger women had put on their ruffled polka-dot flamenco dresses.

The men, too, had dressed for the occasion. Antonio wore a pale pink shirt, tight leather pants and a green vest. He had little to say to Dan, and apparently he had voiced his suspicions to the other men, for they looked at Dan differently and their friendly attitude of acceptance had changed.

Soon the women began to dance. Everyone had a bottle of wine. Before long some of the men were drunk, and their voices raised in minor disagreements.

"Come on," Dan whispered to Elizabeth. "The party's getting rough. Let's go back to our wagon."

He'd just gotten to his feet when one of the younger men, whose name was Manolo, grabbed Lupe around the waist. "Come dance with me, sweetheart," he said drunkenly. "I'm a better dancer than your Antonio." He caressed her bottom. "In fact, I'm better than Antonio at everything I do."

Antonio sprang to his feet. He thrust Lupe aside and began to circle the younger man. *"Cabrón,"* he muttered. "Silly young rooster. It is time someone taught you a few manners."

"Not you, Antonio," the younger man sneered. "You're not man enough to teach me anything."

Antonio growled low in his throat and leaped forward.

Manolo dodged and stuck a foot out.

Antonio stumbled and fell onto one knee.

A woman screamed.

Manolo reached down to his boot. He came up fast. A knife flashed. He raised his arm, but before he could strike, Dan jumped at him. He grabbed Manolo's wrist and twisted hard. The knife fell to the ground, and Dan kicked it away.

Antonio scrambled up. His face was white with anger, his lips drawn back from his teeth. "Get out of here," he screamed at Manolo. "Get out before I kill you!" And when Manolo's brother hustled him away, Antonio turned to Dan and said, *"Gracias, compadre. Muchas gracias."*

"Por nada."

Antonio handed him a bottle of wine. "We will drink together, yes?"

"Yes." Dan tipped the bottle back.

"Manolo was drunk and unsteady on his feet," the Gypsy chieftain said. "But with a little luck, he might have killed me—if it had not been for you. So you are my brother. Yes? There will be no more questions between us."

The talk became more animated. More bottles of wine were brought out of the wagons. The guitars played; the women danced.

The hour grew late. Dan tightened his arm around Elizabeth's waist. She rested her head on his shoulder, and again they felt the fire between them kindle and grow.

Finally Dan said, "My woman is tired. We're going to rest now."

The others nodded their good nights. Some of the men clapped him on the back. Antonio embraced him. "*Buenas noches, mi hermano,* my brother," he said.

"Buenas noches," Dan answered. "Until tomorrow, *amigo*."

When they reached the darkness of trees, Dan continued a few steps farther in, then pulled Elizabeth into his arms.

"I was so afraid," she whispered against his chest. "That knife—"

But Dan covered her mouth with his, stopping her words. He'd waited too long for this moment. He didn't want to talk; he only wanted to hold her, to feel her close to him. He ground his mouth against hers and held her so closely he could barely breathe.

As excited as he now, Elizabeth pressed her body to his. She felt the heat and the hardness of him against her, and for a moment she was afraid and tried to hold back. But when the kiss grew and deepened, she whispered his name in an agony of need as intense as his.

"Elizabeth," he said against her lips, and pulled her down to the ground with him.

On their knees, facing each other, bodies close, Dan kissed her closed eyes, her cheeks, her mouth. With a strangled cry, he eased her down. Her eyes were luminous in the light of the new moon. Her lips trembled and he took the lower one between his teeth to suck as he would a wild strawberry while his hands found the rich fullness of her breasts. He cupped, then caressed them. Running his fingers across her nipples, he felt her shiver under his touch.

"Look at me," he said softly. And when she did he took the shawl from her shoulders and reached to undo the string that laced the front of her blouse together.

She looked up at his face shadowed by the night and watched it change as he lowered the blouse from her breasts. With narrowed eyes and nostrils fluted with desire, his strong white teeth clamped his lower lip.

She felt the heat of her breasts, the peaks hard and tense, waiting... waiting for his kiss.

When it came his tongue was hot and moist, and she whimpered with pleasure.

"Tell me," Dan whispered against her skin, "tell me you want me as much as I want you, Isabela." His teeth closed over one tender nipple. "Tell me," he said again.

She waited for the heartbeat of a second. "Yes," she whispered. "Oh, yes, I want you."

He raised his head to look at her. "My Gypsy lady," he murmured.

And she thought her body would burst with need.

Quickly, impatiently, they fumbled with their clothes. The flowered blouse was pushed up around her waist, her silk panties down over her ankles. He gripped her hips and with a whispered, "Now, my Isabela," joined his body to hers.

It was wild and primitive, as fierce as a thunderstorm, violent yet tender, savage yet sweet. Their bodies quickened and trembled and moved together in perfect cadence.

Elizabeth opened her eyes, and above her, through the trees, she saw millions of stars and the golden sliver of moon.

Dan moved hard and deep and fast. The moon shone brighter; the stars drew closer. In the distance Elizabeth could hear the music of the guitars, and it seemed to her that their beat grew stronger, stronger, until the rhythm of the music became the rhythm of her body and Dan the instrument of her pleasure.

She was one with him and the night and the music, totally free, abandoned to all the feelings that gripped and rent her, surrendering all in that last desperate, seeking, fevered moment.

She cried out and Dan took her cry and mingled it with his own.

Elizabeth opened her eyes and looked up at the moon. And suddenly she thought of Pilar's Gypsy curse, the curse of love.

"May its wings enfold you, bind and hold you," Pilar had said. "You will do things you've never thought of doing."

A sudden chilling wind moved through the trees above them, and Elizabeth shivered.

"What is it?" Dan gathered her close in his arms. "What is it, *querida*?"

"Nothing," she said. She sat up and covered herself with the shawl. "Only the wind."

At noon the next day, the Gypsy caravan reached the village of Cuevarubia. There were others there, too, Gypsy wagons, campers and trucks filled with pilgrims come to celebrate the anniversary of their special saint.

"Tomorrow is the day of commemoration," Antonio told Dan. "Tonight we will celebrate. There will be music and wine, and the women will dance as they did last night. My Lupe is young, but already she dances with great passion." He winked at Dan. "The passion I have taught her; the steps she learned from her mother. What about your woman? Will she dance, too?"

Dan shook his head. "I don't think so. Isabela is shy about dancing in public."

"She doesn't look shy." He nudged Dan. "Maybe she dances only for you, *amigo*."

Dan only smiled. But as he walked away from Antonio, the words, "only for you" buzzed around in his head.

He wished that he had seen this coming, wished he'd been prepared for it. He wasn't sure how it had started, because in the beginning he hadn't been in the least attracted to Elizabeth. All he'd felt was impatience and anger that he was stuck with her. He'd told himself that if she'd been somebody like the beautiful blonde in Puerto Vallarta, he would have been happy to have dragged her along. But she wasn't anything at all like the blonde; she was Elizabeth, and she was different from anyone he'd ever known.

He'd thought her dull and dowdy, a plain gray mouse of a woman in her tailored flannel suit and sensible shoes, and he'd vowed to get rid of her just as soon as he could.

Maybe it had started that night at Pilar and Jonas's when Pilar had danced. He'd looked at Elizabeth. Her face had been shadowed by moonlight, and she'd worn an expression of breathless excitement. He'd felt something stir in him then, something he'd never felt before.

Or maybe it had started that early morning when she'd tried to run away from him. He still remembered the astonishment he'd felt at the softness of her body under his. Her face had been flushed, and she'd been breathing hard. Her breasts had pushed against the red cotton of her blouse, and her hair had been free and tousled around her face. He'd felt a flash of amazement, and he'd suddenly realized that she wasn't plain, that she was, in her own way, a beautiful woman.

He hadn't meant to kiss her, but he had, and what he'd felt had been totally unexpected. She'd fought to get away from him, and the thrashing around of her body under his had excited him as nothing had before. He couldn't stop kissing her, and finally her lips had parted under his, and for a moment she had answered his kiss.

He'd told himself then it wouldn't happen again. He couldn't afford to be distracted by a romantic involvement. He didn't want one; he didn't need one. The only kind of relationships he had were with women like the blonde in Vallarta. Elizabeth wasn't like that; she was different.

God, she was different. He didn't know a lot about her, but he would bet everything he had in the world that she wasn't the kind of woman who tumbled into bed with every man she met. When they had first made love, he'd felt, in his few fleeting moments of sanity, her uncertainty, her endearing awkwardness. But over and above it all, there had been her passion, her consuming female sensuality.

Last night they had made love out in the open, no more than fifty yards from where the Gypsies had gathered around the camp fire. The tension between them had been building all day. His nerve ends had felt raw and ragged; his body had burned every time he looked at her. When finally they were alone, he had to have her. Nothing would have stopped him. He'd taken her there on the ground with the strum of the guitars in the background and the moon overhead. He'd taken her quickly, almost violently, and she'd loved it. She'd whispered his name in smothered cries. She'd been as wild as he was, her body like a bright, hot flame beneath him.

Who was she? Was she Elizabeth, the prim and proper schoolteacher? Or was she Isabela, the wanton Gypsy?

She was a woman, and for the moment, for this time that they shared, she was his woman.

And that was a sobering thought.

Chapter 8

There were more than three hundred Gypsies gathered in the fields outside the Santa Martina Church that afternoon. They had come from near and far to commemorate the day of their patron saint, Martina de Cuevarubia.

It seemed strange to Elizabeth, who was not Catholic, that so many people would come to this medieval village every year to celebrate a saint's day. The village lay in a peaceful valley, amid fields and trees and surrounding farms. There was little here except the church and the crumbled Moorish walls that had once surrounded Cuevarubia; only a few houses, a small market and a bar, where the local men gathered every evening to play dominoes.

Elizabeth didn't understand the current of excitement that ran through the Gypsy camp now that they had finally arrived. But even though she didn't understand, she soon became caught up in it, for this was the kind of sharing experience she had never known before. She had become a part of something; a participant of a joy of living that was both earthy and spiritual.

So much had changed since Dan had come into her life. It was a time of awakening, of a new awareness of everything around her. Every day she discovered something new and saw things differently. Flowers were more aromatic, the song of birds more beautiful, and music stirred her soul. Passion had stripped her of all pretenses, all defenses. She had become a feeling, sensual being, not by choice but by something that had been too long buried deep inside her, something that only Dan Thornton had been able to release.

All she had in the world was her gray flannel suit, this skirt, a pair of sandals, a shawl and two blouses. And Dan. It was enough. It was everything she wanted.

But what did Dan want? She had no way of knowing how he felt about her. Certainly they made wonderful love together, but undoubtedly he'd made love to many women. Why should she think that she was different? What would happen to them when this was over?

These were the thoughts that had tortured Elizabeth the past few days. She was afraid she was falling in love with Dan, and that frightened her, because she didn't think he loved her in return. When this was over, would he, as he had promised, put her on a plane? Would he shake her hand and say that it had been nice knowing her?

Every time they made love, and afterwards when Dan slept quietly at her side, these were the questions that went around and around in her head.

For days now she had not thought of the danger they were in. The names Castro and Sanchez had faded from her memory. There was only Dan and this new, exquisite joy they shared.

But if Elizabeth had forgotten the danger they were in, Dan had not. He had been more relieved than he liked to admit this morning when Antonio said, "After what happened last night, Daniel, you are a part of my family. You and Isabela will stay with our caravan for as long as you like."

"*Gracias*, Antonio, but we must go on to Seville."

"Then come with us at least as far as Estepa. That is where we turn to take the road back to our homes."

Dan nodded. "It will be our pleasure to go that far with you. What has happened to young Manolo?"

"His family has kept him out of my way, but others have told me of the threats he has made against me, and you, too, my friend."

"Against me?" Dan looked surprised. "I have no quarrel with Manolo. I only did what anyone would have done—I disarmed him."

"Nevertheless, the young rooster has told everyone who will listen that he must avenge his honor." Antonio's face darkened with rage. "He has said to others that I am too old for Lupe, that he will take her away from me as soon as my back is turned. But she is *my* woman, *my* Lupe. She belongs to me." He moved closer to Dan, and there was danger in his voice. "I would kill anyone who tried to take Lupe from me, anyone who dared put his hands on her. The thought of it makes the bile rise bitter in my mouth." He took a steadying breath. "But you know. You must feel the same about your woman."

"Yes," Dan said. "I feel the same."

He had not thought before of how he would feel when Elizabeth left him. He had known that she would, of course. She had a job, a life far different from this back in Ohio. Perhaps there was a man, a man she planned to marry.

And suddenly the bile rose bitter in Dan's throat at the idea of another man touching her the way he had touched her.

He didn't know what was happening to him; he only knew that the thought of losing Elizabeth was too painful for him to think about right now.

Dozens of bonfires glowed in the cool night air. The music of flamenco guitars blended with the excited murmur of voices.

"After the celebration we'll go on with the caravan to Estepa," Dan told Elizabeth that night in their wagon. "We'll leave the wagon in Osuna with a cousin of Pilar's and go on from there by bus to Seville."

She took a deep breath and held it. "And in Seville?"

"I'll find Thomason and turn the jewels over to him." He touched the belt that he continued to wear around his waist. "I'll be glad to get rid of this," he said.

"You've never seen the jewels?"

"No." Dan shrugged. "It's funny, I haven't really wanted to. Wars have been fought because of them and men have killed for them. There's a legend about a Moorish caliph who bought the jewels to give to his Gypsy queen. But I don't believe in legends. I'll only be glad when the jewels are out of my hands." He hesitated. "I'll open the pouch if you'd like to see them."

"Not now. Maybe before you give them to your friend, though."

"Whenever you like."

"How soon will we leave here?"

"The celebration's tomorrow. I imagine we'll leave the following morning." Dan saw the question in her eyes.

"This will all be over soon," he said. "I'll find Al Thomason and turn the jewels over to him. He'll alert Interpol about Castro and Sanchez. Once we know we're safe, we'll head down to the coast, maybe to Torremolinos. We'll sun and swim and drink *sangría*." He brushed the dark hair back off her face. "We'll buy some new clothes, and we'll sleep in a big room in an air-conditioned hotel. We'll have breakfast in bed every morning and lie on the beach all day. We'll make love every night and—"

"Make love to me now," she said.

Dan looked at her for a long moment, then he drew her into his arms. "Elizabeth," he said. "Oh, Elizabeth."

At ten o'clock the next morning, some of the men, after fighting for the honor, carried the heavy, carved litter that held the statue of Santa Martina out of the church and through the narrow streets of Cuevarubia. Hundreds joined them, and there was an air of festivity as well as of solemnity in the procession. And when they had paraded through the streets, they came back to the church.

Dan and Elizabeth watched from the sidelines. They hadn't intended to go in, but the crush of people all trying to get into the church carried them along inside. And Elizabeth found herself in a pew near the front.

The congregation sang an off-key, a cappella hymn, and the mass began to the accompaniment of crying babies and murmuring voices. Hundreds of white candles flickered and glowed. The smell of melting wax mingled with the smells of incense and the multitude of flowers that covered the altar.

As the mass went on, Elizabeth, who knelt beside Dan, looked at the people all around her. There were too many of them squeezed into the small, windowless church. The day had grown warm, and the heat inside was suffocating. The aroma of the flowers and incense was too sweetly oppressive. Through half-closed eyes she watched the flickering candles. They merged, wavered and danced before her gaze as the sonorous voice of the priest droned on.

She looked at the dark-skinned Gypsy faces. Some of them she knew, some of them she'd sat around camp fires with. Their faces were different now, solemn and reverent. The statue of the saint was lifted again, this time by robed altar boys. A low murmur ran through the congregation. Expressions became worshipful, fervid. A woman began to weep. From the back of the church, Elizabeth heard the guitars, then the soft rhythm of palm striking palm.

Overwhelmed by the heat and the raw emotion that lived and breathed in the small, overcrowded church, Elizabeth leaned against the back of the pew in front of her and rested her head on her hands.

She thought about the love these people had for a saint who might well be a figment of their imaginations, and of the love these men and women had for each other and for their children. She thought of Dan and knew that she loved him, and she felt hot tears sting her eyes.

"What is it?" he whispered. "Are you ill? Elizabeth, what is it?"

She tried to lift her head and couldn't.

Dan put his arm around her shoulders. "Elizabeth?" he said again. And when finally she raised her head and he saw her face, he pulled her up off her knees and put his arms around her.

"Take a couple of deep breaths," he said. "The mass will be over soon."

Elizabeth leaned back against him. She closed her eyes, but through her eyelids she could still see the flickering flames of the tall white candles.

When it was over she tried to stand, but when she swayed against him, he picked her up and carried her out through the throng of people.

"*Ay, pobrecita*. It is the heat," an old woman said.

"No," another said. "She is a Gypsy and she has felt the spirit of the saint of the Gypsies."

Dan carried her to their wagon and laid her down. He bathed her face and hands with cool water. He opened her blouse and laid the damp cloth against her breasts. When she felt better, he helped her sit up so that she could drink some water.

"I don't know what happened to me," she said weakly.

"It was the heat." He brushed the hair back from her face. "I'm sorry, Elizabeth. I didn't mean to go into the church. We were pushed in by the crowd."

"I know. I'm sorry I made a scene."

"You didn't make a scene." He took her hand. "Why don't you rest now? I'll leave both the front and back open so that you'll get a breeze."

Elizabeth gave a grateful sigh. "Yes, I'm tired." She reached for his hand. "You're very good to me, Dan."

"I have to be." He brought her hand to his lips and kissed it. "You're my prisoner—I have to take care of you."

The shadow of a smile crossed her lips. "I'd forgotten," she said as she closed her eyes.

His prisoner. Yes, she had forgotten. Dan had forced her to come with him. He had taken her to the caves of the Sacromonte. He had made her dress like a Gypsy and ride in a Gypsy wagon. She had tried to run away, and he had brought her back. He had told the Gypsies she was his woman. He had called her Isabela.

Today in the church she had felt like a Gypsy, a woman who loved a man named Daniel.

And with a sigh, Isabela, who had been Elizabeth, drifted into a dreamless, restful sleep.

The celebration went on far into the night, but Dan and Elizabeth stayed in their wagon. He prepared a salad with the vegetables they had bought in the village that morning. They ate it with bread and cheese and washed it down with red wine.

When Dan turned down the lantern and they went to bed, he pulled back the curtains and they watched the flickering of candles, like fireflies in the darkness, and listened to the music of the guitars. When Elizabeth grew tired, he closed the curtains and held her until she slept.

It was late when he heard the soft knock on the wagon door.

"Daniel," he heard then. "Daniel, wake up!"

"What is it?" Elizabeth whispered.

"It's Antonio." Dan grabbed his pants and put them on. Then he opened the door and said, "What is it?"

"The Guardia have been here. They were asking questions about an American and a woman who is traveling with him."

"Did you tell him you knew no such people?"

"What do you think, *hombre*? That I am crazy? I told them nothing." Antonio lowered his voice to a whisper. "I have wondered about your accent, Daniel, and your woman's. But it is none of my business. You are my friend—you saved my life."

"Gracias, amigo."

"There were two men with them, and to me they looked more dangerous than the Guardia. Perhaps they were secret service, but I don't think so. They asked if anyone had recently joined us, anyone who was not of our family."

A muscle jumped in Dan's cheek, and he had to bite back a curse. "Have they gone?" he asked quietly.

"*Sí*, but I am worried, Daniel. That is why I have awakened you." Antonio looked back over his shoulder. "I have not seen Manolo since they were here," he whispered. "I am afraid he has gone after them. I think you should leave."

Dan nodded. "Yes, so do I." He looked back at Elizabeth. She was sitting up in bed, the satin comforter pulled up around her shoulders. Her eyes were wide with fear. He turned back to Antonio. "I can't take the wagon. It's too slow, and besides, if they return and find us gone, they'll look for a wagon. We'll have to go on foot."

"Yes, that would be best."

"I was going to leave the wagon with friends in Osuna. The family of Pilar Fonseca de Belmonte."

"I will see that it is delivered there." Antonio hesitated. "Do you need money, Daniel?"

"No, *gracias*, I have enough." Dan put his hand out. "You've been a friend to us, Antonio. I'm grateful."

"*Por nada*, Daniel." He handed Dan a map. "Now you must go. If Manolo tells them about you, they will come back. If you are not here, they will look for you on the road to Estepa. Do not go that way. Take the woods and head in the direction of Utrera."

"I will, *compadre*."

"*Vaya con Dios*, Daniel."

"And to you, Antonio."

Dan closed the door. "We have to leave," he told Elizabeth.

She swung her legs off the bed and reached for her clothes.

"It'll be all right," he said. "Don't be afraid."

She pulled her blouse over her head and watched him tie the pouch with the $6.5 million in jewels around his waist. She hoped they were worth the risk he was taking.

Dan raised his head and saw her staring at the pouch. Almost as though he knew what she was thinking, he said, "We'll be rid of them soon."

"If they find us..." She looked at him, unable to go on.

"They won't." He pulled his boots on. "Ready?" he said.

Elizabeth looked around the wagon. It was garish and uncomfortable, but in a way she could not explain, she had been happier here than she'd ever been in her life. She touched the pillow upon which her head had rested only a few minutes ago. "Yes," she said, "I'm ready."

The night was cold. Elizabeth looked back at the wagon for a brief moment before she pulled the shawl closer around her shoulders and followed Dan through the darkness of the trees. All she carried was the shoulder bag that held her passport, her airline ticket and a few personal things. Dan carried a knapsack he'd hastily packed with bread and fruit and cheese. There was a knife in his pocket and a gun in his waistband.

She remembered what he had told her about the man named Sanchez. The thought of him and of the other men out searching for her and Dan filled her with fear, as much for Dan as for herself.

They spoke little all through what remained of that night. When morning came they stopped to rest and to eat a bite of cheese and a piece of bread.

"We'd better stay off the roads today," Dan said. "If Castro and Sanchez are anywhere nearby, we're safer in a wooded area. Maybe tonight we'll be able to grab a bus that's going to Seville. I'd like to get you some different clothes, but I don't think we ought to try a town today."

Elizabeth pulled the shawl closer. "The clothes don't matter," she said.

"They do. It was different when we were traveling with the caravan, Elizabeth, but Spaniards have always had a lot of animosity toward the Gypsies. Nobody would harm us, but we might run into a little unpleasantness. I'll be happier when you're dressed in more formal clothes." He smiled. "But no gray flannel, okay?"

Elizabeth stiffened. "There's nothing wrong with gray. I wear a lot of it."

"I bet you do."

She glared at him. "Everybody should know what type they are. I'd look terrible in flashy clothes or something low cut and slinky."

"You're pretty flashy right now, sweetheart, and you look good to me."

Elizabeth blushed, then said, "This is a costume. Can you imagine what would happen if I showed up to teach a class dressed this way?"

Dan raised an eyebrow. "Yeah, as a matter of fact, I can. Those high school boys would never be the same." He reached for her hand and pulled her to her feet. "Come on, Isabela, it's time to hit the road."

"My name is Elizabeth."

Dan looked at her for a long moment. "Is it?" he said.

They walked for a long time that day, staying close to the trees but in sight of the road so they wouldn't lose their way.

It was late afternoon when Dan looked at the map Antonio had given him and said, "We'll have to cross the road here and head south. There's a village a little farther on. Maybe we'll be able to catch a bus there."

He took her hand and started across the road. A small black car rounded a curve ahead of them and hovered like a mirage in the glaring sun. Then it leaped forward, straight at them.

"Come on!" Dan grabbed her hand and ran with her to the other side of the road, down into a ditch, up again and headed for the trees.

The car screeched to a stop. A door slammed. A man shouted at them to stop.

They were almost to the trees when a shot whistled over Elizabeth's head.

"Run!" Dan screamed in her ear, and she sprinted forward.

More shouts came from somewhere behind them. The trees were closer now. Another few yards...then they were in the forest.

It was darker here. She wanted to slow down and catch her breath, but Dan wouldn't let her rest. He urged her on, pulling her after him as he zigzagged through the trees. Finally he let go of her wrist and moved a few paces ahead of her. He was running fast when he broke through a tangle of underbrush. Suddenly he grabbed the trunk of a tree and stopped. But Elizabeth couldn't stop; her momentum carried her forward, and she didn't see the ground ahead of her give way to a gully. She ran toward it before Dan could catch her, and crying out in fear, fell headlong down an incline.

She tried frantically to grab a root, a scraggle of brush, a branch. The world turned topsy-turvy; sky, trees and earth became a kaleidoscope of mixed-up colors and objects as she rolled over and over. Finally she hit a cluster of bushes and stopped.

For a moment she couldn't breathe. She lay where she was, flat on her stomach, gasping for breath.

"Elizabeth!" Dan knelt beside her. "Oh my God, Elizabeth, are you all right?"

She nodded, unable to speak. Finally she gasped. "Yes. Okay."

From somewhere above them there came a shout.

Dan stiffened. "Get behind the bushes," he murmured, and half pulled, half dragged her until they were hidden behind the thatch of brush she'd fallen against.

"Down here!" a man shouted.

"Castro," Dan whispered in her ear. "Don't move."

Move! She was frozen to the earth.

There were scrambling sounds and muttered curses as the men slid down into the gully.

"They went the other way," a man said.

"Then go back up," someone else said.

"No, we'd better stay together."

The voices were closer. Elizabeth saw a pair of shiny black shoes only a few feet from her face.

She held her breath. Dan's hand closed painfully around her shoulder.

A voice said, "Let's look farther on." The shiny black shoes shuffled back and forth, then turned and moved out of sight.

Elizabeth let out a breath she'd been holding, but she didn't move.

The minutes ticked by. The sun went down. She heard the voices again, this time farther off.

"We'll wait until we're sure they've gone," Dan whispered.

She was cold. Her body hurt. Something rustled in the branches in front of her, and then a six-inch lizard slithered through and stopped close to her face.

"Shoo!" Elizabeth whispered. The lazy pop eyes looked around. A thin tongue darted out, in, out again. Filmlike eyelids blinked. The lizard hesitated, then quickly scurried back into the bushes.

Time passed. There were no voices, no sounds.

At last Dan said, "I think it's all right now. They can't find us in the dark, and anyway, they've probably given up." He rolled to a sitting position and helped Elizabeth to sit up. "Are you all right?"

"I think so." She brushed the dried leaves and dirt off her arms and her hands.

"You had a bad fall," Dan said. "You sure you're all right? Nothing broken?"

"Maybe a couple of fingernails." She tried to see his face through the darkness. "What are we going to do, Dan?"

"Walk until we get to a town, then try to find a bus."

"But those men are looking for us."

"We can't stay here forever, and we can't go back to Antonio and his people. We've got to go on."

He helped her to stand, and when she did, she couldn't help a smothered yelp of pain.

"What is it?"

"Nothing," she lied. "I'm just stiff from the fall and from lying on the ground so long." She shivered and pulled the shawl closer around her shoulders.

Dan took his jacket off. "Put this on," he said.

Elizabeth shook her head. "No, it's cold. You need it."

"No, I don't." He held it until she put her arms in the sleeves, then he fastened it up around her neck.

She'd had a bad fall and a scare. She needed to be warm. He wished they could build a fire, but he knew they couldn't, so he put his arms around her and held her closely.

Elizabeth, he thought. Oh, Elizabeth, what have I gotten you into?

Chapter 9

"Why didn't you tell me you were hurt?" Dan asked. He pulled Elizabeth closer to the outside light in front of the small bus station. Her face and hands were scratched and dirty, and there was an angry red abrasion on her right arm.

"It's nothing that a long soak in a tub of hot water won't cure." She forced a smile and stepped away from him. "But I'd better find a ladies' room and clean up before we get on the bus."

The ladies' room was small but clean. She took the shawl off and tied it around her waist so that she could wash. She had just begun to rinse the dirt off her hands when two other women entered. They had been talking, but when they saw her, they stopped, and one of them said to the other one, "I didn't think they allowed Gypsy trash to come in here."

Elizabeth's mouth tightened but she concentrated on washing her hands and face.

"Watch your purse," the other one said.

It was a shock to suddenly find herself one of a minority, part of an ethnic group that other people looked down on. It was a strange feeling, a bitter and helpless feeling.

One of the women went into a stall. The other stood guard in front of it, clutching both their purses to her ample bosom while she glared defiantly at Elizabeth.

Elizabeth wanted to say something, but she didn't. If there was a disturbance, the Guardia Civil might be called, and that would be the end of her and Dan.

So she kept her head bowed and waited for the women to leave.

When they did, she stripped out of the red blouse. She washed with a bar of rough soap in the cold water, then tried to get the stains and dirt out of the blouse. Finally she brushed out her long dark hair, and with a touch of defiance applied the bright red lipstick Pilar had given her.

She looked in the mirror, and the reflection that looked back at her was all Gypsy, right down to the golden earrings.

The two women had disappeared by the time she came out of the ladies' room, and there was no one but Dan in the small waiting room.

"You look better," he said when he saw her. "I was getting worried because the bus will be here in a couple of minutes."

"Does it go to Seville?"

"No, only to Utrera." Dan put his arm around her. "You look so tired."

"I'll sleep on the bus."

It pulled in then, a yellow rattletrap of a bus that looked as though it couldn't go another mile. The door swung open. "Utrera," the driver said.

They boarded, squeezing their way past burlap bags filled with potatoes and onions and grain. A pig, hobbled and tied to an armrest, squealed when they went past it. The other passengers looked at them suspiciously, and four young, rough-looking farmers poked each other, and one said, "I didn't know we'd be traveling with pigs and Gypsies."

Elizabeth stiffened but before she could say anything Dan shoved her ahead of him into a seat. "Don't pay any attention to them," he whispered. Then he pulled the cap down over his eyes and pretended to sleep.

The bus pulled away from the station. Elizabeth, as angry as she was tired now, stared moodily out the window. Then she, too, closed her eyes.

The sun was high in the sky when she awoke. Someone was playing a guitar and a baby was crying.

"Feel better?" Dan said beside her.

"Yes, a lot better." She shifted in her seat. "How soon before we get to Utrera?"

"The way we're going, who knows? I'm not sure the bus will make it over the next hill." He reached into his knapsack and pulled out the bread and cheese. "Hungry?" he asked.

"Starving." Elizabeth broke off a piece of bread and laid a bit of cheese on it. After she'd eaten a couple of bites, she said, "When you told me there was a lot of prejudice against the Gypsies, I thought you were exaggerating. But it's true, isn't it? Nobody seems to like or trust them."

"That's why they keep pretty much to themselves," Dan said with a nod. "And why I'll be glad to get you in some decent clothes."

It grew warmer inside the bus as it chugged on past silvery seas of olive groves and Don Quixote windmills. Twice the driver had to stop and get out to do something with the engine. A few people got off. A very old lady, dressed all in black, got on with two live chickens.

Elizabeth sat back in her seat and looked out the open window. When they passed a sign that read Utrera, 10 kilometers, she said, "We're almost there," and just then the bus coughed, stalled and stopped.

The driver swore. He got out and went around to the front of the bus and raised the hood.

The passengers' voices hummed like a swarm of angry bees, and the baby began to cry again.

"What the hell's going on?" somebody from the back of bus called out.

"*¿Quién sabe?* Who knows?" somebody else said.

The bus driver, wiping oil off his hands with a dirty rag, stuck his head in the door. "This is the last stop," he said roughly. "The damn bus won't go any farther."

"But it's ten kilometers into town," one of the passengers protested. "What are we supposed to do?"

"Walk," the driver said. "The same as I have to do."

The passengers, amid muttered threats against the bus company as well as the driver, gathered their belongings and crowded into the aisle.

One of the farmers, a young man with a cocky grin and a shock of black hair that hung over his forehead, pushed forward toward Dan and Elizabeth. "Hey Gypsy girl," he said. "What did you do? Put a curse on the bus?"

"Go to hell," she snapped.

"Hey! You're a feisty one, aren't you?" He laughed, and to the three friends behind him said, "Watch out for the little Gypsy, *compañeros*, she's a wild one."

"Take it easy, Isabela." Dan pushed her ahead of him up the aisle. "We've got a six-mile walk," he said when he helped her off. "We don't want any trouble."

"I'm sorry but that damned attitude about Gypsies makes me mad." She looked at him, an expression of dismay on her face. "We've got to walk six miles!"

"I'm afraid so." He slung the jacket over his shoulder. "Let's go," he said.

There were seventeen of them, not counting the pig or the chickens. The sacks of vegetables and grain had been left on the bus. One man carried the crying baby, and two of the farmers hitched their guitars over their shoulders. A few of them spoke among themselves; no one spoke to the bus driver.

The trouble started the first time they stopped to rest.

One of the young farmers had a leather *bota* of wine, and he passed it around. Someone said to the two with the guitars, "If you can play those instruments, then play us a tune."

"A *jota* or a fandango," one of the women said. "Something lively."

They nodded, but first each in turn held the *bota* high and squeezed a thin stream of wine into their mouths. Then they began to play while the passengers leaned back on the grass, more relaxed now as they listened to the music.

Someone said, "Let's hear some flamenco."

One of the guitarists reached for the *bota* again. He looked at Elizabeth and said, "Only if the Gypsy girl dances."

The others looked at her.

"Come on," the other guitarist said. "Dance for us."

Elizabeth glared at both of them. "No!" she said. "I don't want to dance."

"It would be better if you did," Dan said quietly. "We don't want any trouble. If they persist I'll have to fight them, and I don't want to do that because it will attract too much attention to us."

"But I..." Elizabeth worried her bottom lip between her teeth. "I've never danced a flamenco," she whispered.

"I think maybe it's time you did."

"C'mon, Gypsy," somebody else said. "C'mon and dance."

She stood up, uncertain and a little afraid.

The guitars strummed an introduction, then began the first stirring notes of a flamenco.

Elizabeth hesitated, then she bent down and took off her sandals. She didn't look at Dan as she stepped forward, away from the trees.

Don't look at the faces, she told herself; listen to the music. Hear the beat of it in your head. Listen and feel. Forget that you're Elizabeth; pretend to be Isabela the Gypsy.

She tossed the shawl aside. She raised her head to the sun and closed her eyes, and as she began to dance she shut out everything except the melancholy strum of the guitars that were playing the haunting song of the Moors and the Gypsies. It was music that stirred the soul, that cried out to all the lost loves. It spoke of loneliness and despair, of loss and separation and tragedy. Of passion and of a love so hot and wild it could not last.

She danced, her body vibrating as the music vibrated, her slender arms above her head, undulating, sensual, sinuous. Her lids were slightly lowered over her pale green eyes; her full lips were moist and parted.

The people on the grass in front of her grew silent.

Dan's heart pounded against his ribs, and a heat unlike anything he'd ever known spread through his body to his loins, a heat as driving and throbbing and hard as the music. His mouth went dry with desire, because he'd never seen anything, anyone, that was as blatantly, vibrantly female as Elizabeth was in this moment. She was a Gypsy. She was Isabela.

As the beat intensified, her body glistened with the sheen of sweat. The dark hair whirled around her face. Her movements were provocative, primitive. She was the most beautiful, the most exciting creature he'd ever seen. She was woman, rejoicing in her sexuality.

The guitars sobbed, then as abruptly as the sudden stopping of the heart, they stopped.

And Isabela the Gypsy stood trembling and still, there in the dirt at the side of the road.

The four farmers were with them when they entered the town. Twilight had fallen and the streets were quiet. For the past three miles the young men had apologized for their behavior. One of them had insisted on carrying Dan's knapsack, and two of them had even wanted to carry Elizabeth.

They were laughing and joking with Dan as they turned into the main street. Dan said, "Can you recommend a hotel? Something quiet and out of the way? We—" Ahead of him he saw two Guardia. He grabbed Elizabeth's hand and pulled her quickly into a doorway.

The four men looked at them, startled, then as though by mutual agreement, they stood in front of the doorway, their backs hiding Dan and Elizabeth, until the Guardia strolled by.

When they were out of sight, one of them said, "*¿Qué pasa, amigo?* Do you have trouble?"

"Yes, I have trouble." Dan hesitated. "There has been a misunderstanding. I'm not running from all of the Guardia Civil, only from one or two who I think have been bought off. Once I get to Seville the matter will be cleared up, but until then my woman and I need a place to stay."

The men nodded. They conferred among themselves, and finally the eldest said, "We will take you and the *señorita* to a *posada* where you will be safe."

The inn was on a narrow back street of the town and set well away from the road in a grove of chestnut trees.

"This is fine," Dan said. "I don't know how we can ever thank you for your help."

"We behaved badly on the bus," one of them said. "We're sorry, *señor*."

"If you have money, they will not ask questions," his friend said.

"We have money."

"Then they will take you." The young farmer turned to Elizabeth. "I have seen flamenco," he said. "Once in Granada and once at a festival in Córdoba. And sometimes our local girls dance. But I have never seen anyone dance as you do, *señorita*. I know we forced you, and I would like to say I'm sorry that we did, but I cannot. It is something I will always remember."

"Thank you." Elizabeth held her hand out for him to shake. He took it, but instead, his cheeks flushing with color, he kissed her hand. Then to Dan he said, "My name is Pedro Algundis. I live on Umaron Street. If you need anything, ask for me there."

"I will, and thank you." Dan shook hands with all of them, and when they turned away, he put his arm around Elizabeth and led her into the inn.

The woman at the desk told Dan there was a room available. He asked if they could have supper sent up, and she said yes, the cook had prepared roast chickens, if that was satisfactory.

The room, while simple, was large and airy. It overlooked the road and the trees in the front. There was a large bed, two chairs and a small table. There was also a bathroom with a big, old-fashioned tub.

"I wish I had some clean clothes to put on," Elizabeth said.

"I'll go shopping tomorrow." Dan put the knapsack down. "I'll be less conspicuous alone than the two of us together."

"How's your taste in women's clothes?"

"You'll find out tomorrow."

Elizabeth smiled. "But no flounces or flowers, okay?"

"Okay." He sat on the side of the bed and pulled his boots off.

"Is something wrong?"

"No, I've just got a lot on my mind."

Elizabeth nodded uncertainly. "I'll take my bath, then."

He answered her with another nod, and Elizabeth went into the bathroom and closed the door. He looked at the boots he was still holding, then shook his head as though to clear it because he'd been in a daze ever since this afternoon when she had danced. This was a whole new Elizabeth, an Elizabeth he hadn't even known existed, not even in their wildest nights of love. He had been spellbound today, unable to take his eyes off her, mesmerized, hypnotized, and he'd wanted her as he'd never wanted a woman is his life. Who was she? Who the hell was she? What had happened to the prim and proper schoolteacher she had been? Where had that woman gone? Where had this other woman come from?

Dan closed his eyes, and when he did he could see her, graceful arms raised above her head, the sheen of sweat on her body, the sensuously parted lips. "Isabela," he whispered, and felt his body tighten with need.

Elizabeth thought that something was wrong but had no idea what it was. She filled the tub with hot water and with a sigh of pleasure lowered herself into it. She washed her hair first, then leaned back for a long soak. She had just finished bathing when Dan knocked on the door and said, "Dinner's arrived."

Elizabeth got out of the tub and wrapped a towel around her damp hair. When she had dried her body, she took another towel and, loath to put her dirty clothes back on, wrapped it around her body.

Dan had laid the food out on the table. "The chicken looks good," he said. "There's a salad and..." He stopped and stared at Elizabeth. A moment passed before he said, "Won't you be cold?"

Elizabeth shook her head. "I couldn't stand to put those dirty clothes back on."

He couldn't take his gaze away. She looked beautiful and fresh, scrubbed so clean he could see the sprinkle of freckles across the rise of her breasts. He gripped the back of a chair so tightly that his knuckles shone white. He wanted to pull the towel away. He wanted to lay her down on the bed and kiss every inch of her body. He wanted to bury himself in her softness. He wanted...

"Sit down," he said, and his voice was harsh in the silence of the room. "The chicken's getting cold."

"Dan?" She looked at him, not understanding. Then she sat down.

The chicken was good. So was the fresh green salad and the bottle of white wine.

They spoke little.

He watched her pick up a chicken leg and bite into it. She looked up and saw him, and her eyes widened with the awareness of his look. Her tongue came out to lick the corner of her mouth.

It was too much.

The chair scraped when he shoved it back. Before Elizabeth could speak, he came around the table and pulled her to her feet. "Isabela," he said, and covered her mouth with his.

"I want you," he said against her lips. "You're driving me crazy. I can't wait." He picked her up and carried her to the bed.

"Dan?" Her dark eyes went wide with alarm. "Dan, wait."

He put her down and began to tear at his clothes. "I can't. I've waited all afternoon. I wanted you then. I wanted to carry you back into the trees and take you the way I did that night with the Gypsies." He leaned down over her. "What have you done to me, Isabela? Have you cast a Gypsy spell on me?" He slowly pulled the towel away from her body. She tried to pull the blanket up to cover her nakedness, but Dan said, "No, I want to look at you."

He kissed her and her lips trembled under his. He took the towel from her damp hair and ran his fingers through it, spreading it out against the white pillow.

When she shivered, he said, "I'll warm you, Isabela. In a little while I'll warm you."

He kissed her again, his lips firm yet soft against hers. She twined her arms around his neck, and her lips parted under his. "I like it when you kiss me like that," she whispered.

"I'm going to kiss all of you like that," he said. He kissed the corner of her mouth and trailed a moist line of fire down to her throat, her shoulders, her breasts.

"Dan," she said. "Oh, Dan."

A fire kindled and grew somewhere deep inside her, and her body grew warm with the heat of it.

He took his time. He touched her breasts tenderly and kissed them sweetly. He played his fingertips over the rosy peaks while he kissed the sprinkle of freckles.

She loved the feel of his lips against her skin, the touch of his hands on her body. Ready for him now, she whispered, "Dan? Come up over me, Dan."

But he said, "Not yet, my Isabela. Not yet, my love."

His mouth was hot. His tongue burned her skin. She couldn't help the small gasps of pleasure that whispered from her lips.

He left her breasts and leaned his head against her belly, then turned his face to rub the scratchiness of his beard against her tender skin. She shivered with pleasure when he nipped her with his teeth and soothed with his tongue. She said, "Please, please, please," and he tightened his hands around her hips, holding her, not letting her move when he leaned to kiss the tender skin of her inner thighs.

Elizabeth tried to stop him, but it was too late. Dan was beyond reason, beyond thought. There was only Isabela, warm and fragrant and his, and he held her there while his mouth took away the last vestiges of whatever restraint she had imposed upon herself. He held her until she became wild and wanton, until she cried his name and trembled like a leaf blown free upon a summer breeze.

And while still she trembled, Dan joined his body to hers, groaning with pleasure when he felt her warm and tight around him. He moved closer, deeper, driven by the desire to mold his body to hers, to make her a part of him.

He said, "Again, Isabela. Again, *mi amor*. My love."

Her body rose against his, and the passion of only a moment ago built again, built until it was past bearing.

Free of all restraint, totally his, she followed where he led, as hungry, as impassioned as he was. And when, in a voice shaking with passion, he whispered, "Now, my Isabela. Now!" she lifted herself to him and cried, "Yes! Oh, yes!"

His body shuddered with pleasure and his arms closed around her, holding her tightly as he whispered her name over and over again.

Afterward, when they lay spent and weak, Dan brushed the hair back from her face. He kissed her forehead, and he said, "I love you."

Her pale green eyes widened.

"I know this is something we didn't count on, but that doesn't make it any the less true. I've fallen in love with you, Isabela."

"But I'm not Isabela," she whispered. "I'm Elizabeth."

Dan shook his head. "Elizabeth has gone away. You're Isabela now and you belong to me."

"Dan? Dan, I..." She raised herself on one elbow and looked down at him. "Isabela is a Gypsy girl," she said gently. "She's as wild as the wind blowing down from the mountains. But I'm not like that, Dan. The real me, the Elizabeth me, isn't like that at all. When this is over, when I leave..." Her breath caught, and she felt the pain of the thought slash through her body, then made herself go on. "When this is over, I'll be Elizabeth again. I'll wear gray flannel suits. I'll pull my hair back and—"

"Never!" He pulled her down beside him and put a finger under her chin to tilt her face up to his. "You'll never be like that again. Not after Spain. Not after me."

Tears flooded her eyes, and for a moment she couldn't speak. But when she did, she tried to smile. "It's Pilar's Gypsy curse," she said at last. But when she saw the pain in his eyes, she said, "And Spain. And you."

Then she drew him into her arms so that his head rested against her breasts. "And you," she said again.

Chapter 10

When Dan found a sign that said *Larga Distancia*, long distance, he went in and placed a call to Al Thomason.

Al answered on the first ring. He said, *"Bueno?"* and his voice didn't sound the way Dan remembered.

"Al," he said. "Is that you, Al?"

"Dan?"

"Where the hell have you been?" Dan asked. "I tried to call you before—so did Maria. Why weren't you in Granada?"

"I...uh...had to go out of town. Something came up." There was a pause, and when he spoke again, his voice sounded hoarse. "Where are you?" he asked.

"Utrera." Dan hesitated. "You all right, Al?"

"Sure, sure. Fine. I've got a cold, that's all. When will you..." And again he hesitated. "When will you be here, Dan?"

"Tonight."

"You've got...everything?"

"Yep."

"Then I'll see you tonight. You know where my apartment is."

"The Barrio of Santa Cruz. I'll be there about ten o'clock."

"It'll be good to see you, Dan. It's been a long time. Since Paris, wasn't it?"

"Paris?"

"Yeah, you remember." There was another pause. Then Al said, "I've got to go now, Dan," and the line went dead.

Dan frowned when he put the phone down. Al Thomason, while capable, had always been a fusty, fidgety kind of man. Just now he'd sounded more fidgety than usual. But he was getting on in years. Soon he'd be due for retirement. It was just as well; the kind of a life somebody in Al's business led was enough to make anybody nervous.

That's why he'd gotten out of it and gone to work as an insurance investigator. This cops-and-robbers stuff wasn't for him anymore. Tonight he'd turn the jewels over to Al, along with the problem of Castro and Sanchez. He'd get Elizabeth to someplace where they'd be safe until things simmered down. Maybe then he'd be able to sort out his feeling for her.

In the meantime he had to buy both of them some clothes so they could get out of here.

There were only a few shops in Utrera. In one of them Dan bought trousers and shirts for himself, and a pair of jeans and a couple of sweaters for Elizabeth. He bought a small suitcase in another store.

There was a women's apparel shop next door to the luggage store. Dan had never shopped for a woman before, and he felt out of place when he opened the door and went in. What he'd do, he decided, was ask a saleslady to pick out a few basic things: underwear, stockings, shoes and some kind of a dress.

But when Dan entered the shop, there were other customers there, all of them women, and the salesperson was busy with them, so he began to look around. Hesitating in front of a display of lacy underwear, he very tentatively touched a pair of black lace bikini panties, then picked up the tiny wisp of satin-and-lace bra that matched it. It would barely cover Elizabeth's breasts. With the flick of a finger he'd be able to open the front snap and shrug it gently aside so that he could touch her, hold her.

His mouth went dry. His body tightened.

A pale ivory nightgown lay folded in display on another counter. He picked it up. It was satiny smooth against his fingertips, and he thought how it would feel on her body and how it would fall whisper soft to the floor when he undressed her.

He bought the gown and the lace panty and bra sets in both black and white. Then a saleswoman helped him pick out a blue wool dress with a matching tweed jacket, a pair of high-heeled beige pumps and sheer stockings.

When everything was wrapped, he thanked the woman and hurried back to the hotel, so anxious to get back to Elizabeth it was all he could do not to break into a run. He'd never felt this way about a woman before. He couldn't keep his hands off her. Every time they made love, it was better than the time before, but not enough, never enough.

He'd had his share of affairs, but no one had ever affected him the way Elizabeth did. That scared the hell out of him.

Last night when she had looked at him across the table, he'd thought his body would explode with need. And the fantastic, the unbelievable part of it was that she felt the same way.

He remembered the first time he'd seen her, when Castro and Sanchez had been after him that day at the Alhambra. He'd caught only a fleeting glimpse of her before he threw her down to the ground, but later in the car, when he'd known he'd have to keep her with him for a while, he'd looked at her more closely and thought, Damn, if I have to be saddled with a woman, why couldn't it have been a gorgeous dark-eyed Spanish *señorita*?

He'd thought her proper and uninteresting, a painfully plain Miss Moneypenny right out of an old James Bond movie.

When had he begun to find her attractive? Had it been when she first put on the red blouse and the flowered skirt and he'd seen the rise of her high, firm breasts, the small waist, the exciting flare of her hips and the long, sexy legs? Or had it started before that?

Dan remembered then how something had stirred in him the day he'd seen her rocking little Paquito. There'd been a womanly softness in her face and an expression in her pale green eyes that had somehow moved him. He had touched Paquito's hair, but it had really been Elizabeth that he'd wanted to touch.

He didn't understand her, couldn't categorize her. Was she an Ohio schoolteacher or a Spanish Gypsy? Was she Elizabeth or Isabela?

Last night he had told her that he loved her, and he'd meant it. But in the cool, clear light of day, that was a sobering thought, because love meant commitment and he wasn't sure how he felt about that.

He clutched the packages in his arms and thought that when he got back to the hotel they would make love again.

Damn, he thought, if I didn't know better, I'd swear she'd put a Gypsy curse on me.

He called her name as soon as he was inside the door and heard an answering call from the bathroom. He put the packages down, and because the door was ajar, he knocked, then went in.

She was in the tub. Her hair was pinned on top of her head, and her face was rosy from the heat. Dan stood for a moment looking down at her. Then he shook his head and said, "Dammit, woman, do you know what you do to me?"

Her eyes widened in that half shocked, half surprised look she sometimes had, and she said, "Dan?" Then her eyes went all smoky with the knowledge of what he was thinking.

He stripped quickly and when he got into the tub with her, she blushed and said, "You make me do things I've never done before."

"Do you like the things I do to you?"

"Yes," she said. "Yes, I like everything you do."

"This?" He cupped her soapy breasts, and she shivered.

"Yes," she whispered. "I like that."

He rubbed his thumbs over the peaked tips, and she said, "Dan. Oh, Dan."

She touched him as she had not touched him before, gently, caressingly, and felt a special thrill course through her body when he whispered his pleasure.

They made love quickly, urgently, their bodies close and tight in the warm, soapy water. When it was over they clung to each other, and after a little while, Dan said, "Let me bathe you."

Elizabeth lay back against the tub and closed her eyes, still afloat in the rapture they had shared. Dan ran his lathered hands over her body, washing, massaging, soothing, while she lay there, somnolent in the afterglow of love.

When they left their bath, each of them with a towel wrapped around them, he handed her the packages. She opened the things from the lingerie shop, and when she saw the delicate nightgown and the underwear, she said, "You . . . you bought all of this for me?" She picked up the gown and held it against her. "It's so beautiful," she said.

"Wear it tonight."

"Yes, tonight."

They looked at each other for a long moment before Dan said, "I got the sizes you asked for, but sizes are different here in Spain. I hope everything is okay."

She held the jeans up and said she was sure they would fit, and the sweaters, too. When she opened the box with the dress and jacket, she said, "I don't have anything blue. I love this, Dan. You have wonderful taste."

He watched her put on the white panties and matching bra. And when she went to sit on the edge of the bed and began to pull the stockings up over her legs, he said, "Wait," and bending to one knee, quickly rolled the sheer stockings back down her smooth, sleek legs. Then he gently laid her back on the bed.

"My Gypsy witch," he murmured as he came down beside her. "What kind of a spell have you cast to make me feel the way I do?"

"Dan—" she started to say, but he covered her mouth with his, and then there was no time for talking, only for feeling. He slipped the panties down over her hips and opened the front hook of the lacy bra before he threw off the towel he'd wrapped around his body.

They came together again, slowly, luxuriously, making it last, allowing sensation after sensation to bring them higher and higher until they reached the crest of pleasure. Dan kissed her then and took her cry into his mouth.

Later, when she had put the blue dress on, Elizabeth looked at herself in the full-length mirror that hung inside the armoire. The dress and the tweed jacket fit surprisingly well. She looked softer than she had in the clothes she normally wore when she was home, but far more conservative than in the Gypsy outfit. She started to pull her hair back, then changed her mind and left it loose around her shoulders.

She thought of the day she had danced barefoot in the earth by the side of the road, and she knew that it was the first time in her life she had ever truly let herself go, to feel and to listen to the music and the rhythm of her own body. When she danced it had been like viewing herself from a distance; Elizabeth standing back to watch the woman who was Isabela dance.

She had felt free then, as free and soaring as she'd felt just a few minutes ago when she and Dan had made love. She wondered if this fire that burned so hot and bright now had always been there, waiting to be released by somebody like Dan. By Dan.

He had told her that he loved her. But which *her* did he love? She knew that in the beginning he had found her dull and drab and uninteresting, that only when she had changed into Adelita's Gypsy clothes had he begun to notice her. That thought distressed her, because she didn't know if it was her that he loved or Isabela, the Gypsy.

He came in then, fully dressed, and said, "I've packed our things. There's a bus leaving at five o'clock."

Elizabeth tried to smile. She looked around the comfortable room and sighed. "I knew this was too good to last."

"There'll be other rooms."

The smile faltered. "Will there?"

"Of course." He took her by the shoulders and turned her to face him. "Of course there will be," he said.

When the bus they were riding on crossed the river of Guadalquivir, Elizabeth saw the Golden Tower of Seville and in the distance the Giralda, the tower that had dominated the Seville scene since 1198. It was a beautiful city, an old city, the heart and the essence of Andalusian Spain.

"We'll find a hotel in the Santa Cruz quarter," Dan said when the taxi they'd taken from the bus station let them off. He hefted the suitcase with one hand and took her arms with the other as they made their way into a labyrinth of alleyways with names like Pepper, Water, Glory and Coffin. Pots filled with bright red geraniums and other flowers hung from the windows of the whitewashed homes that stood side by side facing the alleyways. The balconies, with tiled undersides, overflowed with flowers, too.

Everything was beautiful and mysterious, and to Elizabeth, Seville seemed to personify the soul of Spain as no other city could.

The hotel Dan chose was on the Little Alley of the Water, where Washington Irving had once lived, he told her.

It was after nine when they checked in. As soon as they were in the room, Dan said, "Al Thomason's apartment isn't too far from here. I said I'd meet him at ten."

"I'm going with you."

"No you're not. You're staying here."

Elizabeth shook her head. "You've dragged me across half of Spain, Dan. I want to be with you now."

He shook his head. "No, and that's final."

She lifted her chin. "I'm not going to be left behind if you're in any kind of danger."

"I won't be in any danger."

"Then why can't I go with you?"

Dan glared at her. "Dammit, Elizabeth, will you listen to me?"

But Elizabeth didn't listen. She only grew more determined in her decision to go with him, and finally Dan conceded, not because of her arguments but because of Paco Sanchez. He didn't think they had been followed from Utrera, but the thought nagged that if they had been, if Castro and Sanchez knew they were in Seville, then Elizabeth was in as much danger as he was. That scared him and his stomach knotted in an almost physical pain at the thought of her with Paco Sanchez. So at last, because, after all, maybe she would be safer with him than alone in the hotel, he agreed to let her come along.

The alleyways, lighted by only an occasional lantern, were dark and narrow. In the distance they could hear the sound of a guitar. They passed a small bar and caught the smell of hot sausages, sardines and fried calamari and heard Spanish voices raised in argument.

The night had grown cool. Elizabeth pulled the tweed jacket closer around her body. Her high heels made sharp staccato sounds against the street stones.

"We're not going to stay any longer than we have to," Dan had told her before they left. "I'll turn the jewels over to Al, and we're out of there."

Something nagged at the back of his mind, something about the phone call to Al this morning. He touched the jewels in the pouch around his waist. He'd be glad when they were gone, glad when this was behind him.

They came to Calle de Susone, and Dan said, "This is the street. Number forty-seven."

The alley was narrower here, and as they went farther on, they saw that it was a cul-de-sac. He didn't like that, nor did he like it that number forty-seven was at the end of the blind alley.

Dan reached into the waistband of his trousers for his gun. "Stay behind me," he told Elizabeth.

She saw the tenseness in his face in the dim lantern light. She wanted to say, Let's get out of here. Let's turn around and run like hell. But she touched his back and knew that she wanted to be with Dan, no matter what the danger.

There was no light in the entranceway. Elizabeth gripped Dan's belt in the back and followed him inside.

"It's apartment C," he whispered. He flashed a pencil-thin flashlight, and she saw a door with the letter *A*. And farther back in the hall, another door.

"Wait here," Dan said, and before she could answer, he moved down the hall.

She smelled garlic and she tried to tell herself that everything was all right, that people, ordinary families lived here. But her hands tightened in the pockets of her jacket, and she bit her lower lip to keep it from trembling. She couldn't see Dan, only that pinpoint of light.

He came back to her and said, "Upstairs."

At the top of the stairs, he stopped. There was another flight of stairs after that that led up into darkness. Dan took her hand and led her up to the first step. He put a hand out to caution her to wait there. She saw a thin streak of light under a door, and when Dan moved the flashlight around, she saw the letter *C* and tightened her hand on the newel as cautiously, stealthily, Dan positioned himself at one side of the door.

"Al?" he said softly. "Al? Are you there?"

There was only an answering silence. Elizabeth's heart beat so hard against her ribs that she was sure Dan could hear it, that everybody in the building could hear it.

Dan tapped his knuckles against the door, waited, then began to turn the doorknob.

From inside there was a sound of movement. Then a harsh shout, "It's a trap!"

Dan whirled. He shoved Elizabeth up the stairs into the darkness. He heard a curse, a shot, a strangled cry. The door swung open and a voice shouted, "*¡Agarrenlos!* Catch them!"

For the flash of a second, Dan saw Ernesto Castro outlined in the light behind him. Dan fired once, then turned and ran up the stairs. "Come on!" he cried, and grabbing Elizabeth's hand, he took the steps two at a time.

They came flat up against a door. Dan wrenched it open. A bullet ricocheted off the wall behind them. He heard steps clattering up the stairs, turned, fired and shoved Elizabeth through the door and out onto a flat roof.

They raced across the roof, able to see a little better now. The door banged open behind them. Castro yelled an obscenity. A gun blasted, once, twice. Elizabeth muffled a scream.

"Keep low," Dan cautioned, and ran in a zigzag pattern with her to the end of the roof.

In the dim light from the lone street lamp on the ground, he saw the roof of the next house, five or six feet below. "I'm going to jump," he said, and before Elizabeth could stop him, he crouched low, then vaulted over the side of the building onto the adjacent roof.

"Jump!" he called up to her.

She looked down, hesitated for a fraction of a second, then jumped into his arms. They fell together. He helped her to her feet and raced with her toward the shadows at the side of the roof. He stumbled against some flowerpots, righted one before it fell, then pulled Elizabeth behind the tangled vines and flowers.

She dropped to her knees, as terrified as she'd ever been in her life.

"Where the hell are they?" a man called out.

The voice that he remembered as Castro's said, "Must have jumped onto the next building. Go after them, Armando. Bastard got me in the leg—I can't make it."

There was a clatter of someone jumping. A man stood up, then crouched and began to move toward them.

Elizabeth saw the gun in his hand, and her breath clogged in her throat. She put her hand on Dan's. He shrugged if off, took aim and fired.

The man spun around. Dan fired again. The man dropped hard.

"Come on." Dan reached for Elizabeth's hand and pulled her out from behind the flowerpots. Still in the shadows, they moved slowly, quietly, to the far edge of the roof. Dan looked over. "It's okay," he whispered. "It's only four or five feet down to the next rooftop. Better take your shoes off." He eased his body over the ledge and jumped. "Now you," he said, and when she jumped, he caught her as he had the time before.

They found a door that led down to the first floor, and when they reached it, Dan went to the entranceway to the street. He opened it slowly, looked in both directions. Then he tightened his hand around hers, and together they raced back toward their hotel.

When they were once again in their room, Elizabeth sank down onto the bed. Shaking with reaction, she managed to say, "Won't they find us here?"

Dan shook his head. "Al didn't know where we were staying."

"They killed him, didn't they?"

"Probably."

Elizabeth turned her head in her hands.

"He sounded strange on the phone. I asked him about it, and he told me he had a cold." Dan leaned against the wall and ran a tired hand through his hair. "They were with him then, waiting for me to call. They made him talk to me, made him..." He took a deep, shaking breath. "He said something about Paris, about our being in Paris together. I didn't get it. Damn me to hell, I didn't get it!"

"What about Paris?" Elizabeth asked.

"We were never there together." Dan put the gun on top of the dresser. "Al was there with another agent, a man by the name of Frank Malone. I don't know what they were working on, but Malone was killed. They never pinned it on anybody, but Al told me later that it was Paco Sanchez."

"Maybe...maybe it was him you shot. Sanchez, I mean."

"No." Dan let out the breath he'd been holding. "No," he said again. "Paco is smaller. Five-seven or eight, and skinny. The man I shot was bigger. I heard

Castro call him Armando. He must have been a hired thug."

"Then Sanchez is still..." Elizabeth wet her lips. "Then he's still out there, looking for us."

Dan pushed himself away from the wall and went to her. He sat on the bed beside her and said, "He doesn't know where we are, Elizabeth. He'll figure we'd head out of town tonight. But we won't. We'll stay here in the room for a couple of days. Then we'll head for Portugal."

He put his arms around her. "I'm sorry," he said, "so damn sorry I got you into this. If there was any way, any way I could, I'd get you out of here."

Elizabeth buried her head against his shoulder, holding him as he held her. "I wouldn't go," she whispered.

His arms tightened around her, and for a moment he felt tears sting his eyes because he loved her and because she was beautiful and brave. And because they might not have time to live together and grow old together.

In a little while they undressed and went to bed. But they didn't make love; they only held each other, and finally went to sleep in the warmth and comfort of their closeness.

Chapter 11

The night before they planned to leave Seville, Dan had placed a call to Maria Cortez.

One of the hardest things he had ever had to do was to tell her that Al had been killed.

In a broken voice she asked him to tell her what had happened.

He told her, then said, "They must have had him all the time. He tried to warn me that last second, and they killed him."

Over the sound of her weeping, he said, "Al was a fine man, Maria. I'm sorry."

Sorry. Dan had put the phone down and sat with his hand covering it for a long moment before he picked it up again and placed a collect call to his boss.

It was 4:00 a.m. in New York, and Joe Jewlensky was mad.

"Where in the hell have you been?" he roared. "You were supposed to call in every week. Why haven't you?"

"I've been traveling around."

"And I'm paying for it."

"I got the stuff."

"Oh?" Jewlensky's voice changed. "Great Dan. I told you it'd be a cinch, didn't I?"

"It was a cinch, all right. I've been on the run for two weeks, Al Thomason has been killed and a couple of killers are hot on my tail."

"Jeez!" There was a sound of a match being struck, then Jewlensky inhaling before he said, "You haven't gone to the police, have you?"

"No, but I would have, no matter what you said about publicity, except that some of the local Guardia are in on it. I don't dare ask for help, except from Interpol. Thomason was my only connection."

"Where're you headed now?"

"Portugal. If that doesn't work, I'll try Tangier. I've got to get out of Spain."

"I'll see what kind of connections I can dig up in both places."

"I'd appreciate that." Dan hesitated. "I've got a woman with me, Joe. She—"

"You and your damn women! Send you to outer Mongolia and you'd wind up with a blonde."

"This one isn't blonde. I dragged her into this against her will. I've got to protect her. She comes first, the jewels second."

"You're there to protect the jewels, Thornton, not some dame."

"She isn't a dame. She means a lot to me—one hell of a lot more than the jewels.

"Or your $650,000?"

"You'd better believe it, pal."

There was silence on the other end of the line before Jewlensky said, "Okay, Dan. If push comes to shove, I'll settle for you and the woman getting here all in one piece."

Dan had smiled when he hung up. Joe yelled a lot, but when the chips were down, he backed up his people. The company would lose a lot of money if the jewels weren't returned, but Dan knew Joe had meant it when he'd said he'd settle for Dan getting out all in one piece.

Now, as he drove the rental car the ninety-one kilometers toward Huelva, his biggest concern was for Elizabeth. From Huelva it was only a few more miles to the Portuguese border. Once in Portugal, they'd grab the first plane out of Lisbon for the States.

But first they had to get to Portugal.

As the first rays of dawn lightened the Spanish sky, Dan reached for Elizabeth's hand. "I thought you were going to try to get some sleep," he said.

"I couldn't." She sat up and stretched. "How soon before we get to Huelva?"

"Thirty or forty minutes."

"Do you think it would be all right to stop for breakfast? I'd really like to have a cup of coffee."

Dan nodded. "We'll stop someplace outside of town. I want to buy a newspaper."

She knew he was thinking about Al Thomason. "If they killed him, do you think there'll be something about it in the paper?"

"Probably."

Elizabeth shivered, glad that she'd worn the jeans and sweater Dan had bought for her in Seville. But she knew the chill that ran through her wasn't just from the cold. She was still scared by what had happened two nights ago. Every time she closed her eyes, she remembered the strangled cry that had come from Thomason's room, the race across the rooftops and the way the man whom Dan had shot had staggered and fallen.

She wondered if these past couple of weeks were typical of the life he led, if the other cases he investigated were all this dangerous.

Chilling thoughts for a cold morning. She was glad when Dan pointed out a cluster of buildings ahead and a sign that read *Restaurante*.

There were only three other customers in the restaurant, a mother and a father and a small boy, and they all looked as sleepy as Elizabeth felt.

She and Dan ordered *café con leche* and a plate of toast and sweet rolls. They had just finished and Dan had picked up the check when a newspaper delivery truck rolled up. The driver stopped, got out and tossed a pile of bound newspapers down near the door. A marked car drove up right behind him and two Guardia Civil men got out.

"Cold as a witch's nose," one of them said to the waitress when they entered. *"Café, por favor, y rápido."*

Dan looked across the table at Elizabeth. "Let's go," he said. "But take it easy; don't hurry."

Elizabeth nodded. She stood up and tried to smile. Dan linked his arm with hers. *"Gracias,"* he called to the woman who had waited on them.

They opened the door and stepped outside. Dan said, "Wait'll I get a paper," when all Elizabeth wanted to do was make a run for the car.

He put money down, snapped open the newspaper and looked at the front page. "Dammit!" he whispered harshly. "Dammit all to hell!"

"What is it?" Elizabeth asked, alarmed by the expression on his face. "What is it, Dan?"

"Get in the car." He handed the paper to her, led her to the car, opened her door and forced himself to walk casually around to his door. He made himself start the car slowly. Only when they were once again on the highway did he feel his shoulder muscles begin to relax.

Elizabeth opened the newspaper. Her picture and Dan's stared back at her under a big black headline that screamed "Wanted for Murder."

"Oh my God," she whispered.

"Read it."

She swallowed hard, then began to read.

> Two days ago, an American named Albert Thomason was murdered in the Barrio de Santa Cruz, shot through the heart by a man believed to be Daniel Thornton, who was accompanied by a woman, Elizabeth Kensington, also an American.
>
> The body was found by the downstairs neighbor who reported having seen a man and a woman entering the apartment at number forty-seven Calle de Susona. Other neighbors heard gunfire and spotted the couple running across the roof of the building.

There was more. People were advised to use the utmost caution, because the two Americans were armed and dangerous. The Guardia Civil had set up roadblocks and were sure of a capture within the next few days.

Elizabeth's hands were shaking when she put the paper down. "What are we going to do? What about the American Embassy? They'll help us, won't they?"

Dan shook his head. "Even if we could reach an embassy office, their only involvement would be to see that we had proper legal counsel."

"Then what are we going to do?"

Dan slowed the car. "Portugal is out because that's where they'd think we'd head. Our best bet now is Tangier."

"Tangier!" Elizabeth stared at him. "But we'd have to go through customs there, too. They'd check our passports."

"I know somebody in Algeciras who'll arrange phony passports." Dan covered her hand with his. "Don't worry, we'll make it. We'll stick to the back roads and head down to Cádiz and from there to Algeciras."

"I should have taken my sabbatical in geography instead of folk dancing," she said.

Dan started the car. The road along the coast was full of bumps and potholes for the first twenty-five miles before it came to an abrupt end and branched out into a road that led to the main highway.

Dan swore and Elizabeth said, "What are we going to do?"

"I think we've got to take a chance. It'd take us three days to walk from here to Algeciras. Maybe we'll find another turnoff along the coast before we get to Cádiz. It's the big cities we've got to avoid."

They were lucky; they found a country road only a few miles from Cádiz. The problem started twenty miles outside of Algeciras. Elizabeth was half-asleep when Dan said, "Uh-oh," and slowed the car.

"What is it?"

"Roadblock."

Dan swung the car off the road, but not before Elizabeth had seen the sawhorses and two marked cars. One car had been stopped. Two others and a truck waited in line to be checked. She hung on while the car bumped over furrowed ground toward a stand of trees.

Dry mouthed, she said, "What are we going to do?"

"We'll have to get rid of the car."

They made it well into the trees before Dan said, "Last stop." He looked at Elizabeth. "I'm sorry, honey."

"It's okay, Dan. I'm glad I wore the jeans and sandals, though. I wouldn't have gotten far in high heels."

He reached into the back for the suitcase. "We'll take this." He forced a grin. "I still haven't seen you in that new nightgown."

Elizabeth grinned back. "You took it off before I had a chance to wear it."

Dan kissed her. He wondered how any of the other women he'd known in his life would have acted under these circumstances and knew none of them would have been as staunch or as brave as Elizabeth. She was intelligent, sensible and sensitive. And she had a sense of humor. He liked that in a woman. He didn't remember who had talked about grace under pressure, but whoever it was must have been thinking about somebody like Elizabeth.

They walked all day. Her legs hurt and her back ached, but she didn't complain. Instead, she told him stories about her childhood and about her sister.

"We used to ride our bicycles from Rocky River all the way to Fairview Park and down into the valley. The river flows through there, and in the summer Paula and I would go wading. The water would be clear and cool, and there were trees all around."

Dan watched her face while she talked, her fear forgotten as childhood memories came flooding back. "There was another place," she said, "where there were rapids and a not-very-tall waterfall. We used to climb up the shale into the water and let the rapids carry us all the way downstream. Paula loved doing that, and so did I." She smiled. "She was such a pretty little girl. Everybody loved her."

"What about you? Were you as pretty then as you are now?"

Elizabeth made a face. "Not only wasn't I pretty; I was probably the tallest and the ugliest girl in Rocky River."

Dan stopped. He put his hands on her shoulders and swung her around to face him. "You weren't ugly then and you're not ugly now. You're a beautiful woman and I'm in love with you." Then, before Elizabeth could speak, he kissed her. There was anger in the kiss, anger at whomever had made her feel that she was less than pretty.

It was almost dark before they saw the deserted farmhouse.

"Hey look," Elizabeth said. "A Holiday Inn. Did you remember to call ahead for reservations?" Dan snapped his fingers. "Sorry, I forgot. But let's try the annex. Maybe they've got a room for us there."

The barn was big and red, and inside it smelled of hay and horses, of cows and old leather.

"This isn't half-bad," Dan said as he looked around. "Shall we get a room with one bed or two?"

"One, please."

"That's what I'd hoped." He put his arms around her. "Oh, Isabela," he said against her hair. "Isabela."

They found a place where the straw was thick enough to make them comfortable, then hand in hand they went into the deserted house.

"The barn's in better shape than the house," Dan said as he looked around. "It looks as though whoever lived here hasn't been gone too long. Let's see if we can find something to eat."

They started to look through cupboards. In one they found half a box of stale crackers and in another a can of peaches.

"Supper," Elizabeth said with a smile.

They went back to the barn, and when Dan opened the can with his knife, they sat cross-legged in the straw and ate the peaches and most of the stale crackers. They had just finished eating when it began to rain.

"It's going to be cold tonight," Dan said. "I'm glad we found this place. I'd hate to sleep outside on a night like this." He looked at Elizabeth. "We'll be in Algeciras tomorrow afternoon. It'll be better than this."

"How long will it take to make the passports?"

"A day or two. We'll be able to rest." He paused. "Poor Isabela," he said. "I've dragged you over half of Spain. You've had to sleep in a cave and in a Gypsy wagon and now in a barn." He touched the side of her face. "What have I done to you?"

"You've made me come alive," she said in a hushed voice. "You've made me feel like a woman—a pretty woman—for the first time in my life. You've made me aware of things I've never been aware of before." Her eyes were as soft as her voice. "There've been times when I've been angry and afraid, and as cold and tired as I am right now. But I wouldn't trade these past weeks for anything in the world, Dan."

He put his arms around her and held her close. He didn't speak because for a moment he couldn't. He only held her until he was able to say, "This will all be over soon. We'll be safe again, back home again."

Elizabeth waited for him to say, "And then..."

But Dan didn't say the words she longed to hear; words that spoke of commitment, of a future together.

The rain beat hard against the roof of the barn and dripped through cracks. The wind blew and the cold came hard and biting.

They lay down in the straw, Elizabeth's Gypsy shawl over their shoulders, seeking warmth from each other's bodies.

Dan meant only to warm her, but in a little while just being close wasn't enough. He kissed her and the kiss grew and deepened until her breath mingled with his. There was warmth in her mouth, and that was the warmth he sought. Then the kissing wasn't enough, and he began to unbutton her sweater.

His hands were cold and she shivered because of the cold and because of the passion that grew from deep inside her body. He unsnapped the front hook of the new lacy bra. His cold hands cupped her warm breasts, and cold and heat merged.

Elizabeth warmed her hands in the thickness of his hair, and when his fingers caressed her, she whispered his name.

Lightning streaked across the barn, and there was a crash of thunder. Elizabeth moved close and he put his arms around her bare shoulders. "It's all right, love," he soothed, then his mouth found hers again, and the fear went away. He rolled her under him and covered her body with his.

When their bodies grew warm, he began to kiss her breasts, and for a little while she lay passively in his arms, because she loved to have him touch her this way. But then the heat began to grow again, and she began to move under him while she whispered his name in a voice fevered with desire.

Dan slipped the jeans down over her legs and quickly tossed his own clothes aside, and when he came back over her again, he groaned aloud at the sheer pleasure of feeling her so smooth and lean against him. For a few moments they lay like that, their bodies entwined, then he raised himself up so that he could see her face in the dim light of the barn.

"Elizabeth," he said, then joined his body to hers. They began to move together while the thunder crashed and the lightning lighted the inside of the old barn with jagged streaks of orange flame. And suddenly all of the fear and the danger of the past few days closed in upon Elizabeth. Tomorrow they might be caught by the Guardia Civil or by Castro and Sanchez. Sanchez, who had cut a woman's breasts. He was out there somewhere, looking for them.

She lifted her body to Dan's. She wanted to say, Hold me because I'm afraid. Love me and make me forget my fear.

She whispered his name and he took her lips as he ground his body to hers in the half darkness of the barn, there on the bed of straw.

The fever in her rose until she was exalted by it, consumed in the love she had for this man, following where he led, as demanding as she was giving, yielding all in this life-giving celebration of love.

Their cadence quickened, slowed, quickened. Because she was afraid of tomorrow, of all the tomorrows that were to come, Elizabeth began to plead, "Don't stop. Oh, please don't stop."

Lightning illuminated the barn again, and for a second she saw Dan's face, saw the agony of love there, and she thought her heart would burst with loving him.

"I love you," she cried. "Love you. Love you."

Together they rose higher and higher, while the thunder and lightning crashed all around them.

Afterward she lay in his arms, dissolved by love. He kissed her eyes, her nose and her cheeks. He caressed the silken skin on her back. And when they began to get cold, he helped her dress, then covered their shoulders with the Gypsy shawl and held her in his arms until they slept.

Dan awoke first the next morning. The rain had stopped and the sun filtered through the cracks in the barn, suffusing thc inside with a soft, warm glow. He looked at Elizabeth, still asleep in his arms. Her head was against his shoulder, her arm across his waist. Her face was rosy with sleep and with cold.

He thought of how it had been last night and it seemed to him he could still hear her small whispers of pleasure, her murmured pleas. In the throes of passion and in the darkness of the night, she had told him that she loved him. He wondered if she would be able to say the words now that passion had eased and daylight had come.

He brushed the hair back from her forehead and gently kissed her. "We have to leave now," he said.

Slowly Elizabeth opened her eyes and looked at him. Then she looked around the barn, and he could see that it took her a moment to remember where she was.

"The rain has stopped," she said.

"Yes, love. It's after seven; we've got to get going."

"In a minute." She took hold of his ears and brought his face close to hers. "Give me a kiss," she said.

Dan looked down into the pale green eyes. He felt choked with love, but all he said was, "With pleasure."

He wanted her again and he knew by the way her lips softened and parted under his that she felt the same. But he made himself sit up and say, "We've really got to get started."

"I know." She let him help her up, and when he did, she stretched and brushed the straw off her jeans. "No breakfast?" she asked.

"We'll find a farmhouse or maybe a small restaurant." Dan put his arms around her and kissed her again.

For a reason she could not explain, Elizabeth felt hot tears sting her eyes. Last night had been so special that it had conquered the fear of today and of the days yet to come. She wanted to spend the day here in the barn; she wanted to forget the danger that lay somewhere beyond.

"C'mon," Dan growled in mock severity, "let's get a move on." Then he saw her tears, and he said, "Don't, love. It's going to be all right. I won't let anything happen to you."

"To us," Elizabeth whispered against his shoulder.

"To us." He held her closely, then he looked down at the place where they had lain together and loved together, and vowed that whatever the cost, he would keep her safe.

For she was Isabela, his life, his love.

Chapter 12

They reached Algeciras late that afternoon and found a small hotel near the wharf. Dan registered in Elizabeth's brother-in-law's name, Harold Skinner, and they went out to eat.

Over a steak, French fried potatoes and a big green salad, Dan said, "Feeling better now?"

Elizabeth took a sip of red table wine. "I'm almost ready to walk another twenty miles."

"How about a good night's sleep first?"

"Fine, provided you let me sleep."

Dan reached for her hand across the table. She'd been walking for two days. Her clothes were mud-splattered and there were dark patches of fatigue under her eyes. They were wanted for a murder they didn't commit, and two of the most dangerous men in Spain were looking for them. But she could still joke.

"We'll sleep," he promised. "Some of the time." He poured more wine into her glass. "Tomorrow I'll see about our passports. Have you ever been to Tangier?"

"No, this has been my first trip out of the country." She raised one eyebrow. "I had no idea Europe would be this stimulating, or I'd have come a long time ago."

"But I wouldn't have been here."

"That's true." Elizabeth rubbed a thumb over the back of his hand. "I wouldn't have liked it without you, Dan."

"Even with all we've been through?"

"Even then."

Their eyes met and held, and Dan was filled with a love that almost overwhelmed him.

When they left the restaurant, they walked hand in hand along the wharf and watched the lights of distant ships. Beyond, through the darkness, lay North Africa. What would it be like there? Elizabeth wondered. Would they be safe there? Could they reach Casablanca? Then New York? And after New York, what?

There were so many unanswered questions about tomorrow and all the tomorrows to come. But she wouldn't think about them tonight. She looked out at the dark, still water, and a sense of calm quieted her thoughts because Dan was with her, and that, after all, was all that mattered.

The next morning Dan and Elizabeth slept late, then he called the man who would arrange their passports. After a quick lunch in their room, they dressed and left the hotel. The day was sunny and warm. They found a taxi and were taken to a house in a not-too-pleasant neighborhood.

A woman who looked part Spanish, part Moroccan, and who was at least a hundred pounds overweight, met them at the door.

"Your name," she said without preamble, and when Dan told her, she nodded and took them through the house into the kitchen. "This is George." She indicated an American in his late fifties, who was standing in front of the sink eating a can of sardines.

George turned around. "You have money?" he asked.

Dan nodded. A price was arranged. Money was handed over. George counted it carefully, then said, "All right, let me see your passports."

He studied them a minute or two, then he looked at Dan and at Elizabeth. "She doesn't look like the picture in her passport," he said. "She looks different now, younger, more attractive." He turned to Dan. "Whoever is looking for you, how do they know her? The way she was before or the way she looks now?"

"The way she looks now," Dan said.

George scratched his head. "Maybe if we make her a blonde?"

"No, not blond."

"Then we'll go with the way she looks in the original passport picture, but more so. I got clothes here. Maybe we can find something to fit her."

The conversation went on around Elizabeth as though she weren't there. The words "The way she was before or the way she looks now?" went around and around in her head. Had she really changed that much?

When the conversation turned to how George could make Dan look different, she reached for her passport and opened it. The photograph had been taken only a year ago, but the woman who looked back at her seemed like someone she had known a long time ago. Had a different hairstyle and a bit of makeup made that much difference? Had Pilar's Gypsy curse changed her? Or had she been changed by love?

Whatever it was, it was a scary feeling to look at the woman she had been such a short time ago.

George decided, over Dan's vociferous objection, that Dan would have his hair dyed blond. He called to the woman who'd let them in, and when she came into the kitchen, George said, "Cut the *señor*'s hair and change the color to a dark blond." He scratched a three-day growth of beard. "It's too bad we don't have time to let you grow a mustache, but Magdelena will fix a fake one that will do for the picture and last until you enter Tangier."

Dan put a hand on Elizabeth's shoulder. "I hope you like blond men," he said, and let Magdelena lead him away.

George took Elizabeth into another room. He slid open a closet door and said, "Let's see what we can find."

He looked at outfit after outfit, paused and discarded until he came to a dull gray dress that hung straight from the hanger without shape or any frill to relieve its drabness.

"This should do," he muttered to himself. He held it up to Elizabeth and nodded. "Yes, this is what we want."

It may be what you want, she thought with dismay, but it certainly isn't what I want.

He handed her the dress and told her to put it on. "Come out when you're ready, and Magdelena will fix your hair," he said. "And take off all your makeup. You've got to look like a very plain woman."

But I've been a plain woman all my life, she thought.

Elizabeth put the dress on, and it hung as straight on her as it had on the hanger. She looked at herself in the mirror and didn't know whether to laugh or to cry.

When she went back into the kitchen, Magdelena was waiting for her, and George went to help Dan select suitable clothes.

Hands on saddlebag hips, Magdelena said, "Sit down. Let me see what I can do."

She brushed Elizabeth's hair out, then pulled it straight back and rolled and pinned it into a tight bun. With a dark pencil she thickened Elizabeth's eyebrows. "Yes," she said to herself, "that's better."

Better than what? Elizabeth wondered.

"Perhaps glasses."

Elizabeth groaned.

Magdelena opened a cupboard, and when she found a box, she rummaged through it until she found saw a pair of black horn-rimmed glasses. She handed them to Elizabeth. "Try these," she said. And when Elizabeth did, Magdelena grunted in satisfaction. "Perfect," she said, and handed Elizabeth a mirror.

Elizabeth stared in the mirror at herself, her real self, all except for the horn-rimmed glasses. This is who I really am, she thought with dismay. This is who I've been all along. That other woman, Isabela, was only a figment of Pilar's imagination. There isn't any Isabela—there's only me.

"Well?" Magdelena asked. "What do you think?"

"I think it's perfect," Elizabeth said. "I think it's me."

Magdelena smiled uncertainly, but before she could speak, Dan came in with George. Elizabeth swung around to look at him, and her lips parted in amazement. Dan's hair had been trimmed and styled and bleached. He wore a mustache that was a darker blond, and he was dressed in dark blue slacks, an off-white sweater and a light blue blazer.

He was probably the best-looking man she'd ever seen, and all she could think of was the song from *Funny Girl* about the groom being prettier than the bride.

"I'm glad that's over," he said. "How in the hell women can stand going to beauty shops..." He stopped and stared at Elizabeth. "You look *terrible*," he said.

She wanted to say, I look like me, but didn't.

"We're ready to take the pictures now," George said. He got the camera ready, and Magdelena arranged a backdrop cloth.

And all the while Dan kept staring at her.

Elizabeth went first. She looked straight into the camera, serious and unsmiling.

Then it was Dan's turn—Dan, who looked so handsome and debonair.

"What names will you use?" George asked after the photographs had been taken.

"Harold Skinner," Dan said, sticking to the name he'd registered under at the hotel.

"And the lady?"

Elizabeth wet her lips. "Mildred," she said. "Mildred Thursby."

"Mildred?" It was the first time Dan had spoken since he'd said she looked terrible.

"She was a teacher I had in the fifth grade," Elizabeth explained.

Miss Mildred Thursby, who had never married, had been a dour, unsmiling woman in her late fifties. She taught fifth-grade math, and Elizabeth had been terrified of her. To this day she remembered standing at the blackboard, her sweaty hands dampening a piece of chalk, trying to do a problem in long division while Miss Thursby glared at her and kept repeating, "Well? Well?"

She'd hated Miss Thursby.

They changed into the clothes they'd come in to go back to the hotel. But not her hair; Elizabeth left it the way Magdelena had fixed it.

"Come back the day after tomorrow," George told them. "The passports will be ready then."

"Well, that's done," Dan said when they were alone on the street.

He knew his voice sounded too forced, too hearty. He hadn't meant it to be, but he was still in a state of shock over the way Elizabeth had looked tonight for her passport photo.

She'd looked like that the first time he'd seen her in the gardens of the Alhambra.

For the past few weeks she had been transformed. But was the real Elizabeth the woman who had sat in front of the camera a few minutes ago, or the woman who walked beside him now?

He didn't like the way he was thinking, and he told himself that it was Elizabeth he had fallen in love with. Elizabeth—whoever she was.

But when they got back to the hotel, he said, "Take your hair down.

Elizabeth looked at him. One still-heavy eyebrow raised in question, then she reached around to the back of her head and took the pins out. "I'm going in to shower," she said without looking at Dan.

He knew he was behaving like an idiot. What in the hell did it matter how she wore her hair? She was Elizabeth and he loved her. Didn't he?

When she came out of the bathroom, her hair was loose and shiny around her shoulders, and she'd scrubbed off the thick eyebrows.

"That's my girl," he said, and hated himself for having said it.

Elizabeth didn't answer. She only looked at him for a moment and got into bed.

They lay side by side in the darkness, together yet strangely apart. When Dan put his arms around her, she said, "I'm really very tired," and turned on her side away from him.

She wasn't angry. What she felt went far deeper than anger and was much more painful. She'd had a shock tonight when she'd looked at herself in the mirror. It was as though she'd stepped back in time, back before Spain, back before Dan. But she could have shrugged off her dismay, could even have laughed about the change, if Dan had been able to laugh with her.

But he hadn't laughed. He'd looked at her, and there'd been an expression of almost revulsion on his face, and she'd known in that instant that it wasn't her he was in love with—it was Isabela. And Isabela wasn't real; she was somebody Pilar had invented. For no matter the makeup or the golden earrings, no matter the clothes or the hairdo, she was still Elizabeth. That hadn't changed. That would never change.

Love had made her softer, more attractive. She knew that and she'd been pleased that it had. She'd never go back to the way she'd been before, to the gray and brown and black dresses that had been her basic wardrobe. And yes, she probably would style her hair differently. But she would still be Elizabeth. When she was forty and fifty and sixty, she would still be Elizabeth.

And what of Dan? If he only loved that part of her that could be pretty and attractive, how would he feel when she wasn't? Nobody could look good one hundred percent of the time. What about those times when she might be tired or ill or pregnant? Or when she got older? Would he love her then, or would he find somebody who looked better than she did?

These were the thoughts that troubled Elizabeth all through that long night. Only toward dawn did she fall into a troubled sleep, and when she finally awoke, Dan was gone.

He'd left a note saying he had gone downstairs for breakfast and that if she woke up she might like to come down and join him. But she didn't. She lay in bed thinking and finally went into the bathroom to shower and wash her hair, delaying as long as she could the moment when she would have to see him again.

She was already dressed in a pair of jeans and a sweater when he returned. She'd pulled her hair back, not into a bun, but into a ponytail. She wore no makeup except for a touch of lipstick.

"There you are," Dan said when he saw her. "I had three cups of coffee while I was waiting for you."

"Sorry. I slept later than I intended to." She picked up her purse.

"I'll go down with you."

"No," she said too quickly. "Really, that's not necessary."

He ran a hand through his newly acquired blond hair. "Okay, if you're sure. I've got to call New York, anyway. I'll do it while you're having breakfast."

Elizabeth nodded. "I won't be long," she said, and before he could answer she went out and closed the door behind her.

Dan stared at the closed door. What in the hell's the matter with her? he thought almost angrily. But he knew what the matter was—he'd known it since last night when they'd gone to bed. It had been something in his expression, and yes, in his attitude from the moment he'd walked into George's kitchen and had seen her in that god-awful gray dress.

He hadn't been able to help himself; he'd been appalled at the way she'd looked, and had the terrible realization that she'd looked almost exactly the same the first day he'd seen her.

It had been a startling realization, the realization that she really was Elizabeth Kensington, a schoolteacher from Ohio, not Isabela, his Gypsy lady.

What was wrong with him? Was he really that shallow? Did looks really mean that much to him?

Of all the women he'd ever known, there wasn't a one who could hold a candle to Elizabeth when it came to character. She was bright and strong and wonderful, but...

He slammed his fist on the bureau. Dammit, what was the matter with him? What kind of a man was he?

He told himself then that he wouldn't think about this now. He had things to do. He had to call Joe Jewlensky.

"Where are you?" Jewlensky asked when he heard Dan's voice.

"Algeciras."

"Everything okay?"

"So far."

"The woman still with you?"

"Yeah."

"I got a name for you."

"Go ahead."

"Hassan Ishmael. He has a shop in the Kasbah, Le Rendezvous. He knows you're coming. He'll get you out of Tangier."

"Thanks, Al."

"No sweat. Just be careful, Mr...."

"Skinner," Dan said. "Harold Skinner."

A feeling of relief flooded through him when he put the phone down, because he knew this would all soon be over. They'd go to Tangier, maybe Casablanca, then New York.

And then what?

He didn't know. He had told Elizabeth that he loved her, but who did he really love? The Elizabeth she'd been last night or the wonderfully alive and wanton woman he'd shared a Gypsy wagon with?

He didn't know. Damn him to hell, he didn't know.

Two days later, dressed in the same clothes they'd worn when their passport pictures had been taken, Dan and Elizabeth boarded the boat that would take them across the Strait of Gibraltar to Tangier. As they drew nearer to this city that was the gateway to North Africa, Elizabeth saw the terraced white houses gleaming in the warm African sun and palm trees swaying in the ocean breeze. Morocco was a place she had always wanted to see, but the excitement she should have felt had been replaced by the terrible feeling of emptiness that still held her. Even the fear that she and Dan might be discovered when they passed through immigration had faded.

She looked at Dan standing so confidently at the ship's rail in the clothes he had bought from George. He was movie-star handsome, and she'd seen more than one woman looking at him. When he turned to say something to her, she had seen the shock on women's faces that she and Dan were together. That only made her retreat even further into the protective shell she was already beginning to draw around herself.

Dan took her arm when the ship docked. "It won't be long now," he said. "Nervous?"

"No, I'm all right." And it was true; she really wasn't nervous. Her passport read Mildred Thursby, and she felt like Mildred Thursby.

They passed through customs and immigration without any trouble. Elizabeth didn't know whether to laugh or cry when the immigration officer flipped open her passport, looked at the terrible picture, then at her, nodded and said, "Very well. You may proceed."

Five or six small boys tried to take their one suitcase when they were ready to leave. Dan shooed them away and signaled for a taxi. The taxi pulled up, but before they could get in, a man wearing a dark brown dejellaba, a Moroccan robe, leaped forward to open the door.

"Here you are *sidi*," he said to Dan. "Shall we put your luggage in the front with me?" Without waiting for a reply, he took the suitcase from Dan and placed it on the front seat.

"Hold on a minute," Dan said, but the Moroccan had already taken Elizabeth's arm and was helping her into the cab.

"Just a damn—"

"Please get in, sir," the man said quickly. "I know you are anxious to take the lady shopping. I have just the place for you. Le Rendezvous has the best caftans in Tangier."

Dan drew his breath in sharply. "All right," he said. "Let's go."

He got in the back seat with Elizabeth; the Moroccan got in front with the driver. "*Yallah, yallah*, get going," the man said.

When they were well away from the docks, he put an arm over the back of the seat. "We will take you to your hotel, sir and lady. In the morning I will come and take you shopping. Will that be satisfactory?"

Dan nodded. "What's your name?"

"I am Mohammed Al-Haj, sir, sent by the tourist bureau to help you and your lady."

"*Shukran*, thank you." Dan looked at Elizabeth, who sat on the edge of her seat, poised as though to take flight. "I didn't expect the tourist company to meet us," he said. "Wasn't it lucky they did?"

"Yes." Elizabeth wet her lips. "Yes, it was lucky."

He knew she was frightened, so he took her hand and squeezed it, and to Mohammed Al-Haj he said, "Where is the hotel?"

"Near the Kasbah, *sidi*. It is quite nice. I'm sure you will be comfortable there."

Elizabeth tried to relax. She leaned back in the seat and looked out of the window. It was late afternoon and the sun shone in an almost blinding glare on the white buildings. She was surprised and did not know why she was, to find Tangier so clean and white. Most of the men and women who hurried down the streets were robed; those who weren't wore stylish, modern clothes. The palm-lined boulevards were wide and the promenades along the waterfront were filled with shops and restaurants.

Soon the taxi passed through modern Tangier and entered the older section of the city. The streets were narrower here, the people not as well dressed. The taxi pulled up to a guard post at one side of a tall, black iron gate.

"Hotel Afrique," the driver said, and the gate opened.

The hotel was set far back off the road that led to it, past olive orchards, stately palms and gardens blooming with a wonderful variety of flowers.

The building, when they approached, looked elegantly Moorish. When they pulled into the driveway, two tall Sudanese, wearing long, bright blue robes and bright red fezzes, rushed out to open the taxi doors.

"We have your reservation, Mr. Skinner," the man behind the desk said when Dan gave his name. "May I see your passports?"

Dan put them on the reception desk. The man looked at them and smiled. "Yes," he said, "everything is in order. I'll have someone show you to your rooms."

Dan thanked the man before he turned to Mohammed Al-Haj. "We'll see you in the morning, then?" he asked.

"At ten o'clock, sir, if that is agreeable."

"Ten is fine."

Mohammed smiled at Elizabeth. "There are lovely things to buy here in Tangier, madam. In Le Rendez-vous you will find silk caftans and robes that I am sure will please you. You must buy several so that when Mr. Skinner takes you out to dine you will feel like a Moroccan princess." The words were kindly meant and gently spoken.

And Elizabeth, moved by that kindness, held out her hand. "Thank you, Mohammed Al-Haj. I look forward to seeing more of your lovely city."

She didn't take the glasses off until they were in the elevator. When she did, she closed her eyes and rubbed the bridge of her nose.

"Tired?" Dan asked.

"Yes." Elizabeth wanted to say something to break the tension between them. But it was difficult, as awkward as when two people have had a silly fight and don't quite know how to make it up. But she and Dan hadn't had a fight, not even a silly one. The problem between them went much deeper than that.

Their suite of rooms overlooked the swimming pool. The sitting room, done in shades of ivory and beige, was stiff and formal, but the bedroom more than made up for it. Everything in it had been done in a delicate shade of golden apricot, even to the dainty roses on the bureau and the sunlight that streamed in through the open doors of the balcony.

"This is nice," Dan said. He smiled uncertainly. "Isn't it?"

"Yes, it's beautiful." Elizabeth took a deep breath. Her shoulders felt tight and tense, the gray dress too heavy for her body. She looked down at the glasses in her hand, then went to the wastebasket and dropped them in.

"You might need them when we leave the country," Dan said

"I'll say they were broken." She looked in the basket. "Actually, they are."

"Elizabeth—"

She held up a hand as though to silence him, then said, "I'm too warm, Dan. I'm going to take a bath."

"I'll send down for something cool to drink."

"That would be nice."

So polite, so formal, Elizabeth thought when she went into one of the two bathrooms and closed the door behind her. What had happened to the lovers they had been? What had happened to the two people who had been able to talk and to laugh together? Where had they gone?

She took off the gray dress, rolled it up into a ball and threw it into a clothes damper. When she had stripped, she turned the water on in the shower and went to stand under it. She let it beat hard and long against her body, letting the feel of it, the sound of it, drive everything else from her mind.

At last she came out of the shower and dried her hair with the dryer attached to the wall. When that was done, she put on the terry cloth robe that hung behind the door and went out to face Dan.

Chapter 13

They made love that night, but it wasn't the same and they both knew it. Elizabeth held herself back, not deliberately, but because she simply couldn't help herself.

Dan sensed it. He tried to ease her and to arouse her, but the more he tried the more self-conscious she became. She was relieved when it ended, and when it did she went in to take a shower.

Dan was asleep, or pretending to be asleep, by the time she came back to bed.

The awkwardness between them was still there the next morning. Dan had their breakfast sent up, and when they'd eaten—in almost complete silence—Elizabeth went into the bathroom to dress.

She put more makeup on than she normally used but less that she'd been using in her Gypsy guise. Then brushed her long dark hair and coiled it into a French twist before she stepped into the blue dress. When she looked at her reflection in the mirror, she knew that she wasn't the Elizabeth she had been, but neither was she Isabela the Gypsy.

Mohammed Al-Haj was waiting for them when they went downstairs, and it was a relief for both of them to have a third person present so they didn't have to talk to each other.

The Kasbah dominated the old city, and as they made their way through the narrow streets toward it, it seemed as though a whole sea of humanity surged around them. The women who hurried past were robed and veiled, some of them so completely covered that only the narrow strip of their eyes showed.

As they drew nearer the Kasbah, Elizabeth became aware of an exotic blend of smells: cinnamon and coffee, rose water and mint, herbs and spices.

Mohammed led them down a narrow flight of steps, past robed men and women and children who held out their hands crying "Dirham, dirham. Money, money."

"La, la," Mohammed said, shooing them away as he would a hoard of pestering flies as he cleared a path for Elizabeth and Dan and lead them toward a row of souks.

Here the stands held brass and silver, gold plates and pots and stall after stall of gaily colored beads, rugs, straw baskets, pottery, velvet slippers, gold belts and all kinds of robes. Other stands displayed dates, almonds and figs, pomegranates and oranges, all arranged in intricate patterns. Farther on, when Elizabeth paused to look at the leather wallets and purses in front of a shop, the owner rushed out and grabbed her arm, trying to lead her inside.

Mohammed shouted something at him in Arabic. The man whined but he let go of Elizabeth. But now a crowd of boys and young men gathered around her, shoving their wares at her; strings of beads, wallets like the ones she'd stopped to admire and brass bells that they rang close to her face.

Once again Mohammed stepped in, this time flailing his arms, swatting a boy, shoving the young men. *"Balak!"* he shouted. "Move, watch out! *Baraka*, that's enough!" And to Elizabeth, he said "That will happen if you stop, madam. It is better not to look or to hesitate, or you will be overrun by these small businessmen."

But it was difficult not to hesitate; she'd never seen sights and smells like these before. When a man in a bright red suit adorned with gold ornaments, came toward them calling, *"L'ma, l'ma,"* Mohammed said, "That is the water man." He took a few dirham out of his pocket and handed them to the man in the red suit. In turn the man offered a cup of water, and when it was refused, he sprayed the air with the scent of roses and said "*Shukran*, thank you. *Allah akbar*, God is great."

Finally they came to a shop filled with robes and caftans and jeweled velvet slippers similar to those Elizabeth had seen in the stalls.

"Le Rendezvous," Mohammed said as he directed them into the shop. Once inside he led them toward the back, and when a young man rushed forward to help them, he said, "Tell Hassan Ishmael that Mohammed is here."

The young man disappeared behind heavy drapes before Mohammed turned to Dan and said, "I will wait for you here, and when you leave you must buy something for your lady, sir. Ishmael is a businessman, and he berates his clerks whenever a potential customer enters but leaves without making a purchase."

"I will, of course." Dan turned to Elizabeth. "Look around," he said. "We'll get something after we've seen what Ishmael has to say."

He hoped that the Moroccan had a way out for them. He'd always enjoyed being in Tangier before, but he didn't want to be here now. Was it because of Elizabeth? Was that why he wanted this over and done with? So that he could sort out his feelings for her?

He wanted to tell her that he was sorry, but he wasn't sure what for. Last night had been a fiasco. He'd been bewildered by her lack of response, then angered by it, even though there was a part of him that knew his anger should have been directed at himself instead of her, for he was the one who really had withdrawn. But he hadn't been able to help himself; he wanted Isabela back. He wanted the Gypsy lady he'd fallen in love with.

Now it seemed so damned phony to say, like an unfaithful husband trying to placate a suspicious wife, "Buy something nice for yourself, dear."

But before Dan could say anything, the curtains were drawn aside and a young woman stepped out. In a shy voice, she said, "Good morning. Please come this way."

She held the curtains back, and when Elizabeth stepped closer, she saw that the girl was no more than fourteen or fifteen and that she was quite beautiful. Dressed in a dark blue caftan, long silver earrings dangled from her ears and bracelets adorned her arms. Small stars were tattooed on her forehead and cheeks.

"This way, sir and lady," she murmured, and led them into a spacious room draped with red-and-lavender silk wall hangings. There were two sofas in the room. No, not sofas, Elizabeth corrected herself, for furniture this luxurious had to be called divans. These were done in a deeper shade of lavender velvet, and seated in the middle of one of them, although his huge frame overflowed almost to the sides of the divan, was a bearded man dressed in a dark brown robe, with a hood drawn up over his head. His hands were crossed over his belly, and there was a ring on every sausage-fat finger.

He did not try to rise when they entered with the girl, but he waved one hand and said, "*Marhaban*, welcome. Please sit down." And to the girl, he said, "Zahira, bring tea for our guests."

He smiled when she left the room. "We are only newly married," he told Dan. "She is still shy but she will get over that soon enough." He looked at Elizabeth. "This is your woman?"

Dan nodded. "Yes, this is my woman."

"You must buy her something before you leave my shop."

"I will, Hassan Ishmael."

"And tonight you will take her out to a club."

"I'm not sure that's wise."

"Do you have reason to believe you were followed?"

Dan shook his head.

"Then tonight you will go to El Jadida. It is a fashionable club, very popular, a place you in your country would say is 'in.'"

"Are you unaware of a certain problem that I face?" Dan asked.

"I have been informed of your problem, sir. Please let me assure you that you will be quite safe at El Jadida. Go at eleven. A table will have been reserved for you. At eleven-thirty you will be joined by a countryman of yours. He will make your travel arrangements."

A door in the back of the salon opened, and Zahira entered with a silver tray and three cups of hot mint tea. She knelt on a hassock in front of Hassan Ishmael. He put a fat finger under her chin and lifted her face. To Dan, he said, "She's quite lovely, isn't she? But too thin, of course. I am trying to fatten her with sweets, because it would please me to have her a bit plump."

A flush colored the girl's cheeks. She kept her eyes downcast, but when she handed Dan and Elizabeth their tea, Elizabeth saw that her hands were trembling.

You should be in high school, Elizabeth wanted to tell the girl. You should be going to dances and movies with boys your own age, instead of being married to a man who is surely old enough to be your father. The thought of Zahira, so young and so fragile, going to bed with a man like Hassan Ishmael made her shudder. It was all she could do to drink her tea and not speak. But since she wasn't included in the conversation any more than Zahira was, she didn't need to worry about saying anything.

Elizabeth had read about the lot of women in some of the Arab countries, but she hadn't quite believed what she'd read until now. She knew, of course, that women played a largely passive role in Arab society and that men—fathers, brothers and husbands—had authority over them. While men spent their time in public places, women generally stayed at home behind the walls of their houses. Perhaps, Elizabeth thought sadly, Zahira's life would be easier after she had children, even though she was little more than a child herself.

So involved was Elizabeth in her own thoughts that she was startled when Dan said, "Thank you, Hassan Ishmael. I am most appreciative of your help."

Hassan waved a ringed finger. "Then buy a few lovely caftans for your lady. That will be thanks enough. *Ma'al salama*, friend. Peace be with you."

"And with you, Hassan Ishmael."

"Mohammed will stay with you until you leave Tangier. He is completely trustworthy." Ishmael turned to Elizabeth. "I know this is a difficult time, madam, but nevertheless I hope you will enjoy Tangier. It is an old city, this gateway to Africa. The pleasures to be found here are far more exotic than any you would find in Europe or your own country. I hope that someday you will return under more pleasant circumstances."

"Thank you, Mr. Ishmael. And thank you for helping us."

To the young woman, Elizabeth said, "It was very nice meeting you, Zahira." And though the words stuck in her throat, she added, "Congratulations on your marriage. I hope you'll be happy."

"But I wouldn't bet on it," she murmured to Dan when they left the salon for the shop.

"I know what you're thinking," he said. "And I agree that it's a damn shame for a youngster like that to be married to somebody like him. But I suppose the wedding was arranged and she didn't have anything to say about it."

"That's terrible!"

"Sure it is, but that's the way it still is in a lot of countries. And who are we to say whether it's the right or the wrong way of doing things? Look at the divorce rate in the States. It doesn't seem as though our way of doing this is much better." Dan took her arm. "Now let's buy you something exotic to wear tonight."

So that I can pretend to be somebody else? Elizabeth wanted to say. But she bit back the words and in spite of herself gasped with pleasure when one of the clerks began to lay an array of caftans on the counter in front of her.

They came in a wondrous variety of fabrics and colors. Some were of a heavy material, others of a cloth so sheer and gossamer fine that when she held them to the light they seemed almost transparent.

Elizabeth finally chose five that she liked, then tried to narrow her choice down to one. When she couldn't decide between a gown in variegated colors of green, turquoise and blue, and one in shimmering shades of peach and flamingo pink, Dan said, "We'll take both of them."

"And slippers to match?" the salesman asked eagerly.

Dan nodded. "Yes, of course, slippers to match."

Elizabeth looked at him. "Whatever else fails, you seem to have an endless supply of money."

Dan patted the pouch he wore around his waist. "I've got more in here than the jewels," he said in a low voice.

The packages were wrapped and handed to Mohammed. As they were leaving the store, Elizabeth saw a display of soft leather evening bags. "I'd better get one," she told Dan. "I can't very well carry my over-the-shoulder bag tonight."

They were assailed by more sellers the minute they stepped out of the store, but once again Mohammed cleared the way. He escorted them back to the hotel and said that he would call for them at ten-thirty.

"You will need a dinner jacket," he told Dan before he left them. "There is a shop in the hotel. I'm sure you will find what you need there." Then, after bowing to Dan and smiling at Elizabeth, he left.

They had lunch in their room, and afterward, while Elizabeth rested, Dan went down to the men's shop off the lobby and bought a shirt, a tie and a white dinner jacket.

That night when he dressed, he tucked the small revolver into the waistband of his trousers, hoping he wouldn't need it. He also hoped the man who was to meet them at El Jadida would be on time and that he was competent enough to get him and Elizabeth out of Tangier and on their way back to the States. He didn't think beyond that, because he didn't know what would happen after they were safely back in their own country. Would she leave him then? Would he let her?

That's what he was thinking when Elizabeth came out of the bedroom dressed in the peach-and-flamingo caftan. The garment fell gracefully around her body, and the colors added a wonderful, soft glow to her face.

For a moment Dan couldn't speak. When he did, he said, "You look lovely. The colors are perfect for you, Elizabeth."

She nodded her thanks, not sure why she suddenly felt so self-conscious, and picked up the leather evening bag. "You look nice, too, Dan."

"Then shall we go? It's almost ten-thirty."

He watched her walk ahead of him. No, he corrected himself, it was more like a glide, with the caftan floating around her. This was the woman he'd fallen in love with, not the severe woman in gray.

Mohammed had a car and driver waiting for them in front of the hotel. He held the back door open for Elizabeth and Dan, and sat in the front with the driver.

El Jadida lay some five miles from the city. They took a winding road that followed the coast, and with the window rolled down, Elizabeth could smell the salty sea air of the Atlantic. There was only the gentlest of breezes, and the sky was filled with a multitude of stars that looked close enough to touch. It was a night for lovers,

Elizabeth thought, and wondered at the sting of tears behind her eyelids.

El Jadida, ablaze with light, stood at the top of a rise that overlooked the sea. The driver slowed on the curves that led up to the crest of the hill, and when he stopped, a uniformed attendant hurried forward to open the door.

"I will wait for you here at one-thirty," Mohammed told Dan. "Is that time agreeable?"

Dan assured him that it was, then took Elizabeth's arm and led her up a flight of broad marble stairs. Inside they were greeted by a tuxedoed maître d', who led them down a red carpeted stairway into a salon as beautiful as any Elizabeth had ever seen. Crystal chandeliers, dimmed to a pleasant glow, lighted their way as a waiter escorted them past low tables and deep love seats to a corner table near the dance floor.

Elizabeth sank down into the rose-colored love seat. Dan settled himself next to her, and when the waiter asked if they would like a drink, Dan said, "A bottle of Dom Perignon, if that's all right with you, Elizabeth."

She told him that it was and settled back against the plush cushions and looked around. The ceiling and the walls of the restaurant were draped like a huge Arabian tent. At one side of the room, a small native orchestra played the haunting music of Morocco, but by the time a waiter brought their champagne, the orchestra had given way to a larger one that played American and French music from the 1940s and 1950s.

"Kind of nice to hear that type of music," Dan said. He looked at Elizabeth. "Would you like to dance?"

"No, thank you."

"Oh, come on."

"I'm really not a very good dancer."

"Not a good dancer?" Dan looked surprised. "I've seen you dance. You're fantastic."

Elizabeth shook her head. "You've seen Isabela dance, Dan."

"I really don't see any difference," he said stiffly and knew that he lied, for the Gypsy girl who had danced barefoot on the side of the road was far different from the elegant woman seated beside him now.

The orchestra began to play a medley of old French songs. The lights around the dance floor dimmed so that the dancers were barely visible.

Dan took the glass out of Elizabeth's hand, and before she could protest, he eased her up out of the love seat. "Just one dance," he said.

At first her body was tense. She moved to step away from him, but he tightened his arms around her, and little by little Elizabeth began to relax.

The music evoked memories of a kinder, more romantic time, when men and women danced close in each other's arms, as she and Dan danced now.

She rested her face against the smooth fabric of his white dinner jacket and gave herself up to the music and his warmth and the faint, smoky scent of incense permeating the air.

She felt his lips against her hair, and when he tucked her hand to his chest and brought her closer, his warmth became her own. And the warmth grew into a flame when he pressed his hand against the small of her back to urge her closer still. She felt the tightening of his body, the pressure of his maleness, and her body went weak with desire.

He nuzzled her hair aside and found the softness of her ear. He took the lobe between his teeth and gently nipped before his hot, moist tongue darted around her ear. And all the while he held her tightly, as they moved to the sensuous rhythm of the music.

They could have been alone in the dim light of the dance floor, alone in each other's arms, while desire, like a bright, hot flame, grew and grew.

Elizabeth trembled in his arms, clinging to him because she was afraid if she didn't her legs would barely support her.

The hand against her back pressed her closer.

She raised her face to tell him to let her go, but when she did he brushed his lips against hers, tentatively, slowly. Her eyes drifted closed, and he kissed her again, so passionately, so deeply that everything around them faded and blurred. There was only Dan—Dan, whose mouth consumed her. Dan, whose body burned so hotly against hers. She was lost in him, unmindful of the music or the other dancers.

Until the music stopped.

They looked at each other.

Elizabeth stepped away from him, her lower lip caught between her teeth, and her eyes, normally so pale a green, were now the color of a deep, pure jade.

The other couples left the dance floor, and still they stood, held by all they were feeling, until finally Dan took her arm and led her back to their table.

A man was seated there, waiting for them.

He rose when they approached. "Mr. Skinner," he said. "How nice to see you again."

Dan held his hand out, measuring the other man as he did. An inch or two shorter than Dan, probably in his late forties, he had pleasant brown eyes and a shock of hair that fell over one eye.

"James Montgomery," he said to Elizabeth. "At your service, ma'am." And leaning closer, he said, "I must say, Miss Thursby, you don't look anything at all like your passport photo."

Then, as though he were the host, he took her hand to seat her on the love seat and said, "I've taken the liberty of ordering our dinner. I hope you don't mind."

Dan raised one eyebrow. "Not all all, Jim."

"James. I've always detested 'Jim'." He raised his glass of champagne. "Let's drink a toast, shall we?" He touched his glass to Elizabeth's.

"To what?" Dan asked, not at all sure he liked the way Montgomery was looking at Elizabeth.

"To your trip to Casablanca," Montgomery said. "Have you been there before, Miss Thursby?" And when Elizabeth shook her head, he said, "Charming city. Very cosmopolitan, not at all like the place where Bogart romanced Miss Bergman. More likely to find a Hilton or a Sheraton there, instead of a place called Rick's."

Montgomery looked up as a waiter approached. "I hope you like what I've selected," he said to Elizabeth. "I chose typical Moroccan dishes rather than French. I'm sure you'll enjoy everything..." He hesitated. "Mildred?" He grinned at Elizabeth. "Somehow that name doesn't seem to fit you."

She grinned back. "Thank you, Mr. Montgomery. That's the nicest thing anybody's said to me in a long time. My name is Elizabeth."

Montgomery reached for her hand and kissed it. "Pleasure to know you, Elizabeth."

Dan frowned. He frowned all through dinner, which included a rich soup called *harira*, a pigeon-meat pastry known as *bstilla*, made of dozens of different layers of thick, flaky dough and *djaja mahamara*, chicken stuffed with almonds, semolina and raisins.

It wasn't until their pastries were served that Montgomery hunched closer to Dan and said, "I've had you watched since the moment you and Elizabeth stepped off the boat from Algeciras. You haven't been followed. I'm pretty sure you're home free. You'll leave Tangier the day after tomorrow by private car. On Friday you'll fly out of Casablanca for New York."

"With our original passports?" Dan asked

James Montgomery nodded. "You're to carry the jewels with you."

"But I assumed I was to turn them over to you and that you'd have them taken out by private courier."

Montgomery shook his head. "No, they want you to do it. I have the letters of transit, so there'll be no problem with customs." He took another sip of the strong Moroccan coffee. "I understand you ran into some trouble."

Dan nodded. "They killed Thomason."

"Damn! Al was set to retire next month. Nobody told me. Who did it?"

"Castro and Sanchez and a couple of Guardias who are working for them." Dan hesitated. "There's something else you need to know. Elizabeth and I are wanted for Al's murder. Our pictures have been plastered all over the newspapers."

"Holy nelly! No wonder you had to get out of Spain." James looked at Elizabeth. "I can see why you had to disguise yourself." He glanced around the dimly lighted room, then back to her. "It's probably all right tonight, but if you go out tomorrow, you'd better go back to being Mildred." Then, as though to reassure her, he added, "But I honestly believe you're all right here in Tangier. In a few more days you'll be back home, wherever that is."

"Ohio," Elizabeth said.

"Oh? I'm from Cleveland."

"Rocky River," she said with a smile.

"I'll be damned. I knew we had something in common."

Dan glowered and looked at his watch. "It's getting late," he said.

"Not for Tangier." James looked at Elizabeth. "Ever been in a gambling casino?"

"There aren't too many of those in Rocky River."

"There's one here. Let's go take a look at it."

"Would it be all right?" Elizabeth asked Dan.

"Sure it would," James said before Dan could answer. He signaled for the waiter and handed him a credit card. As soon as the man returned, James stood up and took Elizabeth's hand. "Come along, let's give the wheels a spin." He linked Elizabeth's arm through his and waited for Dan to stand.

The casino, reached through a golden-draped doorway, was a place of glittering lights, whirring roulette tables and elegantly dressed men and women.

"Hold on," James told Elizabeth. "Let me get some chips."

"I don't think we should be doing this," Dan said when Montgomery disappeared into the crowd.

"But he said we weren't being followed."

"I don't care what he said; this isn't a good idea. We should have gone back to the hotel. We—"

"Here we are," James interrupted. "Let's try our luck at roulette."

He put three chips on red. The croupier spun the wheel while Elizabeth watched in fascination.

"Red!" the croupier said, and placed a stack of chips in front of Elizabeth.

"Let it ride," James said.

She won three more times. James handed her half the chips she'd won and said, "Pick a number."

"Nineteen, because it's my birthday."

He placed the stack of chips there, the croupier spun and Elizabeth watched, fascinated, until the small red ball stopped—on number nineteen.

"You've won again!" With a laugh James scooped up the chips and poured them into Elizabeth's hands, then kissed both her cheeks.

She looked at all the chips in her hands. "That was wonderful, James, but these are yours." She tried to give them back to him.

But James wouldn't take them. "Buy yourself something special while you're here. Something to remind you of Tangier." He leaned closer. "Something as lovely as the outfit you're wearing tonight, Elizabeth."

Dan stepped between them. "I hate to break this up," he snapped, "but it's time I took Elizabeth back to the hotel. Mohammed must be waiting for us."

"At least let her cash in her chips." James indicated the far corner of the room. "Over this way, Dan."

Dan took Elizabeth's arm, glancing around as they made their way through the crowded casino. A feeling he didn't like, a sense of danger he couldn't shake off, made him uneasy. The lights were too bright; the place was too crowded. He looked around at the well-dressed men and women, past the blackjack tables and the roulette wheels. Not being a gambler, places like this made him nervous. He'd be glad when they got back to the hotel. He didn't—.

Suddenly he froze. He looked at the croupier at the wheel on their right. The croupier looked back at him.

"What is it, Dan?" Elizabeth looked at him, then at the man who stared at Dan, a man with a face as white as his hair, a man whose eyes were so pale that they, too, looked white.

The man's glance swept over her, and a chill ran like an icy finger all the way down her spine.

When they were past the man, Montgomery said, "What's the matter?"

"I know the guy," Dan said quietly so Elizabeth wouldn't hear. "His name is Nathan Janss. He worked the casinos in Cuba in the days before Fidel. I had a run-in with him when he worked the Bahamas."

Montgomery muttered an oath. "Maybe he didn't recognize you, Dan."

"He recognized me."

"But that doesn't necessarily mean trouble. He's probably never even heard of the men who're after you."

"Maybe not," Dan said.

But all the way back to the hotel, he worried about Nathan Janss and knew he wouldn't draw a relaxed breath until he and Elizabeth were safely on their way to Casablanca.

Chapter 14

The car that Mohammed had engaged was waiting for them when they left El Jadida. Dan had agreed to meet James Montgomery at one o'clock the next afternoon in the lobby of the hotel, at which time Montgomery would have finalized their plans to leave Tangier.

Dan and Elizabeth spoke little on the ride back to the hotel. The night was soft with the scent of the sea, but Dan seemed unaware of it. What had begun as an evening of promise had been going downhill from the moment they'd returned to the table to find James Montgomery.

Dan had never met Montgomery, but he knew something of his reputation. He was a good field man, good enough at what he did to have been promoted long before this. But Montgomery had a weakness for women that had gotten him into trouble with the agency more than once. Tonight he'd fallen all over Elizabeth, and dammit all, she'd liked the attention.

Was that why he didn't like Montgomery? Dan glared out into the night. He'd never been jealous before, but he'd been jealous tonight. It had been all he could do not to throttle Montgomery every time the other man touched Elizabeth.

He'd be glad to get out of here, because even though Tangier was an exotic city, there was an air of decadence that he didn't like. It was as though an unseen evil lay hidden behind the glamour of the place.

He thought about Nathan Janss and swore under his breath at the turn of luck that had made him run into Janss tonight. It had been almost ten years since he'd seen him on Grand Cayman Island. Janss had been working in a casino then, too, but that had only been a sideline. His real business had been smuggling coke. Dan had tipped off the local police. They'd busted Janss and that was the last Dan had heard of him, until now. He'd never known for sure whether or not Janss knew it was him who'd tipped off the police, but if he had known, and if he knew that Dan was in trouble now, this was the perfect time to settle the score.

His thoughts were still troubled when the car pulled up in front of the hotel. Mohammed jumped out of the front to assist Elizabeth, and Dan followed.

"I am to bring Mr. Montgomery here at one o'clock," Mohammed said. He handed Dan a card. "If you need any assistance before that, please do not hesitate to call me."

Dan thanked him and when the car drove off, he took Elizabeth's arm and led her toward the door.

"Gardenias for the lady, *sidi*?" A robed woman wheeled a small cart in front of them. "Buy a flower for the beautiful lady," she said, and held up one of the flowers.

"Give me what you have," Dan said.

"All of them, *sidi*?"

"Yes, all." He handed the woman a few bills. "Will this cover it?"

"Yes, yes." She grabbed the money and shoved it in the pocket of her robe before she filled a basket with dozens of flowers and handed it to Elizabeth. To Dan, she said, "*Barakallahoofik*. Thank you, God bless you, *sidi*."

When they were up in their room, Elizabeth picked up a handful of the fragrant flowers and held them to her face. "They're lovely, Dan. Thank you." When he didn't answer, she said, "Why are you angry?"

"I'm not angry."

"Are you upset about the man we saw in the casino?"

He wanted to tell her that he knew Nathan Janss. He even thought he should tell her that because Janss had recognized him there might be trouble. But instead, because he didn't want her to be afraid again, and because he *was* angry, he said, "I'm upset about the whole damn evening."

"You didn't like James, did you?"

"I didn't like the fact that he couldn't keep his hands off you."

"It wasn't like that," Elizabeth protested. "He was only being nice."

Dan gave an ungentlemanly snort. "Nice, hell!" he muttered.

He knew he was being unreasonable, but he couldn't seem to help himself. Elizabeth had looked lovely tonight. When they danced and he held her closely, when he'd felt the heat of her response, he'd wanted her with a fierceness that had shaken him. If James Montgomery hadn't been waiting for them when they'd left the dance floor, he'd have slapped some money on the table and taken her back to the hotel.

But Montgomery had been waiting for them, and his eyes had damn near popped out of his head when he'd seen Elizabeth. Dan had hated the way he'd looked at her, hated the way he'd kissed her hand. If that was jealousy, then so be it. And that, coupled with running into Nathan Janss, had put him in a foul mood. He'd even bought the gardenias in a juvenile attempt to outdo Montgomery.

Dan glanced at Elizabeth. She was sitting in a high-backed wicker chair, the basket of gardenias on her lap, one hand fingering the flowers.

He wanted to say something to her, something to recapture what had been between them earlier in the evening. But because he was at a loss for words, he said, "I'm going to take a shower." He tried to smile. "Maybe that'll help my disposition."

Elizabeth smiled uncertainly, then she got up, and taking the ivory silk nightgown from a drawer in the dresser, she went into the other bathroom.

She showered and put on the nightgown, but she hesitated when she heard Dan moving around in the other room. Last night's lovemaking had been unpleasant for both of them, and she had no wish to go through that again. It would be better to tell Dan that she was tired rather than try to pretend as she had last night.

When Elizabeth went out into the room, she saw that the overhead chandelier had been turned on and that Dan, wearing one of the short, heavy terry-cloth robes the hotel provided, was standing beside the bed.

"Come here." He motioned her toward the bed. "I want you to see these."

She looked down at the bed and a gasp escaped her lips, for spread out on the apricot satin sheet were the jewels that Dan had carried around his waist in a pouch for the past few weeks.

There was a diamond and a sapphire necklace set in the purest filigree gold. Matching earrings and bracelets. Emerald earrings, necklaces of two or three rows of diamonds. And rings, at least a dozen of the most beautiful rings she'd ever seen. She picked up a diamond and ruby necklace that was almost too beautiful to be real and held it up to the light. The jewels, like stars sparkling in the sun, winked back at her in an unbelievable blaze of light.

"I've never seen anything so magnificent," she whispered.

Dan held his hand out, and she placed the necklace in it.

"Turn around," he said, and when she did, he fastened the priceless necklace around her neck.

It was cool and heavy against her skin. Each of the rubies set between the diamonds was the size of the fingernail on her pinkie. The center ruby that rested against the cleft between her breasts was the size of a robin's egg.

She touched it, too awed by its beauty to speak. She wanted to see it in the mirror, but when she turned toward the dresser, Dan said, "Wait."

He found the matching diamond and ruby teardrop earrings and fastened them in her ears before he stepped back and looked at her, then took her hand and led her to the mirror.

And as he gazed at her reflection, he was seized by the strangest feeling, the feeling that at another time, in another place, he had stood as he was standing now, watching the woman he loved as she laid one pale hand on the priceless ruby that rested between her breasts.

"They're so beautiful," she said.

Dan rested his hands on her shoulders. "You make them beautiful."

He kissed her then, kissed her the way he had wanted to ever since they'd danced earlier in the evening, and because he had to feel her nearer, he took his robe off and pulled her closely to his naked body. His hands explored the smoothness of her back through the silk nightgown and his tongue explored the warm moistness of her mouth.

Elizabeth clung to him. She heard the whisper of his breath and knew that he wanted her as she wanted him. All that she had thought before ceased to matter. There was only the hardness of his body against hers and the crush of his lips.

When Dan let her go, his eyes were narrowed with desire. He led her back to the bed, and when she said, "Wait, let me take off the jewels," he said, "No, keep them on."

Quickly he scooped the other jewels off the bed and onto one of the chairs, all except for a single-strand diamond bracelet.

"Sit down," he told Elizabeth, and when she sat on the edge of the bed, he took one foot in his hand and fastened the diamond bracelet around her ankle.

"Now you belong to me." He kissed the ankle he had fastened the bracelet on.

The breath caught in Elizabeth's throat. She placed her hands on his shoulders and rested her face against the thickness of his hair.

He urged the ivory gown up over her hips, then over her head before he eased her back against the apricot satin pillows.

For a moment Dan only looked at her, and again he was seized by the feeling that all this had happened before. Then he reached up and turned out the chandelier light so that the room was bathed in only the soft glow of the two bedside lamps.

Her heart pounded against her ribs, and her body felt swollen with need. She looked up at Dan, standing so still beside her. His body was lean and hard. His shoulders were broad, his hips narrow, his stomach flat. He had a thatch of brown hair on his chest, hair that curled sensuously downward. He was so strikingly masculine, so strong that he almost frightened her.

Holding out her hand to him, she said, "Come make love with me."

With a smothered sigh, Dan came down beside her and gathered her into his arms. He kissed her, gently at first, his lips tentative against hers. Then the kiss deepened, and when her lips parted and her tongue met his, she felt his body strain against her. He caught her lower lip between his teeth and ran his tongue back and forth across it. He kissed the corners of her mouth and whispered her name in an agony of desire.

When he let her go, he leaned over her and looked down into her eyes. He touched the ruby that rested between her breasts and ran his fingers across the peaked tips.

Her lips parted. Her eyes went smoky with desire.

"Yes," he said softly, and gently tugged and stroked the ready tips. Then he took one between his teeth to lap and tease, and she whispered, "Please, oh please," not knowing that she did or what it was she pleaded for.

Dan wanted her badly now, and though he knew that she was warm and moist and ready, he hadn't yet had enough of her, and so he left her breasts and teased his way down across her rib cage to her belly. He stroked her gently, and when he felt her quiver at his touch, he murmured, "Wait, love. Wait."

He encircled her hips with his hands and began to kiss her thighs.

Her legs trembled and he felt the faint scratch of the diamond bracelet he'd placed around her ankle. Was it a slave bracelet? he wondered. An expensive bauble given to a slave girl by her king to show that she belonged to him?

The thought excited Dan. As though in a dream, he thought, If I were a king or a caliph...

His servant said, "There is a girl you should see, a Spanish Gypsy more beautiful than any I have ever seen."

Because he would not deal with a slave trader, his servant brought the girl to him.

"She is beautiful, is she not?" his servant said.

"Beautiful," he agreed in a voice already trembling with passion.

She would not look at him or speak when spoken to, so his servant grasped her shoulder roughly and with the hard butt of a whip prodded her forward.

"Leave her alone!" He grabbed the whip and threw it away. "Touch her again and I'll kill you," he threatened.

He asked her price, and without bargaining, he paid what was asked. Then he took her hand and said, "Come, woman, you belong to me now."

When she had been dressed in the finest clothes in Arabia and her skin perfumed with the most expensive perfumes from the Orient, he had her brought to him.

He had had many women in his life. Some had come to him willingly and some had not. Now, for a reason he could not explain, it became important to him that when the Gypsy came to him, it would be willingly. But time passed and though he touched her and kissed her in a hundred different ways, though he called upon all his skills of seduction the Gypsy would not yield.

When he knew that he would never possess her, he set her free. But before he let her go, he placed a priceless necklace around her throat and a diamond chain around her ankle. And when he had fastened it, he kissed her gently, then released her and said, "Go now, for you are free."

For a moment she did not speak, she only looked at him with her Gypsy-green eyes. Then she raised her arms and said, "Come, sire. Come make love with me."

He tightened his hands around her Gypsy hips. "If you were mine," he said, "I'd never let you go." He kissed her inner thigh. "I'd mark you so that if another man ever touched you, he would see the mark and know that you belonged to me."

"Dan?" His name trembled on her lips.

"Here," he whispered, and holding her still he nipped the tender skin there, and when she cried out, he soothed it with a kiss. And then he set about making her forget the feel of his teeth against her delicate skin, and he began to kiss that warm and secret part of her. He held her, though her body tightened with passion and she cried, "Oh, oh, please" and writhed in an agony of pleasure. He did not let her go until he knew she could no longer bear the heat of his kiss.

He came up over her then and quickly, urgently, his body shuddering with need, thrust himself into her softness.

Elizabeth clung to him, past all thought, her body on fire, meeting him thrust for thrust, pleasuring him as he pleasured her, reaching higher and higher for that final moment. And when it came she cried his name and heard his answering cry, "Isabela! My Isabela!"

The shock of it cut like a dagger through her heart.

But Dan didn't know. He said that name again and again while his body still throbbed with reaction. "My love," he whispered. "my lovely, my passionate Gypsy."

And fell asleep, his head against her breast, his body still joined to hers.

But it was a long time before Elizabeth went to sleep.

Dan awoke in the faint light of the near morning. In the distance he heard the low, plaintive call to prayer floating upon the morning air. He drifted, half asleep, half awake, in the dim light of the room. His body had never felt so relaxed, so satisfied. He was afloat on a wave of contentment unlike anything he had ever known.

There had been a dreamlike quality about last night's lovemaking, and even now, in the comfort of this half sleep, it seemed unreal to him. Never before had he known a woman so giving in love, so completely attuned to everything he felt. Her passion had risen with his. She'd given as much as she had received. She'd softly whispered indistinct words of passion and the knowledge that he was exciting her had filled him with a pleasure unlike anything he'd ever known.

With the thought of the way it had been, his body began to tighten with need. Without opening his eyes, he reached for her. He touched her pillow. She wasn't there.

Dan came fully awake then. He said her name, "Isabela?" and when she didn't answer he sat up in bed and saw a faint streak of light from the bathroom.

He got up, put the terry-cloth robe on and tightening the belt around his waist, crossed the room. He started to call her name, but held back when he saw that the door was partly open. He looked in and saw her lying there in the black marble tub. Her head rested against the back of it. Her eyes were closed; her hair was pinned atop her head. The water came just to the strawberry tips of her breasts.

Dan watched her for a moment without speaking. His pulse quickened and his loins grew hot and heavy with desire. He went back to where she'd placed the basket of gardenias, then returned to the bathroom and opened the door.

Elizabeth opened her eyes, but before she could speak, Dan held the basket over her half-submerged body and showered her with gardenias. Then he took his robe off, and when he did, her gaze ran down his body and a flush crept into her cheeks.

"Dan?" she said, in a trembling voice.

He stepped down the two marble steps into the tub and eased himself into the hot, gardenia-scented water.

"Why did you leave me?" he asked.

"I woke up. I couldn't go back to sleep."

"I missed you." He touched her throat. "You took the jewels off." He closed his hand around her ankle. "Even the bracelet?" He smiled, remembering how it had been. "Last night I pretended it was a slave bracelet."

"Diamonds would be an expensive present for a slave."

"Not if the slave were someone so special, so beautiful that the man she belonged to wanted the whole world to know she belonged to him." He cupped her chin. "You're that beautiful, my Isabela."

And again the dagger twisted in her heart.

Dan plucked a gardenia out of the water and stuck it behind one of her ears, then he brushed aside the flowers that floated up over her breasts so that he could touch her.

She looked at him, then sank deeper into the water and let the flowers float up around her, covering her with their soft petals, their sweet aroma, while Dan stroked her breasts and whispered words of love.

He moved closer so that their bodies were touching. He brushed the gardenias aside and moved her legs apart so he could cup her with his palm. And after a while it didn't matter that he called her Isabela or that he said, "My darling, Gypsy," for she was lost in the magic of his touch, the warmth of the water and the seductive, overwhelming scent of the flowers.

For a little while she did nothing; she simply submitted to the hands that stroked her body and the fingers that grazed her breasts. When he cupped her chin, she lifted her face for his kiss, and when the kiss ended, there was a fever in her blood and she reached to touch him.

Now it was she who stroked, stroked until the breath rasped in his throat and a harsh groan escaped his lips.

"Yes," he said, "like that. Oh, yes. I love it when you touch me." He put his arm around the back of her neck and pulled her to him. "But no more, Isabela, or I won't be able to wait. And I want to wait, love, because I want to kiss every sweet inch of you. I want to taste you and tease you until you cry my name and beg for me. And when you do I'll start all over again, until it's too much for both of us. I want it so hot, so good, so much that neither of us will ever forget it."

He took the fingers that had so gently stroked him and kissed each one. "Now lie back and let me bathe you," he said.

Like a person who had been drugged, Elizabeth gave herself up to the ministrations of his hands as he lathered her breasts, and when he flicked a dollop of soap off one tip so that he could kiss her there, she moaned aloud with pleasure.

By the time he helped her out of the black marble tub, her body was on fire with a need unlike anything she'd ever known.

But Dan pulled the full length of her slick body against his only for an instant, just long enough for her to feel his strength and his tumescence. Then he held her away from him, and with agonizing slowness dried her with a big fluffy towel, lingering in the places already afire with longing, kissing her with lips that singed and burned.

"Please," she whispered over and over again, and arched her body to his.

"Not yet." He trailed fire across her belly.

"I can't stand it," she moaned.

"Neither can I." He tightened his hands on her hips and pulled her closer.

"Oh, please..." She dug her nails into his skin, and he shuddered with pleasure but did not release her.

Only when her body began to shake and he knew she could bear no more did he pick her up and carry her to their bed.

"Isabela," he whispered, and joined his body to hers. And as he felt her warmth and her softness close around him, he cried aloud with the pure joy of it. For this was his Gypsy love who moved so wildly, so wantonly beneath him. Isabela who lifted her body to his, who murmured sweetly abandoned words of love.

He felt the heat of her breasts against his chest, and because he hungered for them, he raised his head and captured one small tip between his teeth.

It was too much. Her body quivered and she cried, "Oh, yes, darling. Yes!" and clung to his shoulders as she spun further and further out of control.

He took her mouth. He answered her impassioned final cry with his own as together they tumbled over the brink of foreverness.

It was the most perfect moment in Elizabeth's life. Until, still caught in the throes of passion, Dan said, "I love you, Isabela. Only you, my Gypsy lady. Only you, my Gypsy love."

Dan didn't wake until almost eleven o'clock. Without opening his eyes, he reached out his hand, but as he had earlier, he found only empty space. He smiled sleepily, thinking that if he found her in the tub again, they'd certainly be the best-scrubbed and best-loved couple in Tangier.

He wasn't sure what it was she did to make him feel this way. He had only to look at her to want her. There were times when he almost believed that Pilar really had cast a spell on him. He smiled again when he thought of Pilar with her Gypsy potions and portents.

He listened for the sound of running water or for the footsteps that would tell him Isabela was coming back to bed. He knew that he had to get up to meet James Montgomery, but still he lingered, hands behind his head, the satin sheet pulled up around his waist, waiting for his Gypsy lady.

He smoothed his hand over the satin pillow where her head had lain. It was then that he saw the gardenia resting there and the note that lay beside it. He picked it up and his mouth went dry with a premonition he would not allow to form.

My dearest Dan,

It's ten o'clock and I've been awake for hours. You're sleeping so peacefully. You didn't even stir when I slipped out of bed.

I'm going out for a while because I need to be alone, to think about so many things.

Dan, what has happened between us is very new and strange to me, and I have a feeling it is to you, too. You've said that you love me, but I wonder if you know which me it is that you love. Whatever or whoever you think I am, there is only one me, the Elizabeth me. I'd like to be Isabela, the Gypsy girl you've fallen in love with, but I'm not, Dan. I'm really not.

I wish I had the courage to say these things to you face-to-face, and perhaps after I've walked and thought a bit I'll be able to come back and say all the things that need to be said.

If you want to talk about how you feel after you read this, we will. But if you don't, we'll talk about the weather and maybe I'll tell you how I felt last night in that wonderful black marble tub with those dozens and dozens of fragrant gardenias. And you. For a little while last night, Dan, I belonged to a sisterhood of women who have truly loved, as I truly love you.

Whatever happens, Dan, I thank you for the wonderful moments you've given me. I'm sorry that I can't be the woman you want me to be, but I'm only Elizabeth, and I honestly don't think she's the woman you're in love with.

Dan stared at the letter. As he'd read it, he had, without knowing, rubbed the petals of the gardenia between his fingers. Now when he looked at the delicate flower, he saw that the leaves were bruised and torn.

He paced the room, hands knotted into fists. What in the hell was she talking about? he asked himself. Of course he was in love with her. So he fantasized—what was the harm in that? What did it matter that he called her Isabela instead of Elizabeth? There were one and the same, weren't they?

He'd have it out with her when she returned. There'd be no small talk about the weather or any other damn thing until this had been straightened out between them.

Angry now, as much at himself as with her, Dan suddenly realized that he had crushed the gardenia in his clenched fist.

He showered and shaved, listening all the while for the knock on the door that would tell him she had returned. But she still wasn't back by the time he was dressed, and it was noon already. Afraid he would miss her if he went down to the restaurant, he picked up the phone and ordered his breakfast sent up. But when it came he found that he couldn't eat. He drank two cups of coffee and paced the room.

One o'clock came. She'd been gone for three hours.

At ten minutes after one, the phone rang. He crossed the room in two strides and grabbed it. "Elizabeth?"

"Not likely," James Montgomery said. And with a chuckle added, "You haven't let the little lady give you the slip, have you?"

Dan swore under his breath. Trying to control his temper, he said, "She went out shopping this morning. I expected her back before now."

"She really shouldn't have gone out alone, Dan. Not that there's any cause for alarm, but the men in the souks are fierce salesmen. You have to beat them away with a stick. Besides, there's always the danger..."

Dan heard the hesitation in the other man's voice, then Montgomery said, "Look, why don't I come up to your room. We can talk there, and if she comes back, you won't miss her."

"Yes, that's a good idea. I'd feel better about it." Dan hung up and took a deep breath. She's shopping, he told himself. She'd be back any minute now, and when she got there he'd raise hell with her for going out without telling him.

Montgomery came in. Dan sent down for more coffee. They exchanged small talk. They said what a nice guy Al Thomason had been. Montgomery told him what the travel arrangements would be. He asked Dan why he'd left the agency and how he liked his work as an insurance investigator.

At two-thirty, Dan said, "I'm going to call the police."

But Montgomery stayed him. "No," he cautioned. "That isn't a good idea. Better let me take care of it."

He picked up the phone, asked for a number, and when it answered, he spoke in rapid French that was incomprehensible to Dan. When he put the phone down, he said, "I've got men close by. They'll start looking for her right away."

Dan reached for his jacket. "I've got to get out of here and go find her myself."

"But what if she calls?" Montgomery shook his head. "Look, Dan, maybe we're both unduly alarmed. She went shopping, right? You know how women are when they get into a store." He forced a laugh. "Maybe she ran into a sale."

"She didn't go shopping." Dan looked at the other man. "She was upset about something. She said she wanted to be alone for a little while to think things out." He looked at his watch. "God," he said, "it's almost three. Where in the hell could she—"

The phone rang. He grabbed it and shouted, "Elizabeth?"

"I'm afraid she can't come to the phone," a voice said.

The color drained from Dan's face. "Where..." He fought for control. "Where is she?" he asked. "What have you done with her?"

"Nothing yet, *amigo*." The voice on the other end, the voice that he recognized now, laughed.

Dan tightened his grip on the phone. "Paco," he said.

Montgomery shot up out of his chair. "Sanchez?" he whispered. "Paco Sanchez?"

"It's been a long time," Sanchez said. "Your taste in women has improved, Daniel. This one is choice."

"Damn you! If you've harmed her..." He made himself stop and take a deep breath. "Okay," he said. "What do you want?"

"The jewels, *compadre*. What else?"

"You'll get them when I get Elizabeth."

Montgomery covered the mouthpiece with his hand. "Tell him you won't discuss anything unless you talk to her."

Dan nodded. "Let me talk to her," he said into the phone.

He heard Paco say something to somebody else, then he heard Elizabeth's voice.

"Dan?" she said. "Oh, Dan."

"Are you all right? He hasn't hurt you?"

"No." He heard the fear in her voice. "Dan, I'm sorry. I shouldn't have gone out. I shouldn't have—"

There was a muffled cry of protest, then Sanchez came on the line and said, "The jewels, Dan. Or believe me, you'll never seen her again."

"Where?" Dan said. "When?"

"I'll let you know."

"Dammit, Paco—"

"Easy, *compadre*. Take it easy. I'll work things out and get back to you."

"Now!" Dan shouted. "I—"

The line went dead. He stared at the phone in his hand, then slowly he replaced it. He looked at James Montgomery. "He hung up," he said. "The bastard hung up."

"He'll call back, Dan."

"But when? Oh my God, James, he's got Elizabeth." Dan put his head in his hands. "Paco Sanchez has got Elizabeth."

Chapter 15

Elizabeth was alone with a fear she had only imagined in her worst nightmares. She heard voices from the other room and put her ear to the door in a vain attempt to hear what the two men were saying. But she couldn't hear anything; she could only visualize them. Castro, who was bigger than Sanchez, had a heavy stomach which bulged over his belt. He wore a wrinkled dark suit. He had short gray hair, and his nose had red veins running through it.

Paco Sanchez was a small man, no more than five feet eight, and he couldn't have weighed more than 135 pounds. His face was thin and foxlike; his greased hair hung in a ponytail down his back. At first glance he did not inspire fear so much as distaste, but when you looked into his eyes and saw the evil there, you knew how dangerous he was and you were afraid.

She'd even seen the fear in Castro's face.

When they'd brought her to this place, Castro had said, "I'll lock her in the other room."

"Lock me in with her," Sanchez said with a vile grin. "I haven't had a woman like her in a long time." He pulled Elizabeth up against him and laughed when she struggled and tried to strike out.

"Leave her alone," Castro had said. "All we want are the jewels. Let her be."

Paco turned on him. He hadn't said anything, but she'd seen the color drain from Castro's face, the sheen of sweat break out on his upper lip, and she'd known that he wouldn't help her.

But he had changed the subject when he'd said, "Damn lucky thing about Nathan Janss spotting Dan last night. Funny, we haven't heard from him in a couple of years. I didn't even know he was here in Tangier until he called. It was a lucky break. We owe him one."

"Luckier still that we spotted her out for her morning walk." Paco grabbed Elizabeth's chin and forced her to look at him. "You're going to help us get the jewels, sweetheart. When we get 'em, I might decide to keep you, too. There's nothing Danny boy can do for you that I can't do a hundred times better." He brought her face closer. "And I will *muchacha*, but right now I've got other things to do." He'd shoved her toward Castro then. "Lock her up," he said. "I'm going out for a while."

Castro had locked her in this small, dirty room then. There was a mattress on the floor and nothing else, except a small window with two iron bars.

Why had she left the comfort of Dan's arms this morning? She tried to remember, but her reasons seemed so unimportant now, and she would have given her soul to be back with him. A few minutes ago when she'd heard his fear and coupled it with her own, she'd wanted to scream, "I love you. Nothing matters except that."

The sun had been shining this morning when Elizabeth left the Hotel Afrique. She'd walked along the boulevard until she found a sidewalk café. She'd taken a table in the sun and ordered a coffee and a croissant, and her thoughts turned to Dan and the way it had been with them last night.

She had never even imagined the kind of ecstasy she had found in his arms. Again and again he had taken her to the heights of passion and whispered of his love. Somehow this morning, sitting in the sunlight, it didn't seem as important as it had last night that he had called her by her Gypsy name. For, after all, maybe there was a part of her that *was* Isabela, and if that was the woman Dan had fallen in love with, then she would be that woman.

He'd said nothing about a commitment, of course. She had no idea what would happen when they left Morocco, but surely he did not mean for it to end here, not after all they had shared.

When Elizabeth had paid for the coffee and croissant, she went to walk along the waterfront. The sea was calm, and far across the water she could see the coast of Spain. Spain, where it had all begun.

It had been a few minutes after eleven when she'd started back to the hotel. Rather than walk along the boulevard, she had decided to try the adjacent narrow streets, which she was sure led back to the hotel. For now she was in a hurry to get back to Dan. She hoped he hadn't awakened. If he hadn't, she would undress and come into bed beside him and awaken him with a kiss. When he stirred in his sleep, she would begin to caress him. And she smiled because it still seemed so strange to her that she could touch a man like that. That it gave her such pleasure to know that she was pleasuring him.

He would open his eyes and bring her down to kiss his mouth, and when the kiss wasn't enough, perhaps he would pull her up over him, as he sometimes liked to do. She would settle herself there, and when he was warm and firm within her, she could begin to move against him. She would . . .

She hadn't even seen the long black car until it was alongside her, but she stopped when a voice said in English, "Excuse me. Can we reach the Hotel Afrique this way?"

Elizabeth had paused. "I think so," she'd said with a smile. "I hope so, because that's where I'm going. If I'm not mistaken it's just around—" She'd stopped and the breath had caught in her throat, because looking at her from the back seat was the man she'd seen in the casino last night, the man whose face was as white as his hair.

Fear had clutched at her, and she'd turned to run. But not fast enough, because the door of the car opened and a man vaulted out. He'd grabbed her, slapped a hand over her mouth, and though she fought, he'd dragged her back to the car and shoved her in.

She broke free and screamed, though there was no one on the street to hear her. Then Paco Sanchez struck her across the face, and she'd fallen back against the seat.

She didn't know where she was or how far they had come, because they had covered her eyes. Now she was here, locked in this narrow, dirty room. Alone with her fear.

A man from James Montgomery's office came to hook up a telephone extension. Mohammed was notified to keep a car ready in front of the hotel. The police, as well as Montgomery's men, had already begun to comb the city.

Dan wanted to go with them. He wanted to tear Tangier apart with his bare hands, to look on every street and alleyway, in every souk, café, warehouse and store. He knew he couldn't, knew he had to stay here and wait for a call from Paco Sanchez.

He thought back to those days seven years ago when he'd first met the man who was now his enemy. Paco had been working in a casino much like El Jadida. Dan had still been with the agency then, and he'd been in Tangier for a week trying to get a line on the man he was after, when somebody told him about Paco.

"He knows everybody," the man had told him, "every back alley, every crooked game in town. If there's anything bad going down, you can bet your Aunt Tilly that Paco knows about it."

So Dan had contacted Paco, and for a price, which the agency agreed to pay, Paco had eventually led him to his man. But it had taken a while, and during the time he'd waited, he and Paco had hung around together. Eventually Paco had introduced him to Yolanda.

She was one of the most exquisite women Dan had ever seen. She was small and delicately made, perfection from the top of her head right down to her toes. He didn't understand what she saw in Paco, and the night that they were alone, the night she'd come on to him, he'd asked her.

"He's the only man, besides you, Daniel, who hasn't been easy for me. Other men have treated me as though I were a fragile flower, but not Paco. He's rough and he's just dangerous enough to be interesting. I like that in a man."

"You're right about his being dangerous," Dan had said. "And if you know that, why in hell would you risk coming on to me? If you've tried it with me, I've got a hunch you've tried it with other men."

Yolanda raised her naked shoulders. "Once or twice," she said.

"Were they more receptive than I've been?"

She smiled her slow, secret smile. "Of course."

He had tried to warn her. He'd said, "Be careful. This isn't a game you're playing."

But Yolanda hadn't listened, and a few months later, Paco had found her with another man. He'd killed the man and he'd disfigured Yolanda.

A couple of years ago, Dan had gone back to Tangier with another agent. The man asked to be shown the other side of Tangier, and Dan had taken him down to the waterfront, where they'd crawled a few low-life pubs. It had been almost three in the morning before his friend had had enough. They came out of the bar, and when they did, a woman approached them. In explicit language she offered herself to both of them, one at a time or both at the same time, she said. It didn't matter.

The other agent, half-drunk, began to bargain with her. Her price dropped from fifty to twenty, then to ten, and finally to the price of a bottle. She'd come closer to pull on the agent's sleeve, and in her anxiety the shawl had fallen from around her face.

Dan hadn't recognized her at first, but in the lights of a passing car he saw her more clearly and knew that she was Yolanda. Yolanda, who had once been so beautiful.

Dan had never forgotten that moment or the look on her face when she recognized him, or when she'd taken the money he had pressed into her hand.

That was what Paco Sanchez had done to her.

And now Paco had Elizabeth.

* * *

In the late afternoon, the door opened and Castro came in with a sandwich and a thermos of coffee. He was limping and when Elizabeth glanced at his leg, he said, "Yes, that is where your friend Daniel shot me. I have a score to settle with him, and when I have settled it and I have the jewels back, I will let you go."

"But will the other man?"

"Paco?" Castro shrugged. "He has said he will once he had the jewels, but I don't know. I'd take no pleasure in seeing you hurt, but Paco and I are partners. I can't control what he does."

He went out and locked the door behind him. Elizabeth listened. She couldn't hear anything. Castro was still alone.

She looked desperately around the room. She yanked at the two iron bars at the window and knew they were too solid to yield. She wasn't hungry but she ate half of the sandwich Castro had given her. When she tried to take a sip of the coffee, it burned her mouth. She held it away and watched the steam rise, then her eyes widened. She stepped closer to the door and pounded on it. "I've finished but I'm still hungry," she called out. "Can I have another sandwich?"

Castro said something she didn't hear. The door opened and he started in.

She threw the hot coffee in his face, and when he screamed and covered his eyes she pushed past him.

And ran. Ran out of the place where she'd been held without really seeing it, pulled open a door and darted outside into a maelstrom of humanity that crowded the narrow passages leading to the souks.

Elizabeth paused for only a fraction of a second before she turned and ran down one of the passageways.

She wasn't sure where she was, but if she headed into the souks, perhaps she could find Le Rendezvous. If she could, if she could find the safety of the shop, then surely Hassan Ishmael would help her.

Sobbing in fear Elizabeth pushed past the sellers who tried to block her way.

"Beads," they cried, "wallets, purses, robes."

A boy of no more than ten grabbed the sleeve of her dress. "Hashish, madam," he hissed. "The finest in Tangier."

She brushed past him and sprinted into an alleyway that led to small shops not unlike Le Rendezvous. She hesitated and looked frantically around for a phone.

A robed woman passed her, and Elizabeth said, "Please, can you tell me where there's a telephone?"

The woman held out her hands, not understanding. Elizabeth tried the same question in Spanish, but before she'd even finished the sentence the woman shrugged and moved away.

Elizabeth paused in front of a store. The seller came out. "Do you have a telephone?" Elizabeth cried.

"No phone but pretty dresses." He motioned her into his shop.

"Le Rendezvous," she said. "Where is Le Rendezvous?"

"No good. My shop better. Come in."

"Please. I have to go to Le Rendezvous. How do I get there? Which way do I go? I must—"

She stopped because the man was looking over her shoulder, and there was a sudden expression of fear on his face.

Elizabeth whirled around.

Paco Sanchez, lips drawn back from his teeth in a snarl, pushed his way through the throng of people and ran toward her.

She looked at the shopkeeper, but he hurried into his shop and closed the door behind him. She glanced around frantically, seeking a way to escape or someone to help her. With a low cry she turned and began to run.

Urchins and sellers tried to block her way. She darted around them. A snake charmer, three long snakes around his neck, stepped in front of her. He lifted a snake and held it high as though to put it around her neck. With a muttered curse, she knocked him aside.

Footsteps were coming closer behind her. She heard Paco call her name and spurted ahead, fear rasping hard in her throat. It was hard to breathe. She had a pain in her side. Run! she told herself. Run!

She felt a hand on her shoulder and yanked away. Sanchez grabbed the sleeve of her dress, and she felt it tear. His hand clamped down on her shoulder, more firmly this time. She tried to spin away from him, and he shoved her hard up against a building, grabbed one wrist and twisted her arm halfway up her back.

She screamed.

People stopped to stare.

"*Es mi mujer*, my woman," Sanchez said. "She is trying to run away, to leave me and our children for another man. I must make her come with me."

"That's not true!" Elizabeth cried. "Call the police! Please—"

He pressed Elizabeth's arm higher, and she cried out in pain. He pulled her away from the wall. "I'll take her home now," he told the curious bystanders.

"She needs a good beating," an old man said.

"I will see to it, friend," Sanchez propelled her ahead of him through the crowd, and when he had turned into a dark alleyway where there were no people, he brought her around to face him.

"You're hurting me," Elizabeth cried.

"Behave yourself or I'll really hurt you," he snarled, and drew his hand back as though to strike her.

Elizabeth had never known pure evil before, but she knew it now, for evil shone in every line of Paco Sanchez's face.

His hand went to his waist, and she saw the knife.

It was then that she fainted.

The phone rang at ten o'clock that night. A man with earphones nodded for Dan to pick up the other phone.

"Yes." Dan's voice strained with tension.

"That you, Danny boy?"

Dan gripped the phone so hard his knuckles turned white. "Is Elizabeth all right?"

"A little bruised, Danny. She tried to get away, and I had to knock her around a little. But yeah, she's okay. Prime stuff, even if she is a hellcat. It'll take me a while to train her."

Dan's face went white. "Damn you—"

"Uh-uh, Dan take it easy *hermano*, if you want to see her again." Paco chuckled. "You'd better give me the jewels before I change my mind. I'm not so sure I want to make a trade."

Dan clenched his fist. Calling upon every bit of his self-control, he said, "I'm sitting here with $6.5 million in jewels, Paco. They're yours for the asking. All I want is Elizabeth. Unharmed. Understand? You touch her again, you can kiss the jewels goodbye."

"Okay, *compadre*, I'll try to restrain myself. You got a driver?"

Dan looked at Mohammed. "Yeah, I've got a driver right here."

"Ask him if he knows where Al Mahbas is."

Dan turned away from the phone. "Do you know Al Mahbas?" he asked Mohammed.

The Moroccan nodded.

"He knows it," Dan said into the phone.

"Have him take you there. It's a club. Wait inside by the phone booth. I'll call you there in thirty minutes. You bring anybody with you, you can say *adiós* to the woman."

The line went dead.

"Let's go," Dan said to Mohammed.

"We'll be right behind you." Montgomery nodded to the man with the earphones.

"No." Dan shook his head. "I won't take the risk. I've got to do what he says." He strapped the pouch with the jewels around his waist, picked his revolver up off the dresser and shoved it into his belt.

Mohammed opened the door.

"Wait a minute," Montgomery tried to say, but Dan and Mohammed were already running for the stairs.

Dan climbed into the front seat with Mohammed. They sped down the street, around the corner and shot out onto the boulevard.

"It isn't far from here," Mohammed said. "No more than ten minutes."

"Make it eight." Dan's muscles were bunched tightly. He could still hear Paco's voice saying, She tried to get away, and I had to knock her around a little. A sickness rose in Dan's stomach, and he put his fist against his mouth to keep from moaning aloud.

Elizabeth. Oh my God, if he'd harmed her... If he'd touched her... If he'd forced her...

He had to stop thinking about it. Had to stop being emotional so that he could think clearly and call upon every bit of his resources to get Elizabeth out of this. The jewels didn't matter now; neither did his cut. All he wanted was for Elizabeth to be safe.

Elizabeth—his life, his love.

Chapter 16

There were two phone booths just inside the door of Al Mahbas. Dan stood next to them, feeling as though his insides had been shredded by broken glass. He wanted to smash his hand against the wall and cry out in frustration and fear for Elizabeth.

Be calm, he told himself. You can only help her if you're calm.

His stomach tightened when the phone rang.

"Yes?" he said as he grabbed it.

"You bring anybody with you?" Castro asked.

"Only the driver."

"You'd better be telling the truth."

"I am."

"Paco wouldn't like it if you're lying."

"Dammit, Castro—"

"Okay, okay. I'm just warning you, that's all. You bring the cops, the woman is dead. Understand?"

Dan gritted his teeth. "I understand."

"Let me talk to your driver."

Dan handed the phone to Mohammed. The man listened, nodded, then said, "Yes, I know where that is. It will take us fifteen or twenty minutes to get there, depending on the traffic." Mohammed put the phone down. "It's near the Kasbah," he told Dan.

When they were in the car, Dan said, "I'll have to go in alone."

"They might kill you the minute you set foot in the door."

Dan thought for a minute, then he unstrapped the pouch from his waist. "We'll go in together, but you stay in back of me. I'll tell them the jewels aren't on me but that they're close by. I don't want to hand them over until I know that Elizabeth is safe." He hesitated. He knew little about Mohammed, but he had the feeling the big Moroccan was a man he could count on. "Do you have a gun?" he asked.

Mohammed nodded. "I have two, *sidi*," he said with a slight smile. "And I know how to use them."

"Good." It helped to know he had a backup, because he didn't trust either Castro or Sanchez. Either of them would take pleasure in blowing him away. And if they did, Elizabeth would be at Paco's mercy. "If anything happens to me," Dan said to Mohammed, "I want you to get Elizabeth out of there. I don't care about the jewels, understand? If I'm hit let them have what they want, only get her out of there."

"Nothing will happen, Daniel. There are two of them and two of us, and I am an excellent shot."

"You don't know Paco Sanchez."

"No, but I know of him, and it would not trouble my conscience to help him into his journey to the other side, *inshallah*, if it is God's will."

"Inshallah," Dan said, and crossed his fingers.

They were close to the Kasbah now. The streets were narrow and dirty, and they smelled of garbage.

"We are almost there," Mohammed said.

Dan touched the gun he'd stuck in his belt.

There were no streetlights. Mohammed stopped briefly to make sure they were on the right street. There were no stores, nothing; only a small, dark building at the end of the street.

"It is like this at night when the souks are closed," Mohammed said when he eased the car forward again. He looked up and down the silent street, then indicating the small, dark building, said, "That must be it, Daniel."

"Stop here." Mohammed did and Dan got out. "Take the jewels and stay behind me," he said.

They moved quietly through the darkness until they reached the building. Dan found a door and eased it open. He hesitated, then stepped inside.

The room was dark except for a dim light at the far end. Dan, with Mohammed a few steps behind him, went farther in.

"Castro?" he said softly. "Paco?"

"Come in, *amigo*," Paco said. "We've been waiting for you. Do you have the jewels?"

Dan motioned Mohammed back into the shadows. "They're here," he said. "My driver has them. You'll get them when I have Elizabeth."

"Then we can do business." Paco's voice was friendly, almost jovial. "Come into the light, where I can see you, Danny. You got a gun in your hand, and your lady love is as good as dead."

Dan moved into the light. "No gun," he said. "Where is she? I want to see her."

"Of course." Paco turned to Castro. "Bring the woman out," he said. Then he laughed. "I'm tempted to keep her, Dan. The jewels are priceless, but she's an exceptional woman. There is a place I know where I could get a good price for her, after I myself have tired of her."

He laughed while Dan's fingers curled into fists.

"But common sense has prevailed," Paco went on. "I will take the jewels, and you may have the woman."

Dan heard a door open. He saw Castro holding Elizabeth by the arm, pushing her in front of him.

She blinked, trying to adjust to the light, and Dan knew that she'd been locked up in a dark room.

"Elizabeth?" he said quietly.

"Dan?" She saw him then, and before Castro could stop her, she broke away and ran to Dan and threw her arms around him.

He put one arm around her. He didn't take his eyes off Castro or Sanchez. "Are you all right?" he said.

She trembled against him so violently he was afraid she would fall if he let her go, but she managed to say, "Yes, I'm all right." She took a deep breath, and he knew she was trying to steady herself. "I'm sorry," she whispered. "This is my fault."

"No it isn't." He eased her away from him.

"Give me the jewels." Paco snapped the safety off his gun.

Dan gestured behind him. "Hand them to me," he told Mohammed.

Mohammed stepped out of the shadows and gave the pouch to Dan.

It was heavy in his hand.

Paco, eager now, stepped closer. "Give 'em to me!"

"Here you are, pal," Dan said, and threw them as hard as he could, right into Paco Sanchez's face.

Castro fired. Elizabeth screamed and Dan shoved her out of the way, then reached for his gun.

There was another shot.

Castro reeled backward and went down.

Paco rolled, fired from the floor, and Dan heard the sound "Zfft!" and knew that Mohammed had fallen.

Dan's fingers tightened around his gun, but before he could raise it, another shot cracked and what felt like a two-ton truck slammed into his shoulder and knocked him off his feet. The gun spun out of his hand and skittered across the floor.

In slow motion he saw Sanchez take aim. Desperately Dan stretched out his good arm to try to reach his gun. He knew he couldn't, not in time. He knew... dear God he knew Paco Sanchez was going to kill him, and his brain screamed, Goodbye, Elizabeth. Goodbye, my love. Love...

He rolled onto his back. He saw the gun pointed at his head. He heard Paco laugh, saw the evil and the malice in his enemy's face, and then... then... A shot! The laughter stopped. Paco's eyes went wide. He pressed his hand to his chest and looked down at the blood that flowed through his fingers. Like a cartoon character, his knees folded and he fell, face forward, down to the cement floor.

Dan turned his head. He saw Elizabeth. His gun was in her hand, and he knew that she had killed Paco Sanchez and saved his life.

Dan went to the hospital to have his arm treated, but though James Montgomery and the doctor insisted, he refused to stay. Mohammed had taken a bullet in his side, Montgomery told him, but he was going to be all right.

Another doctor had examined Elizabeth, and although she was bruised, she wasn't hurt.

"But the doctor wants to talk to you," Montgomery said, "about Elizabeth."

Then Montgomery helped him button his shirt over the sling that held his bandaged shoulder, and he went to find the doctor who had taken care of Elizabeth.

"It's obvious she's had a bad time of it," the doctor told Dan. "She has a few bruises, but it's more than that. She's been traumatized. I've tried to talk to her but without success. Perhaps you'll be able to when she leaves here." He pushed his glasses up on his forehead. "I presume you know what's bothering her?"

Dan took a painful breath. "Yes," he said. "I know what's bothering her."

For the rest of her life, Elizabeth knew she would have to live with the knowledge that she had killed a man. And the most terrible thing about it was that if she had it to do over again, she would.

It had happened so fast. Dan had been hit, the gun had flown out of his hand, and Paco Sanchez had raised his gun to fire again.

She hadn't stopped to think. She'd grabbed for the gun, raised it and fired. She'd taken a man's life; she would never be the same again.

Like two walking wounded, she and Dan went back to the Hotel Afrique. It was over; they were safe. In another few days, Dan would be well enough to travel.

James Montgomery cleared up everything with the Spanish police. Dan and Elizabeth were no longer wanted for murder. Dan called Joe Jewlensky and told him he had the jewels and that he'd be flying back with them as soon as he was able to, and that things had been cleared with the Moroccan authorities.

He simply took it for granted that Elizabeth would fly back to New York with him.

But Elizabeth wasn't sure that was what she wanted to do. She couldn't think; she felt as though the bullet that had ripped through the body of the man she had killed had ripped through her body, too. Every time she closed her eyes, she could see Paco Sanchez—the surprised look on his face, the blood seeping through his fingers, his eyes growing dim.

Dan tried to talk to her about it. "You did what you had to do," he said again and again.

"I know. And I'd do it again, but..." Tears choked her and she began to tremble.

"You saved my life, Elizabeth." He put his good arm around her and held her while she wept.

But it didn't help. Nothing helped. She tried to tell herself that Paco Sanchez had been an evil man, a vicious man. He'd ruined the young Moroccan woman's life when he'd disfigured her. He'd almost killed Dan. He had terrorized her. He *was* evil and vicious, but he'd been a human being. A woman had borne him and loved him, and now he was dead because she had killed him. She didn't think she'd ever get over it.

James Montgomery came to the hotel to see them. He told them that all of the travel arrangements had been made, for her as well as for Dan. He told her she was a terrific woman and one hell of a good shot.

She got up and went into the bedroom.

After James had left, Dan followed her in. She was lying on top of the spread, her forearm over her eyes.

Dan sat down beside her.

"James is a fool," he said.

"I know."

He moved her arms so that he could see her face. He saw the anguish and said, "Elizabeth, oh, Elizabeth," and very gently he brushed his lips against hers.

At first she didn't respond, then she lifted her arms and brought him close. "Hold me," she whispered.

She wanted to be close to him, to burrow herself against the warmth of his body, to smell the freshness of his skin and feel his arms around her.

Dan sensed her need, and though his body grew taut with desire, he only held her. He smoothed the dark cloud of hair back from her face. He kissed her cheek and caressed her shoulders. After a little while, Elizabeth sighed against him and he could feel some of the tension recede from her body. She unbuttoned his shirt so she could touch his chest, and a quiver ran through his body.

She realized his need then, and wanting to please him, she curled her fingers in his thatch of chest hair and, careful of his arm, pushed his shirt aside so that she could kiss his chest.

Dan closed his eyes and his good arm tightened around her.

"Yes," he whispered. "Please, yes."

She found his mouth in only the shadow of a kiss before she began to nuzzle his ear and trace the lobe with her tongue.

Her breath was hot and sweet, and it took every ounce of his will not to take her then.

But Dan made himself wait until Elizabeth wanted this as much as he did.

Her fingers were so warm, so satiny soft against his skin. He tried to hold himself back, tried to smother the low moan of need that whispered from his lips.

Slowly, slowly, a fire began to kindle somewhere deep inside Elizabeth. Her senses sharpened. Dan touched her breasts and the fire grew and she moved closer to him, raising herself so that she could kiss his mouth.

And in a little while that's all there was, that's all that mattered—Dan's mouth on hers, fierce and gentle, demanding, giving.

All the while they caressed each other, and when Dan said, "I can't wait," she helped him undress and quickly removed her own clothes.

"Elizabeth," he said, "oh, love." He tried to raise his body over hers, but he gave a cry of pain.

"Wait, darling," she said.

She came up over him then, and he saw the love and the passion in her eyes, and his heart filled with loving her.

Elizabeth began to move against him, and when she did she began to forget her unhappiness. There was only Dan now; he was alive and she rejoiced in his being alive.

It was a gentle loving, a quiet, healing passion. When it ended Elizabeth rested her body on his, and for the first time since Paco Sanchez's death, she slept without dreaming.

"What do you mean you're not going back with me?" Dan faced her, shocked and angry. "Of course you are."

Elizabeth took his hand. "I can't go back, Dan. Not right now. I still have three months left of my sabbatical."

"Your sabbatical?" So much had happened in the past few weeks that he'd forgotten Elizabeth's reason for being in Spain. Now, in a strange way that he couldn't explain, it seemed as though she had always been with him, a part of him, and he couldn't conceive that she wanted to leave him or what life would be like without her.

It was true that they hadn't talked about what would happen when this was over and it was time for Dan to return to the States, but he'd assumed... What? That Elizabeth would go with him? That she would stay in New York with him? Live with him?

They hadn't talked about any kind of a permanent relationship, but surely Elizabeth knew how he felt about her. He thought then of the letter she had written on the morning when Castro and Sanchez had kidnapped her, about his being confused about who she was, Elizabeth or Isabela. That was nonsense, of course. He was in love...with *her*. The thought of being away from her was unthinkable but... Yes, the big "but." Did he want to commit himself to marriage? Was that what she wanted?

Palms only slightly damp, Dan looked at her. "Listen," he said, "I know we haven't talked about—" he swallowed "about any kind of a permanent relationship."

"Like marriage?" Elizabeth smiled. "I love you Dan, and I think you love me." She shook her head. "But I'm not sure which me it is you love."

"What in the hell are you talking about?"

"Darling..." Elizabeth hesitated, trying to find the words to make him understand how she felt. She took his hand and led him to the bed, and when they were seated side by side, she said, "So much has happened to us in such a short time, Dan. We were thrown into this so suddenly. You came crashing through the gardens of the Alhambra, and my life hasn't been the same since."

Elizabeth smiled. "I've led a fairly sedate life, Dan. Suddenly men were shooting at me, and this tough-looking stranger grabbed me, hustled me into a car, tied my wrists and sped off down the mountain road."

She still remembered how terrified she'd been that day, how much like a nightmare it had seemed. How frightened she'd been of Dan.

"You took me to the Gypsy caves," she went on, "and you made me go with you in a Gypsy wagon." There was a hint of both humor and sadness in her pale green eyes. "You turned me into a Gypsy, darling, and it was the Gypsy, Isabela, you fell in love with. Not me."

"That's not so," Dan protested.

"Isn't it?" Elizabeth shook her head. In a gentle voice, she said, "I'm not Isabela, Dan. I'm only plain Elizabeth Kensington." She tightened her hand around his. "I wish I were the Gypsy girl. I'd love to be that free, that uninhibited, that filled with the joy of life. But I'm not. I'm a schoolteacher from Rocky River, Ohio. And I don't think that's who you're in love with."

Dan looked at her for a long moment. He wanted to shout his denial, to say that she was crazy, that it wasn't so, that of course it was her he was in love with. But he didn't say anything, because in a strange way what she'd said was partly true—he had fallen in love with Isabela. Until he met her, he'd never really known what it was to truly love. She had been the answer to all of his fantasies, all of his dreams.

Had she only existed in his imagination?

He thought back to those wonderful days and nights they had spent together in the Gypsy wagon, days when he'd been so overwhelmed with love that he had only to look at her or touch her hand to have his body grow hard with desire. And, oh, how his Gypsy lady had responded. Her green eyes would widen, and her lips would part. He'd see the tip of her pink tongue touch the corner of her lip, and he'd know that the same heat that coursed through his veins coursed through hers.

He remembered the day she had danced barefoot on the side of the road. In his mind's eye he could still see her slender arms raised above her head and the way her body moved—slowly, sinuously, sensually. His heart had pounded hard against his ribs and heat had spread through his body into his loins. And he'd thought he would die with wanting her. Isabela, his Gypsy lady.

He looked at Elizabeth, but before he could speak, she said, "It's all right, darling. I understand."

He knew then that he'd lost her. He'd lost his Gypsy lady.

James Montgomery drove them to the airport, because Mohammed was still recovering from the wound he'd received the night they had rescued Elizabeth. Dan had visited him in the hospital. "I'll come back to Tangier someday," he'd told the other man. "When I do, we will see each other again."

"Inshallah," Mohammed had said. He shook Dan's hand. "It has been a pleasure to know you, Dan Thornton. And your lady, too. Please tell her goodbye for me and that I hope she, too, will return someday."

"We both will," Dan had said.

But when they walked into the airport, he wasn't so sure that they would ever return, at least not together. Elizabeth had remained adamant. She would fly to Málaga with him so they could be together a short while longer. From there he would take the plane to Madrid, then on to New York.

He shook hands with Montgomery. He still didn't like James, but he was sincerely grateful to him for taking care of all the time-consuming details. Because of his help, Elizabeth had only been questioned briefly about her kidnapping and the death of Paco Sanchez. Both the Spanish and the Moroccan governments had been after him for a long time.

As for Castro, though badly wounded, he would survive to spend the next twenty years in a Spanish prison. And so would Nathan Janss for having been a part of the kidnap conspiracy.

Montgomery, as he had done the first time he met her, kissed Elizabeth's hand, lingering longer than Dan liked as he brushed his mustache against her skin.

"I hope that's the last we see of him," Dan told Elizabeth when they boarded the plane.

She smiled, remembering his earlier jealousy of James.

They spent two days in Málaga. They wandered up and down the palm-lined avenues, and they went down to the beach to eat sardines that had been roasted over a fire on the sand. They ate inch-thick steaks, drank good red wine and toasted each other across candlelit tables.

On the night before Dan left, they held each other closely. It seemed to Dan that he could not get enough of her or she of him. They made love again and again, and the last time, though he tried not to, in that final moment of passion, he cried, "Isabela! Oh, Isabela!"

Elizabeth went to the airport with him the next morning.

"Please come back to New York with me," Dan said.

"I can't" She tried to hold back the tears that threatened to fall.

"I love you."

"And I love you."

He put his hands on her shoulders. "I'll come back," he said. "There's going to be a lot of paperwork and things I'll have to take care of after I turn the jewels over to the authorities. But I'll be back, darling. Wait for me."

She nodded against his jacket, clinging to him, unable now to hold back the tears.

"Oh, God," he said as he crushed her to him. "I don't want to leave you."

They called his plane.

"I have to go."

"I know."

"Where are you going when you leave here?"

"I don't know," she managed to say through her tears. "Seville. Arcos de la Frontera, Ronda. Probably back to Granada."

"I'll find you."

"If you come back."

"I'll come back.

The final call came.

"This is crazy," Dan said. "I can't leave you like this."

Elizabeth touched his face. "You've got to go," she said weeping. "You'll miss your plane."

"Por favor," an attendant said. "You must leave immediately, *señor*."

Dan looked at Elizabeth and there was such a look of anguish on his face that her tears began anew.

"I love you," he said. "Whoever you are, I love you."

"Please, *señor*," the attendant said.

Dan pulled Elizabeth close. He kissed her hard, then he let her go and without a backward look ran down the jetway to the plane.

Chapter 17

Elizabeth was in Málaga for a week. From there she went back to Seville, where she wandered the narrow, winding streets and shopped in the stores along the Sierpes. She saw three flamenco shows, and though they were good, it seemed to her that the dancers had little of the wondrous passion Pilar had shown when she'd danced.

She thought often of Jonas and Pilar, of little Paquito and Rosalia.

She tried not to think of Dan.

From Seville, Elizabeth went to Arcos de la Frontera, because she had heard there was to be a folk dance festival there. She attended the three days of the festival, took voluminous notes and photographs and worked on her dissertation.

Someone in Arcos de la Frontera told her about the ballets that were held in Nerja in August, and although it wasn't summer, she went to that small town on the sea in the hope of finding out more about the kind of dancing from that area. She went through the caves where ballets were held, amazed at their immensity, and tried to visualize what it must be like to see something as beautiful as *Swan Lake* performed here on a stage that nature had built.

And while Elizabeth made her notes and took her pictures, she pretended not to think about Dan or how it had been with them. But often she awoke in the night, weeping and alone, and touched the empty pillow where his head would have lain had he not gone away.

Again and again she told herself she had been right not to go with him. They had shared something wonderful, but it was over. She was not the woman he wanted; she was only Elizabeth. Elizabeth, who would love him for as long as there was breath in her body.

By the end of the third week she was so miserable she could barely stand it. She read her notes over and over. She tried to work on her dissertation, but her mind kept wandering back to Dan. Finally she knew that it wasn't any good in Spain without him, and she decided to go home.

But first she would go back to Granada, where it had all begun.

Dan didn't remember ever having been this restless before. He had turned the jewels over to Joe Jewlensky, who returned them to the State Department, who gave then to Señor Calderon so that he could at last make the formal presentation to the Smithsonian. Two weeks later Jewlensky had given Dan a check for $650,000.

"Maybe this'll take that sour look off your face," Dan's boss said. "What's the matter with you? You got what you went to Spain for, and I've just handed over the biggest check this insurance company has ever given an investigator." He raised a bushy eyebrow. "Whatever happened to the woman you told me about?"

"She's in Spain."

"Spanish gal?"

"No, she's an American."

"You're so crazy about her, why didn't she come back with you?"

"She had to stay for a while. She's on a sabbatical."

"A sabbatical?"

"Yeah, she's a schoolteacher."

"A schoolteacher?" Joe leaned back in his chair and laughed. "I'll be damned. Dan Thornton's fallen for a schoolteacher."

"I don't see what's so funny," Dan said.

"You are, Dan. I thought your taste ran more to model or showgirl types. This gal must be something to have frazzled you like this."

"She *is* something," Dan growled.

"Then why didn't you bring her back with you?"

"I told you, she's on sabbatical."

"Uh-huh." Joe looked at the younger man and tapped his hairy fingers on the top of his desk. "You've got vacation time coming," he said. "After you clear up all the paperwork, why don't you go on back to Spain?"

"I'm planning to."

Jewlensky nodded. "Bring the lady in to meet me when you get back."

"If she'll come back, to New York, I mean. Her home's in Ohio."

"I've got confidence in you, Dan. Like I said, bring her in to meet me."

Maybe Joe had confidence in him, Dan thought that night when he went back to his apartment, but he wasn't so sure how much confidence he had in himself as far as Elizabeth was concerned.

A hundred times in the past few days, he'd thought about what she'd said and wondered if there was any truth to her words. Certainly he'd been more attracted to Elizabeth in her Gypsy dress than he'd been the first few days they were together. But after all, wasn't that understandable? He hadn't even known her then; it had only been in the closeness of the Gypsy wagon that he had really become aware of her as a woman.

What did it matter when love began? The important thing was that he had fallen in love with her and she with him. He didn't want to make light of her fear that he'd fallen in love with the illusion that was Isabela, but he knew now that she had been wrong, for he loved her, whoever she was, and he wasn't going to let her go.

Another two weeks passed before Dan finished everything that had to be cleared up. He answered hundreds of questions and filled out innumerable forms. But at last the day came when everything had been taken care of.

He didn't know where Elizabeth was; he only knew that he was going to Spain and that he was going to find her. She'd said she was going to Granada; that's where he would look first.

The taxi that Elizabeth was in came to a stop in the Sacromonte.

"Are you sure you want to get out here?" The taxi driver looked concerned.

"Yes, I'm sure," Elizabeth answered with a smile. "The people who live here are my friends." She paid the man, then picked up the packages she had brought with her.

"Here come the kids," he said, and tried to wave them away with shouts of "Get out of here! *No moleste a la señorita.* Don't bother the lady."

"It's all right." Elizabeth laughed. "I can handle it." She got out of the taxi and said to the children, "I'm going to the house of Pilar and Jonas Belmonte. Will you take me there?"

They gathered around her like lilliputians, a group of ragged little people, all chattering at once as they reached for her packages.

As they approached the cave-house, Elizabeth saw Pilar standing in the doorway. The Gypsy shaded her eyes against the afternoon sun and squinted. Then with a cry she shouted. "Eleezabet! Is it you? *Dios mío*, I cannot believe it."

Before Elizabeth knew what was happening, Pilar had embraced her and kissed her cheeks. When she let Elizabeth go, she motioned the boys away, but not before Elizabeth filled their hands with pesetas.

"Come in," Pilar said. "Jonas will be surprised. And Rosalia! All she's done is talk about you these past few months. She told me you'd come back, but I didn't believe her. Now here you are. She'll be home from school soon. You must meet her at the door and watch the expression on her face when she sees you."

"Is she well? And Paquito? How is he? He was ill the last time I was here."

Pilar frowned as she rested her hands on her broad hips. "He has gone away with Adelita."

"Gone away?" Elizabeth stared at the other woman. "But where?"

"*¿Quién sabe?* That daughter of mine took up with another no-good fellow. She took Paquito with her when she left, but she did not take Rosalia. One of these days she will come back. She has before." She motioned Elizabeth ahead of her into the house. "But come in, come in and let us have a glass of wine to celebrate your return."

It all looked so familiar to Elizabeth; the richly colored rug that covered part of the linoleumed floor, the framed photographs and the bullfight banderillas, the picture of the Virgin Mary, the dozens of gleaming copper pots hanging from the whitewashed walls.

She took a sip of wine and knew that she was glad to be here, that she felt strangely, comfortably at home.

"We have wondered what became of you and Dan," Pilar said. "Our friends in Osuna brought the wagon back to us, but they knew nothing about you. The man who left it with them was named Antonio. Were you and Dan traveling with him? Where is Dan now?"

"He went back to New York."

Pilar raised her dark brows. "I see."

But it was obvious to Elizabeth that she didn't see. Pilar probably had lots of questions she wanted to ask, but before she could, they heard some of the children returning from school. "Rosalia will be here soon," Pilar said, and Elizabeth went to the door to wait for the little girl.

At first Rosalia didn't see Elizabeth. She walked a little apart from the others, schoolbooks clutched in her arms, head bent, looking far too serious and sad for a child her age. Her shoulders were narrow, her arms and legs too thin.

Elizabeth smiled, remembering herself at that age. She'd been all arms and legs, too, and oh, how she'd longed to be like the cute, chubby little girls with big blue eyes and dancing curls. It's going to be all right, she wanted to tell Rosalia. Someday you're going to grow up and you'll be beautiful.

"Rosalia?" she called.

The child looked up, puzzled, then she saw Elizabeth and an expression of delight crossed her face.

"Eleezabet!" she cried, as her grandmother had, and began to run toward her. But when she reached Elizabeth, she stopped, suddenly shy, then said, "*Buenas tardes, Señorita Eleezabet.*"

"*Buenas tardes*, Rosalia." Elizabeth dropped to her knees and drew the little girl to her. "*Un abrazo,*" she said, hugging Rosalia. She felt warm and wonderful when the little girl's thin arms crept up around her neck and she buried her face against Elizabeth's hair.

"I thought you were never coming back," Rosalia whispered.

"I told you I'd be back, didn't I?" Elizabeth stood up and took her hand.

"Mama and Paquito went away."

"Your grandmother told me." Elizabeth's face was as solemn as Rosalia's. "But they'll come back, Rosalia, and meantime you have your grandmother and your grandfather." She smiled down at the child. "And me, for a little while, at least."

When they went into the house, Elizabeth indicated the packages she'd placed on the sofa. "I brought you a few presents," she told the little girl.

Rosalia's eyes widened. "For me?" she whispered.

"Yes." Elizabeth handed her a gaily wrapped box. "Open this one first," she said.

Rosalia, though Elizabeth could see she was in a fever of impatience, carefully untied the red satin bow and unwrapped the package. Then, small white teeth clamped on her lower lip, she opened the box and pushed the white tissue paper aside. With a soft "Oh" she lifted out a blue organdy party dress.

"It's got puffed sleeves," she whispered. "I love puffed sleeves."

"So did I when I was a little girl."

"It's the most beautiful dress I've ever seen."

"I'm glad you like it, sweetheart." Elizabeth handed her another package, then another and another and smiled with pleasure when Rosalia oohed and aahed over two pretty school dresses, a pair of blue jeans, white pants, a red sweater and two blouses, also with puffed sleeves. When everything had been opened, Rosalia sat among her packages as though unable to believe her eyes.

"I bought a few toys for Paquito," Elizabeth said, "but we can put them away until he comes back."

There was also a new shawl for Pilar and a bottle of Manzanilla for Jonas, which they opened as soon as he came home.

"You are staying here in Granada?" Pilar asked over supper that night.

"Yes, for a little while. I came to Spain to study dancing, Pilar, so that I could write about it. I thought I knew a lot about dancing, and I suppose I do, technically, but I never really understood it until I watched you do the flamenco. That's why I've come back to Granada. I want to see you dance again. I hope you'll let me come here sometimes so that I can watch you and the others."

"Of course you must come here," Jonas said. "Did I not tell you that *mi casa es su casa*, that my home is your home?"

"Yes, you did, Jonas, thank you."

"If this is your home, then you must be here with us," Pilar said.

"Oh, I couldn't do that," Elizabeth protested.

"Why not? The room you had is empty now. Jonas and I use Adelita's room. Tomorrow you will move out of your hotel and come to stay with us. You cannot learn all there is to know about flamenco unless you learn about the Gypsies." Pilar smiled. "It is settled. Yes? Tomorrow you will come back, and you will stay for as long as you are in Granada."

And so it was. The next morning after breakfast, Elizabeth packed her suitcase and took a taxi back to the Albacín.

A week passed. She was happy there, but each night when she lay alone in the room that she and Dan had shared, she remembered that first morning when she'd awakened in a strange bed with a stranger. "Dan," her heart cried, and again, as she had hundreds of times since they parted, she wondered if she had been wrong not to have gone back to New York with him.

Every day Elizabeth told herself that it was time to leave, but still she lingered on. She wore Gypsy clothes now, off-the-shoulder blouses, gaily colored skirts, and sandals. The other Gypsies accepted her, and at night she sat with them outside the Gypsy caves and watched and listened while the men played their guitars and sang the haunting songs of the *canto hondo*. She hadn't understood this strange music before, but she did now. She understood the mournful cry of sadness and of loss, and sometimes when the evenings were over and she went to her room, she lay in bed and wept for Dan and for all lost loves.

One night when the moon was full, and after some of the others had danced, Pilar said, "It is your turn, Eleezabet. Come and dance for us."

She hesitated, then stood and went to the place where the women danced. For a few moments she only listened to the strum of the guitars while she let the music seep through her bones into her heart, then slowly, eyes closed, Elizabeth began to dance. She could feel it now, feel this music of the Gypsies coursing through her veins, feel the sadness and the tragedy, the pride and the passion.

She barely heard the palms that beat in time to the music, the soft "*Olé*'s" the whispered words "*¡Mucho! ¡Éso!*"

The music came faster. Elizabeth's dark hair cascaded around her bare shoulders, swaying as she swayed, sinuously, sensuously. Then abruptly the music stopped. Elizabeth's head was bowed. Her body quivered and her breasts rose and fell with each breath she took.

Then with a shuddered sigh she raised her face and saw Dan coming toward her through the crowd of Gypsies.

"Hello, Isabela," he said. "Hello, my love."

"How did you know where to find me?" She asked later when they were alone.

"I knew you'd come back to Granada, back here to the Sacromonte."

Elizabeth clung to him. She found that special place against the hollow of his shoulder and burrowed closer.

He lifted her face to his and gently kissed her lips. "I'm never going to leave you again," he said.

The kiss deepened and grew, and their bodies caught fire with a passion too long delayed. The breaths came fast as they undressed each other and fell upon the bed in this cavelike room in this Gypsy house.

And when in the deepest throes of passion, Dan cried, "Isabela! My Isabela!" she did not feel a dagger pierce her. Instead, she felt pierced by a love so strong her body rose to his and she cried her own sweet cry of ecstasy against his lips.

The next morning when she awoke, Dan was no longer beside her. She got up and dressed in her Gypsy clothes and went to look for him.

There was no one in the house except Rosalia. "Where is everybody?" Elizabeth asked the little girl. "Where is Señor Thornton?"

Rosalia giggled and covered her mouth.

"What is it?" Elizabeth asked. "What's going on?"

"Señor Thornton and Grandma and Grandpa are outside." Rosalia took her hand. "Come," she said, and giggled again.

Elizabeth opened the door. She looked out and gasped, scarcely able to believe her eyes, for there before her was the Gypsy wagon that she and Dan had escaped in, the wagon where their love had begun, where they'd spent so many happy hours.

It was decorated with all kinds of flowers: roses and daisies, carnations and orange blossoms.

Elizabeth's eyes filled with tears as Dan came toward her. "Dan," she said through trembling lips. "Oh, Dan."

He drew her into his arms and kissed her. "Will you marry me, Elizabeth? Will you come with me and be my Gypsy lady?"

So overcome she could barely speak, Elizabeth managed to whisper, "Oh, yes. Yes, Dan. I'll be your Gypsy lady or anybody else you want me to be."

For it was true; it didn't matter. Let him call her Elizabeth or Isabela. It really didn't matter. She was his love; that was all that was important now.

He kissed her again and held her away from him. "I've arranged everything," he said. "We're going to be married in the church here in the Albacín this afternoon. Tonight we'll leave for our honeymoon."

Elizabeth pointed to the wagon. "In that?" she said, laughing through her tears.

"Yes, love." For a moment a look of doubt flickered across Dan's face. "Unless you'd rather go to a hotel."

She threw her arms around him. "What do Gypsies want with a hotel when they can have a beautiful wagon like this?"

Her smile was radiant. "Oh, Dan," she said. "Dan, what a lovely way to spend a honeymoon."

As the Gypsies watched, they kissed again, then Dan took Elizabeth's hand and led her toward their Gypsy wagon.

That night when the hour grew late and the only sound was the low, sweet cry of a night bird calling to his mate in the branches of the tree that sheltered them, they looked at each other across the fire that Dan had built.

When he saw the yearning in her eyes, he said, "Come, love," and led her into the Gypsy wagon.

They kissed and when the kissing was not enough they undressed each other and Dan carried her to their bed. "I have a present for you," he said, and handed her a blue velvet box.

Elizabeth looked at him questioningly. Then she opened the box and gasped, for on a strip of dark satin there lay a diamond bracelet exactly like the one from the collection of Anzaran jewels.

"I had a replica of the original made for you," Dan said as he fastened the chain of diamonds around her ankle. "I remembered how it was the night you wore it, Elizabeth. I remembered..."

And somewhere in time a handsome caliph and his Gypsy queen smiled down upon the lovers.

* * * * *

COMING NEXT MONTH

#309 THE ICE CREAM MAN—Kathleen Korbel

Could the handsome new ice cream man in Jenny Lake's neighborhood be selling more than chocolate and vanilla? She didn't want to believe the rumors that he could be a drug dealer, but there was something strange about an ice cream man who clearly disliked children. For undercover detective Nick Barnett, this assignment was unrelieved misery—except for Jenny, who was charmingly capable of making his life sweeter than it had ever been.

#310 SOMEBODY'S BABY—Marilyn Pappano

Giving up custody of her infant daughter to care for her critically ill son had been Sarah Lawson's only choice. Now, a year later, she was back to claim Katie from her father, Daniel Ryan, as per their custody arrangement. But Daniel had no intention of giving up his adorable daughter, agreement or not! Then, through their mutual love for Katie, they began to learn that the only arrangement that really worked was to become a family—forever.

#311 MAGIC IN THE AIR—Marilyn Tracy

Bound by events in the past, Jeannie Donnelly tried to avenge an ancient wrong and become the rightful leader of the Natuwa tribe. But she found her plans blocked by Michael O'Shea, surrogate son of the man she had to depose. The pain of yesterday could only be put to rest when they learned that trust and compromise—and love—were the only keys to the future.

#312 MISTRESS OF FOXGROVE—Lee Magner

The hired help didn't mix with the upper class—at least that was what stable manager Beau Lamond believed before he fell for heiress Elaine Faust. Surrounded by malicious gossip and still hurting from a shattered marriage, Elaine turned to Beau for the friendship and love she so desperately needed. But Beau was not what he seemed, and the secret he was keeping might destroy their burgeoning love.

AVAILABLE THIS MONTH:

#305 DEVIL'S NIGHT
Jennifer Greene

#306 CAPRICORN MOON
Barbara Faith

#307 CLOUD CASTLES
Kaitlyn Gorton

#308 AT RISK
Jeanne Stephens

INDULGE A LITTLE SWEEPSTAKES

OFFICIAL RULES

SWEEPSTAKES RULES AND REGULATIONS. NO PURCHASE NECESSARY.

1. NO PURCHASE NECESSARY. To enter complete the official entry form and return with the invoice in the envelope provided. Or you may enter by printing your name, complete address and your daytime phone number on a 3 x 5 piece of paper. Include with your entry the hand printed words "Indulge A Little Sweepstakes." Mail your entry to: Indulge A Little Sweepstakes, P.O. Box 1397, Buffalo, NY 14269-1397. No mechanically reproduced entries accepted. Not responsible for late, lost, misdirected mail, or printing errors.

2. Three winners, one per month (Sept. 30, 1989, October 31, 1989 and November 30, 1989), will be selected in random drawings. All entries received prior to the drawing date will be eligible for that month's prize. This sweepstakes is under the supervision of MARDEN-KANE, INC. an independent judging organization whose decisions are final and binding. Winners will be notified by telephone and may be required to execute an affidavit of eligibility and release which must be returned within 14 days, or an alternate winner will be selected.

3. Prizes: 1st Grand Prize (1) a trip for two to Disneyworld in Orlando, Florida. Trip includes round trip air transportation, hotel accommodations for seven days and six nights, plus up to $700 expense money (ARV $3,500). 2nd Grand Prize (1) a seven-night Chandris Caribbean Cruise for two includes transportation from nearest major airport, accommodations, meals plus up to $1,000 in expense money (ARV $4,300). 3rd Grand Prize (1) a ten-day Hawaiian holiday for two includes round trip air transportation for two, hotel accommodations, sightseeing, plus up to $1,200 in spending money (ARV $7,700). All trips subject to availability and must be taken as outlined on the entry form.

4. Sweepstakes open to residents of the U.S. and Canada 18 years or older except employees and the families of Torstar Corp., its affiliates, subsidiaries and Marden-Kane, Inc. and all other agencies and persons connected with conducting this sweepstakes. All Federal, State and local laws and regulations apply. Void wherever prohibited or restricted by law. Taxes, if any are the sole responsibility of the prize winners. Canadian winners will be required to answer a skill testing question. Winners consent to the use of their name, photograph and/or likeness for publicity purposes without additional compensation.

5. For a list of prize winners, send a stamped, self-addressed envelope to Indulge A Little Sweepstakes Winners, P.O. Box 701, Sayreville, NJ 08871.

DL-SWPS

INDULGE A LITTLE SWEEPSTAKES

OFFICIAL RULES

SWEEPSTAKES RULES AND REGULATIONS. NO PURCHASE NECESSARY.

1. NO PURCHASE NECESSARY. To enter complete the official entry form and return with the invoice in the envelope provided. Or you may enter by printing your name, complete address and your daytime phone number on a 3 x 5 piece of paper. Include with your entry the hand printed words "Indulge A Little Sweepstakes." Mail your entry to: Indulge A Little Sweepstakes, P.O. Box 1397, Buffalo, NY 14269-1397. No mechanically reproduced entries accepted. Not responsible for late, lost, misdirected mail, or printing errors.

2. Three winners, one per month (Sept. 30, 1989, October 31, 1989 and November 30, 1989), will be selected in random drawings. All entries received prior to the drawing date will be eligible for that month's prize. This sweepstakes is under the supervision of MARDEN-KANE, INC. an independent judging organization whose decisions are final and binding. Winners will be notified by telephone and may be required to execute an affidavit of eligibility and release which must be returned within 14 days, or an alternate winner will be selected.

3. Prizes: 1st Grand Prize (1) a trip for two to Disneyworld in Orlando, Florida. Trip includes round trip air transportation, hotel accommodations for seven days and six nights, plus up to $700 expense money (ARV $3,500). 2nd Grand Prize (1) a seven-night Chandris Caribbean Cruise for two includes transportation from nearest major airport, accommodations, meals plus up to $1,000 in expense money (ARV $4,300). 3rd Grand Prize (1) a ten-day Hawaiian holiday for two includes round trip air transportation for two, hotel accommodations, sightseeing, plus up to $1,200 in spending money (ARV $7,700). All trips subject to availability and must be taken as outlined on the entry form.

4. Sweepstakes open to residents of the U.S. and Canada 18 years or older except employees and the families of Torstar Corp., its affiliates, subsidiaries and Marden-Kane, Inc. and all other agencies and persons connected with conducting this sweepstakes. All Federal, State and local laws and regulations apply. Void wherever prohibited or restricted by law. Taxes, if any are the sole responsibility of the prize winners. Canadian winners will be required to answer a skill testing question. Winners consent to the use of their name, photograph and/or likeness for publicity purposes without additional compensation.

5. For a list of prize winners, send a stamped, self-addressed envelope to Indulge A Little Sweepstakes Winners, P.O. Box 701, Sayreville, NJ 08871.

© 1989 HARLEQUIN ENTERPRISES LTD.

DL-SWPS

INDULGE A LITTLE—WIN A LOT!

Summer of '89 Subscribers-Only Sweepstakes

OFFICIAL ENTRY FORM

This entry must be received by: Sept. 30, 1989
This month's winner will be notified by: October 7, 1989
Trip must be taken between: Nov. 7, 1989–Nov. 7, 1990

YES, I want to win the Walt Disney World® vacation for two! I understand the prize includes round-trip airfare, first-class hotel, and a daily allowance as revealed on the "Wallet" scratch-off card.

Name ______________________________

Address ______________________________

City ____________ State/Prov. ________ Zip/Postal Code ________

Daytime phone number ______________________________
Area code

Return entries with invoice in envelope provided. Each book in this shipment has two entry coupons—and the more coupons you enter, the better your chances of winning!

© 1989 HARLEQUIN ENTERPRISES LTD.

DINDL-1